Freddy's War
A NOVEL

JUDY SCHULTZ

Brindle & Glass Publishing Ltd.
www.brindleandglass.com

LIBRARY AND ARCHIVES CANADA CATALOGUING IN PUBLICATION
Schultz, Judy
Freddy's war / Judy Schultz.

Issued also in electronic formats.
ISBN 978-1-897142-55-4

I. Title.

PS8637.C5775F74 2011   C813'.6   C2011-904185-5

Editor: Lynne Van Luven
Proofreader: Heather Sangster, Strong Finish
Design: Pete Kohut
Front cover: Army soldier by Darren Hunt, istockphoto.com
Chinese lanterns by Donald Johansson, istockphoto.com
Author photo: Lori Demers

Brindle & Glass is pleased to acknowledge the financial support for its publishing program from the Government of Canada through the Canada Book Fund, Canada Council for the Arts, and the Province of British Columbia through the British Columbia Arts Council and the Book Publishing Tax Credit.

MIX
Paper from
responsible sources
FSC® C016245

The interior pages of this book have been printed on 100% post-consumer recycled paper, processed chlorine free, and printed with vegetable-based inks.

1 2 3 4 5 15 14 13 12 11

PRINTED IN CANADA

For Ed, forever.

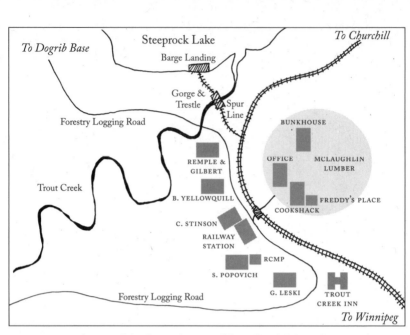

A map of the fictional town of Trout Creek, Manitoba.

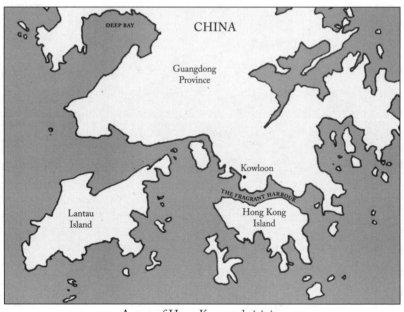

A map of Hong Kong and vicinity.

BOOK ONE

There's a War On

ONE : Ghosts

Vancouver, October 1960

THE GREY MAN SHUFFLES ALONG East Pender Street, checking the payphones for change, but people in Chinatown don't leave dimes behind. By the bus stop in front of Tai Hing Supermarket he pauses, watching the girl in the red coat.

Something familiar about her. Her face, the way she holds her head. That mop of hair. He stares at her, watches while she pulls her collar around her chin, hunches her shoulders against the wind, juggles grocery bags.

It couldn't be her. Could it? He turns away, back to the phones.

The girl watches him slam the coin returns. Hears him swear. No luck. No forgotten dimes today.

Grey hair, grey skin, dirty-grey sweater that must once have been white. He shuffles, as though his shoes are too big. Moves close to her bench, and she gets a whiff of something stale, as though his clothes haven't been washed in a long time. She glances sideways, checking. Wary.

Just keep moving, don't stop, don't look at me.

He pauses in his shuffle, fishes in his pocket for a cigarette butt. Tries to light it, shields it with a shaky hand, but the wind plays with the match, blows it out before the flame can catch.

Now she's certain.

If he remembers me, what will he say? Any spare change, kid? How's your mother?

Finally, her bus. Hurrying to get on, she jostles an old Chinese woman lugging overstuffed shopping bags. The woman yells at her in rapid, high-pitched Cantonese. Rude Canadian female, no respect.

His head jerks toward the sound. Turning the shrill tones over in

2

GREENWOODS' BKSHOPPE

7925 - 104 ST. EDMONTON, AB T6E 4C9
439-2005 SMALL WORLD 439-5600
CALL US TOLL FREE 1-800-661-2078
FINE BOOKS FOR ALL AGES - ALL INTERESTS
G.S.T. #R102194735

306313 Reg 2 ID   1 8:57 pm 21/09/11

```
S FREDDYS WAR          1 @  19.95    19.95
SUBTOTAL                             19.95
DISCOUNT -  10%                      -1.99
     SENIOR CITIZEN Discount
DISCOUNTED SUBTOTAL                  17.96
VAT: GST - 5%                          .90
TOTAL VAT                              .90
TOTAL                                18.86
CASH PAYMENT                         20.01
CHANGE                                1.15
```

List 19.95 Sell 17.96 Your Savings 1.99

THANK YOU FOR SHOPPING AT GREENWOODS'
Independent books for independent minds
****
Have you joined our e-mail list?
Talk with any staff member!

his mind, he grins. Even with his bad ears he can still appreciate the eloquent insults of a furious Cantonese woman in full sail.

His eyes follow the red coat into the bus, along the aisle, all the way to the back.

She falls into the last seat, relieved.

He didn't know me, he doesn't remember.

The bus begins to move. She turns her head to the window and his face is there, inches from hers. He looks into her eyes.

▲ ▲ ▲

FROM THE BUS stop she walks the long block, scuffling through damp yellow leaves, hearing the screech of seagulls in the rising wind. It's past six o'clock, and lights are already on in the three-storey brick building.

"David? I'm home! I shopped."

Hope smells garlic frying. She hands her grocery bags to the tall Chinese man emerging from the kitchen. His black T-shirt bears a fluorescent orange slogan, *You and WHOSE army?* An improvised apron, lacy at the edges, flaps around his knees.

"Did you get my fresh chicken? Oyster sauce? Rice stick?" He checks the bags, kisses her over a bunch of leafy greens.

"Hey, vino," he says, pulling out a bottle of wine. "Good girl. We'll make a cook of you yet."

"You're welcome. Is that my mom's tablecloth you're wearing? How was your exam?"

"Duck soup! Two long essays on torts, but I think I aced them."

"Wish I had your confidence. My worst exam is tomorrow, wills and estates."

"No worries, babe, Big Dave is here to help you. Now outta my way, woman, while I cook. Lady lawyer can't write exam on empty stomach."

Hands on her shoulders, he steers her into the living room with its board-and-brick bookshelf, sagging couch, and two desks. David's desk is pin-neat and organized. The other one is awash in textbooks, a too-high stack of manila filing folders, and a small typewriter.

From the kitchen, steam hisses in the wok and David sings as he cooks, "Pretty woman, don't walk away from mee-ee . . ."

Hope snaps on a gooseneck lamp, lifts a sleeping cat off the ominous-looking pile of books, and rolls a blank sheet into her Corona Portable.

Vancouver. October 27, 1960

Dear Mom,

I saw Freddy today.

He was at a bus stop in Chinatown, near Su Li's old place. At first I wasn't sure it was him. His hair is grey, and he's so thin. He looks sick. I think he recognized me.

TWO: On Dieppe Road

Edmonton, December 1924

THE LAST HOUSE ON DIEPPE ROAD is a grey stucco two-storey, identical to all the others but separated from them by an empty lot. It sits apart, as though it had fallen off one of the passing trains.

In the early morning, men in striped overalls walk the tracks toward the rail yards, carrying their lunches in black tin pails. Egg sandwiches, oatmeal cookies, a Thermos of sweet tea.

The mornings are filled with the shunting of big steam engines back and forth along the tracks. The shrill whistle of trains and the rumble of their passage goes on day and night, so the people of Dieppe Road no longer notice it, in the same way they no longer feel the shaking and quaking of their houses, until some china knick-knack, souvenir of the Calgary Stampede, goes crashing to the floor.

The smell of coal smoke lingers in the Monday wash, in bedsheets and towels, in the best Sunday tablecloth hung out to dry. After dark, cinders along the tracks wink red in the night, their small glow pulsing briefly as they cool.

In this house, in the early hours of Christmas morning 1924, Frederick McKee is born. Doctors don't make house calls on Dieppe Road, and the midwife has seldom seen a scrawnier infant, nor a noisier one. His squalling is feeble, but it's persistent.

"Poor scrap, you wouldn't even make a good roasting chicken," she mutters as she swaddles him in a torn sheet, restraining tiny fists and spindly legs so he lies in the clothesbasket like a flannel-wrapped sausage, howling.

Gradually, the howls grow weaker. At the other end of Christmas Day, when most of Edmonton is sitting down to roast turkey and mince pie, the midwife hustles through falling snow to hammer at a certain door.

The parish priest answers her insistent knocking. A warm odour of goose grease issues from his black gown, and the midwife can smell fresh coffee. Her stomach rumbles.

"I wouldn't be bothering you, Father, if not for the infant," she wheedles in the obsequious tone reserved for priests, landlords, and bill collectors. "Not with you being so busy, and it being Christmas and all. It's only that the infant needs baptizing. He's puny, and neither he nor his ma will last the night. You're needed, Father."

Her words float over her shoulder, almost inaudible to the fat priest trudging behind her through the drifted snow of Dieppe Road.

"The baby's ma. She's in a bad way."

Even as he administers the last rites, and well before young Freddy has a chance to identify his mother's touch or smell or voice, she gives a small sigh and quietly dies. She's not quite twenty-six. Freddy had been her seventh child.

▲　　▲　　▲

THE BOY'S FATHER is not a railway man. He's a peddler, a smooth talker selling brushes and cleaning products out of an old brown suitcase. This venture takes him away from home as often as possible, away from Edmonton and Dieppe Road and his miserable brood of brats. It takes him through the back doors of other men's houses, into their kitchens, and on the odd lucky occasion into their bedrooms.

Louis McKee didn't like children. Each time another little McKee appeared in the household he took it as one more misfortune. His wife's untimely death while giving birth to her last child on a Christmas morning is a final burden laid upon him by an apparently vengeful God. He ignores his brood of unruly and unkempt children, and the neighbours are right when they tell one another that the McKee tribe lives on the sharp edge of squalour.

Now and then, when things get too much out of hand, Father Francis calls a social worker.

The older siblings administer a kind of custodial care, tolerating the little boy as they might tolerate a stray pup who wanders in and stubbornly refuses to leave. Still, it's soon clear to everyone, including the priest, that if young Freddy McKee is to survive, he'll have to be a fighter.

The winter Freddy turned six, a new neighbour moved in next door. Her house sat on the far side of the double lot. A garden sprawled across the empty space between the backyards, further separated by giant spruce trees and an overgrown caragana hedge that billowed out in all directions, a haven for bees in summer and sparrows in winter.

Serena Hume, a woman in her late forties, had short curly hair the colour of steel wool, eyes dark as maple buds, and a face deeply lined from the sun and wind of central Alberta, for gardening was her passion. Winter and summer, her daily uniform was a pair of long overalls and a man's plaid shirt. Though he'd been gone for thirteen years, she'd never been able to discard her late husband's favourite clothes. He and Serena had had no children, so now she was alone.

On the January day when she saw the little boy hanging around her gate with no toque or mittens and nobody visible next door, she invited him to come in and get warm. She gave him a cup of sweet milky tea and a thick slice of bread with butter and brown sugar, and kept him there until she saw that a light had finally appeared in the McKee house.

"Come back any time, Freddy," she called after him. "Any time. Don't forget."

After that, the boy often leaned on her gate, and she'd ask him to come in for a minute and help her with some small project. By the time he was seven, he was staying for supper two or three nights a week, apparently never missed by his own family.

In Serena's tiny kitchen he'd help her make brown sugar sandwiches, and sometimes she'd fry an onion in a big cast-iron pan and dump in a can of mushroom soup while he was delegated to make toast. He'd lay thick slices of bread in the wire camp toaster and, taking one lid off the wood-burning cookstove, he'd turn them carefully, so the yellow flames licked up around the bread and the smell of the browning toast made his mouth water.

The hot soup flowed like pale lava over the toast, and they'd carry their bowls into the crowded living room because the kitchen table was invariably covered with gardening books, seed catalogues, and tin cans full of leggy geraniums waiting for spring.

On those winter nights they'd sit in two overstuffed chairs by Serena's piano with one small lamp burning between them, listening to *The Shadow* on her radio while the wind rattled through the spruce trees. He loved the familiar creepy voice, and those chilling words, *The Shadow knows!*

When Freddy had trouble reading, Serena taught him to unlock the baffling symbols of the alphabet. The day they finished reading *The Adventures of Tom Sawyer* together, she gave him his own copy, and it was inscribed: *To Freddy, from your friend, Serena Hume.* The next book they read was *The Adventures of Huckleberry Finn*, and later she gave him that book too, and others, *The Legends of King Arthur and His Knights, The Merry Adventures of Robin Hood, Treasure Island*, until he had a shelf full of his own books, and his own heroes.

Serena had hundreds of books, stuffed into the assortment of sagging shelves and mismatched cabinets that lined the walls of her small house, floor to ceiling. Her books spilled off end tables, propped up a plant stand, acted as doorstops. Their jackets lent colour to the walls, and they had a certain smell, the slightly musty odour of old paper that Freddy grew to love.

Years later, drawn to second-hand bookshops, he would remember the woman in her book-filled rooms, and the heroes she had given him.

When he is eight, arithmetic confuses him, so Serena gets out her late husband's old cribbage board and teaches him to play.

"Fifteen two, fifteen four, and a pair are six," he yells. They spend many evenings hunkered over the cribbage board. By the time he's nine, Freddy can shuffle and deal cards as though he'd been born with a deck in his hands. He relishes every game she teaches him: gin rummy, penny-ante, honeymoon bridge, two-handed solitaire. He develops a particular talent for poker.

On the best nights Serena plays her mandolin, strumming the steel strings with a pick, singing in her strong contralto,

"'Froggie went a-courtin' and he did ride, uhuh . . .'"

Freddy admires the beautiful beetle-back mandolin with the mother-of-pearl butterfly inlaid on the top, and he loves the delicately tinny sounds she wrings from its eight steel strings as their voices rise together, filling the little house with music, Serena making up her own words when she forgets the original version.

"'Froggie went a-courtin' and he did go
To Miss Mousie's house singin' ho ho ho . . .'"

She taught him to pick out a few chords, and then a few more, and soon he could play "Froggie Went a Courtin'" as well as she could. They began playing duets, the boy strumming on the mandolin and the woman thumping away on the piano, which she played by ear, making up for her lack of technique by holding the loud pedal down throughout the song.

"'Pack up your troubles in your old kit bag . . .'"

"Sing with me, Freddy," she'd say, and they'd sail through the verse together. "'While you've a lucifer to light your fag . . .'"

"What's a fag, Serena? What's a lucifer?"

That spring they raked the newly turned soil in her garden until it was as smooth as fine-ground coffee, and the boy held a stick with twine tied around it while she measured the rows. They planted peas and beans, two seeds by two seeds. "One for us, one for the birds," she explained. When the garden came up, they gloated over the first onions and ruffles of new lettuce.

▲   ▲   ▲

ONE HOT JUNE morning in his tenth summer, Freddy ducked through the hole he'd made in the caragana hedge and found Serena in the garden with a stranger, a man with a different kind of face. Something about his eyes, maybe. He couldn't be sure, but he thought it was the eyes.

"Freddy, this is my friend Mr. Lee."

Serena and Yip Lee wore broad-brimmed straw hats to keep off the sun, and each of them had a hoe. She looked tired. When she wiped the back of her hand across her forehead, it left a streak of mud.

"Mr. Lee is helping with the garden, Freddy."

"Why?"

"Because it's too big for me now."

Freddy stood close to Serena, tugging at her sleeve so she bent low to hear him whisper.

"We don't need him. I'm helping you."

"But you don't have time, Freddy. You have to study for exams."

Man and boy eyed each other in mutual distrust. The boy wriggled back through the hedge and stayed away for a week. When he returned, Serena told him she had a surprise for him.

"Godfrey's pension cheque is burning a hole in my pocket, Freddy."

"Who's Godfrey?"

"He was my husband. He was a soldier, and every month the government sends me his pension money. So let's splurge!"

"What's splurge?"

Serena laughed and rumpled his hair. He didn't mind. He liked the feeling of the woman's hand on his head, and he liked hearing her laugh.

"We'll go out for supper!"

They caught the streetcar south along 101st Street and walked four short blocks along Jasper Avenue.

"Where are we going?" asked the boy, who had never been out for supper anywhere but in Serena's kitchen and wasn't sure what to expect.

"You'll see," she told him.

On the corner by the WW Arcade Hardware, they cut north along 97th Street, into Edmonton's scattered Chinatown. They passed a small confectionery, a grocery store, an herbalist, and a laundry before Serena stopped at a two-storey brick building with *Elite Eats* arched across its front window in big red letters, and *Yip Lee, Prop.* in smaller letters underneath. A fat porcelain Buddha grinned out at them, its face almost lost amid overgrown begonia foliage on the window ledge. Freddy could see people sitting along a counter, hunched over plates.

The restaurant was crowded, noisy, the air a fog of hamburger grease, fried onions, and strong tobacco. Serena led him all the way to the last booth, just outside the kitchen where Chinese waiters rushed back and forth through two swinging doors. She seemed to know them all by name.

A few minutes later, a familiar face appeared at their booth. The man from Serena's garden put a plate in front of Freddy.

"Egg roll," he told Serena. "For the kid."

The boy gazed solemnly up at the Chinese man, fascinated by the length of grey ash quivering at the end of a chewed-looking cigarette.

"Do I eat them?" Freddy asked Serena, looking at three log-shaped pastries still sizzling on the plate.

Yip spoke to him for the first time.

"Yeah, kid. You eat."

"All of them?"

Yip looked thoughtfully at Freddy, taking in the small, thin face, the dark circles under the boy's eyes.

"Sure, kid. You too skinny. Fatten you up, maybe."

Yip hadn't brought him a fork, and he eyed the pair of sharp sticks being wielded by a man in the booth across the aisle.

"How do I eat them?"

"How you think? Use fingers."

The hot oily rolls were filled with things he'd never tasted. "Bean sprouts, bamboo shoots, Chinese cabbage, and ginger," she explained.

"What's the yellow stuff?"

"Plum sauce. Like ketchup."

He bit into the first log and the filling burned his tongue, but Freddy had never eaten anything so delicious. He polished off all three while Serena and Yip smoked roll-your-owns, talking of gardens and plants and the recent rain, which had done wonders for the peas.

After that, Serena and Freddy often went to Yip's, sometimes for Coke floats on a hot afternoon, sometimes to drop off a basket of something from her garden, onions, cabbage, or the funny-looking plants she grew from seed Yip supplied. Sometimes in the early mornings Yip would be in Serena's garden with his straw hat and his hoe, but he always left when Freddy arrived.

"Freddy, just look at these beans! Run and get my tape measure. I'll bet a nickel they're at least eight inches, and Yip says they'll grow twice that long."

The remarkable beans were even longer than predicted.

"Yip calls them dau gok. It means 'long bean.' Good name, don't you think?"

Woman and boy viewed each unfamiliar vegetable as an event for celebration, exulting over size and colour as she recorded the Chinese and English names in a coil-back notebook, jotting culinary use and such cooking tips as she was able to glean from Yip. As the vegetables matured, she sketched them.

Beside a drawing of five large leaves on a single thick stem, the boy read the following entry in Serena's small, neat script.

Saan choi. Plant May 24. Pick July 2. Dark green leaves, rubbery texture. Use in soup with fresh ginger, chicken stock, bean curd. Cooks up slippery. Good laxative.

Daily she consulted the boy on weeding and watering, asked his opinion of this or that. Did he think the tomato stakes would hold if the wind kept up? Should they give the peas a drink? He began to look forward to measuring the length of a bean, or checking the potato leaves for bugs.

Gradually Freddy grew less wary of the Chinese man with the funny name, and a pattern was established for those nights when Serena's pension arrived in the mail. They'd take the streetcar to Elite Eats and head for the back booth. If he'd finished cooking, Yip would be there with a pair of glasses propped on his nose, reading his Chinese newspaper. It fascinated the boy that Yip read from back to front, and the strange symbols were a curiosity. He pointed to one of them.

"Is it a letter or a number?"

"Whole word," Yip told him. "This mean teahouse." He waved his arms around the room. "Teahouse, café, all same thing."

The boy stared at the symbol a long time until he realized that he was looking at a pictograph of a small house, composed of five brush-strokes—one for the floor, two for the walls, two for the roof. Suddenly it made sense to him, and he was excited by his new knowledge.

On these evenings Yip would always bring out three egg rolls with plum sauce, and he and Serena would smoke while the boy ate. Their conversation seldom varied. In summer, the garden; in winter, the weather.

Then Yip would disappear through the double swinging doors and cook his own favourite dishes especially for them. By this time Freddy had mastered chopsticks, and he loved dry-fried chicken, the crisp brown skin dipped in cinnamon-laced salt. Sometimes they ate spicy minced pork wrapped in leaves of Serena's saang choi and a pancake so thin you could see through it. Sometimes there'd be a whole fish, steamed with green onion and ginger, bathed in rice wine and soy sauce, the fish sizzling in its broth. On those nights, Yip would sit with them, cautioning the boy to remove the backbone without turning the fish over because if that happened, a fishing boat somewhere in the China Sea would capsize and he'd have the whole drowned crew on his conscience.

A picture behind Yip's counter, beside the operating certificate for Elite Eats, showed Yip in a dark suit, sitting stiffly in a chair, with a woman beside him. Freddy thought she was pretty, in a stern way. Her black hair was pulled tight against her head, and earrings dangled nearly to her shoulder. Her dress had a high collar that stood up under her jaw line. Behind Yip, a tall girl with fuzzy hair and two smaller girls. Nobody was smiling, not even the little one with the big hair bow. Freddy didn't ask about the woman or the girls.

Photographer Wing Soon had suggested the family portrait, and Yip wrote to his wife, instructing her to have a picture taken exactly the way Soon described. She was to wear her best cheongsam, the black one he liked so much. He had been back to China three times in fifteen years, and his wife had produced three females. Bad luck. The last one, born after his last visit five years ago, he'd never seen. Still, they were a family, and they were his.

"You must place an empty chair beside you," he'd written to his wife. "It must be a good chair, of carved rosewood. Your daughters must be arranged like the half moon, around the empty chair."

So on the following Monday morning Yip put on his white shirt, carefully knotted his only tie, brushed the jacket of his only suit with a clothes brush. It was a good-looking suit, dark blue with a fine red pinstripe. He'd found it in Eaton's bargain basement when he first arrived in this country, full of youthful dreams, and he was happy to have a reason to wear it. He felt good in this suit. Successful. There was a spring in his step as he walked the three blocks to Soon's small Chinatown studio to have his picture taken.

Yip sat bolt upright on a kitchen chair, staring poker-faced at the camera while Soon huddled under the dark cloth draped over his head. Suddenly a blinding flash, and all Yip could see were blue and white spots.

Four months later, the photograph of Yip's wife and daughters arrived from China, and it was exactly as Yip had instructed. Mr. Soon cut, pasted, carefully retouched, and two days later, there they were: Yip Lee and family looking prosperous and united, with Yip seated beside his wife, surrounded by his three daughters. Only an expert could tell that Yip's image had been cut out with a razor blade and pasted into the good rosewood chair. Mr. Soon was a master of his craft.

THREE : Rumours of War
Edmonton, November 1935

IN THE WINTER OF FREDDY'S eleventh birthday, an ex-house-painter with a funny moustache began making political speeches in the beer halls of Germany. Adolph Hitler's book, *Mein Kampf*, had already been translated into English, disturbing the sleep of thoughtful people in several countries.

"What does that mean?" Freddy asked when he found Serena reading the book for the third evening in a row.

"In German, it means 'My struggle.'"

"You can read German?"

"It was my first language." She showed him the book full of incomprehensible words, and he saw that she'd almost finished it.

"Are you a German?"

"My parents were from Munich. So is Adolph Hitler, the man who wrote this book."

For Freddy, most books had only two important characters: the good guy and the bad guy. All others he considered window dressing.

"Is he the good guy?"

"He's the bad guy, but it doesn't seem to matter."

"How come, if he's bad?"

"He tells the German people things they want to hear. Things they want to believe."

She put the book down and rubbed her eyes.

Serena tells the boy to get her atlas, she'll show him something, so he fishes the heavy green book down from a shelf, enjoying the feel of the leather binding, rough and cool under his fingers. Together they read the names of countries he didn't know existed, cities he's never heard of. They look up Germany, Poland, Czechoslovakia. The

15

vast space with the long name, the Union of Soviet Socialist Republics, and a patchwork of countries she calls the Balkans. The names of their cities are like a foreign language, and he whispers new words to himself, searching for those that begin with B.

"Belgrade, Bucharest, Berlin, Budapest, Bratis . . ."

"Bratislava."

"It's kind of like a game, isn't it, Serena? War, I mean."

"Some people think so. Except for the Poles. The poor Poles won't think it's a game."

She watches the boy as he bends his head over the atlas, searching for new cities, new worlds.

"And the Jews," she says thoughtfully. "God only knows what'll happen to the Jews."

▲　　▲　　▲

FOR FREDDY AND his friends, war is a game they never tire of playing. Billy Sanderson, Siggy Helfritz, Bucky Girard, they all have fathers or uncles who fought in the last war. Mikey Prochuk's older brother, Johnny, is in the army right now.

The boys see the possibility of another war in some comfortably distant future as one of their rites of passage, like driving a car or getting drunk, or feeling up their first girl. The idea of wearing a uniform excites them too. The next war will be theirs, they tell each other. Their turn to show everybody in the whole world exactly who's boss.

Wars were the only parts of social studies that didn't bore them half to death. On Remembrance Day, after reciting "In Flanders' Fields" in the gym and standing still through the interminable two-minute silence between "The Last Post" and "Reveille," during which Freddy giggled nervously and got his ear yanked by a teacher, they headed for the vacant lot behind the school to play their favourite game.

There among the leafless poplars they spend hours planning imaginary campaigns, shooting each other with imaginary guns, stabbing each other with imaginary bayonets.

They draw straws to see who gets to wear Mikey Prochuk's brother's

16

steel helmet and be the general, and Freddy often wins. They are an uneven number, so he commands both armies and acts as referee.

The battle rages until, accepting his wound (staggering, groaning, clutching his chest), the boy whose turn it is to die that day expires magnificently at the feet of both armies. Then they all go home for supper.

△　　△　　△

NOW SERENA ASKS the boy to stand on a chair and hand down the framed medals. The ones her husband, Godfrey Hume, won in his war. The boy has admired them, hanging there in solemn procession, pinned on black velvet that has begun to sag with the passage of time and their own weight.

"That's how Godfrey's mandolin got broken, you know. He had it with him in the trenches, and somehow it broke. See? Right here."

Tenderly she runs her fingers over the glued scar on the neck of the instrument, remembers opening the trunk that was returned to her after Godfrey's war had ended. Long, long after the telegram.

She turns her attention back to the medals. Five of them, each one suspended from a striped ribbon, each ribbon's stripes in different colours.

"The battle of Passchendaele," she says, tapping the glass over a round medal with a red ribbon on top. It's as though she's forgotten the boy, forgotten that he's in the room.

"Did he win?"

"Win what?"

"The battle. At that place you said. Pash-something."

"They won the battle, but Godfrey was wounded. At least, we think that's what happened. When the battle was over, nobody could find him."

"So what did they do? Did they go home without him or what?"

The possibility that fellow soldiers might abandon a wounded buddy in the field seems monstrous to the boy. His heart beats faster, he hears the sound and fury of battle raging around his ears, smells the smoke, hears the cries of the wounded. He sees himself leaping out of a trench, plunging bravely through the mud of no man's land to rescue Bucky or Siggy.

"Did they go back and get him after the battle?"

Serena lifts a cigar box off the top of the piano. Inside is a thin stack of pale blue papers tied together with garden twine. "Godfrey's letters," she says. She undoes the twine, selects a letter, unfolds it carefully, as she has so many times. The writing is small, without separate paragraphs, but the boy has no trouble reading it.

Belgium, Oct. 14/17

My Dearest Serena, Your parcel arrived, thanks for the socks. The trenches are cold, and warm socks feel good. By now the garden will be finished. I wonder how you managed with the potatoes, how many bags you got. Wish I'd been there to help. Be sure you clean the spade before you put it away for the winter. We're camped near a farm, and yesterday a woman gave us some cheese and a loaf of fresh bread. It was still warm. It reminded me of home, and you. The weather stays cold and wet, with rain every day and mud up to our ears. Sometimes I wish the rain would just wash this whole place into the ocean. Surely it must end soon and I'll be home again. Take care my dearest wife.

With love, Godfrey

"That was Godfrey's last letter," she tells the boy.

"But who told you about that fight, the one where he gets wounded?"

She hands him a thin yellow envelope with a see-through paper window. The telegram is dated Feb. 23, 1918.

From: Adjutant, 29th (Vancouver) Battalion
To: Mrs. Godfrey Hume, Lethbridge, Alberta, Canada
Corporal GODFREY HUME missing in action. Presumed killed.
J. Franklin Cobb, Major. A/Adjutant, 29th (Vancouver) Battalion

"I made quite a stink because nobody would tell me anything more about what happened to Godfrey. He was just missing, presumed killed, that was all they'd say. But I was his wife, I needed to know. So I made a fuss. I wrote to everybody I could think of. The premier, the Governor General. I even wrote to the prime minister. After that the army got the wind up. Sometimes, that's what you have to do, Freddy. Make a fuss."

There is another letter, on thin blue paper folded into the shape of an envelope.

Edinburgh, Scotland
Feb. 7, 1918.
Dear Mrs. Hume,

I am writing to express my sympathy on account of the loss of your husband, Corporal Godfrey A. Hume, who was a Lewis gunner in my platoon and was with me at Passchendaele, in which battle he was officially reported as missing, believed killed.

About 6:00 PM on Nov. 6th, the day the Canadians took Passchendaele, he went to visit another part of the trenches to get some equipment. I did not see him again.

We searched all the trenches in the vicinity, but he was not among our dead. There is not the remotest chance of your husband having been taken prisoner because the firing was so heavy from both sides. His body was most probably buried by flying debris during the shelling.

Corporal Hume was a brave soldier, liked and respected by the entire company. You must take comfort in the fact that he died for King and Country, which is what we're all fighting for.

Yours truly, J.R. Hamilton, Lieutenant, #7 platoon, 29th Batt.

P.S. His mandolin, which was in our trench when he left, is being forwarded to you.

"Wow."

It's all he can think of to say, but the boy feels again that ripple of excitement, like a moth fluttering somewhere under his ribs. He sees the trenches in the smoky half-light of battle, hears the shellfire, *rattattatt, kaboom*! Smells the cordite. He wants to find some of the guys in the neighbourhood, Bucky or Siggy, to play war. He wants them to know about this, but something in the woman's face stops him.

"What does 'take comfort' mean?" he asks because she seems so far away and he wants to bring her back.

"It means I was supposed to feel good because my husband died. For King and Country."

"Did you feel good?"

Serena takes a deep breath, more like a sigh.

"No, Freddy. I hated it. I still hate it."

The boy thinks about the soldier he's never seen and wonders what he was like, this man she had married, this hero adventurer.

"I guess you missed him a lot?"

"Yes, Freddy. I still miss him."

▲   ▲   ▲

TWICE DURING THE following year, Serena disappears into Grey Nuns Hospital. Once she stays for a week, and the second time she's gone nearly a month. Freddy and Yip visit her, take her grapes and Crispy Crunch bars, but Freddy hates the hospital smells, hates seeing her like that, a plastic tent over her head so she can breathe, her face so pale and tired, her voice so weak. It scares him more than anything has ever scared him before.

When she comes home, the three of them return to the garden on those days when she feels well enough. Yip shows Freddy how to brew a special tea with herbs and roots, "for strength," he says.

She sips it and says she feels better, much better. A little stronger every day, she says. They talk of entering their biggest cabbage in the horticultural show at the Edmonton Exhibition, but as July draws to a close she loses more weight and her skin takes on a strange yellow pallor. The garden is forgotten. She is too tired now to play cards or thump on the piano.

One October night when the boy slips through the hedge, he finds her asleep in her chair and he can't wake her. The mandolin that belonged to her husband is in her lap, as though she's been playing it and nodded off in mid-song.

"Froggie went a-courtin and he . . ."

Yip and the boy go together to St. Joseph's Church, Yip in his blue pinstriped suit, the boy in a white shirt and striped tie that Yip has found for him at the Salvation Army Thrift Store.

"Have to show respect, kid."

They sit in the back of the church, in the very last pew, well apart from the handful of mourners, people they don't know. Father Francis mumbles through a short eulogy.

"Serena Hildegard Hume, nee Steinberg . . ."

The priest drones on about the forgiveness of sins, the resurrection of the body and life everlasting, but the boy has stopped listening.

"Froggie went a courtin' and he . . ."

After the funeral, Father Francis bends over the boy, muttering condolences. The priest's breath smells sourly of sacramental wine, and Freddy notices grease spatters on the front of his robe.

Later that night, a tall woman knocks on the McKees' door and the boy answers it. She's holding the mandolin.

"Are you Freddy McKee? Aunt Serena left a note, that you were to have this."

The woman seems uncertain.

"I don't suppose you want it," she says. "It's not worth anything."

Freddy holds out both hands.

FOUR: At the Elite
Edmonton, April 1938

SERENA HAD REPLACED THE MOTHER Freddy never knew. Her songs became his songs, her house had been his home, in ways that his own joyless house had never been.

For Yip, Serena had been the only female in his world of men, the soft-spoken, feminine yin, essential balance to the yang of his masculine nature. They had shared a strange friendship over Serena's garden, and he'd cherished those mornings with her as he had their occasional evenings over supper in the back booth. As he now cherished her garden sketch book.

It arrived by special delivery mail, addressed in her own hand, as though she hadn't trusted the grieving relatives to pass it along. He couldn't read the fine English script, but the drawings were delicate and lovely. He wrapped the book in a large piece of red silk and put it in his trunk where he kept papers of great importance. It was there now, along with the letters from his Chinese wife, one for every year of his sojourn in this country.

Of course he had never so much as touched Serena's hand. Not possible. She was a white woman.

There was a female, one who lived in a seedy rooming house in the north end of town. Humiliating, his occasional visits to the pockmarked woman who was always half drunk.

Hell, I don't mind chinks. Their money's as good as a white guy's, eh? They're all the same in the dark, eh?

But in her own way Serena had been like the good Chinese wife in a long marriage. Friend, adviser, companion. She had replaced the woman in his family picture, and she had brought him Freddy, a surrogate son.

A month after her death, without saying goodbye to anybody in his family, Freddie walked away from the house on Dieppe Road. The day he packed up his things, nobody asked about the cardboard box in the hall. If he was missed, it wasn't mentioned.

Freddy moved into a small room above Yip's café, where he kept everything he owned: a few clothes, his modest collection of men's magazines, his books. Serena's mandolin.

He often touched the worn spot on the top where her fingers, flying lightly over the wood for so many years, had worn away the shiny finish. It helped him remember her voice, the warmth of her messy kitchen, the lines in her face when she smiled. Then he'd lean back on the cot, picking out melodies on the eight steel strings, singing to himself, "Froggie went a courtin'. . ."

Now and then he played it in the kitchen, late at night after the restaurant closed. Yip and the other guys liked his music, and sometimes the old men from upstairs, the ones who never talked, would come down and sit on the stairs to listen, smiling wordlessly.

He spent his days in school and his evenings doing homework in the back booth of Elite Eats. Sometime around midnight, after the last customer wandered out the door, he'd join the waiters at the big round table.

▲   ▲   ▲

STANDING OVER THE stove, Yip begins to cook. The stale fog of hamburger grease recedes, eclipsed by the whoosh of yellow flame and billowing steam, lost in the sweeter smells of garlic and ginger, five spice and hoisin sauce.

At the table the men break into Cantonese, the language of their birth, and the boy loves to hear their rapid chatter with its risings and fallings and sudden shouts and barks. He learns a few words, and a few more, and gradually acquires enough of the language to be included in their circle.

He'd have been surprised to know that he speaks with the recognizable accent and peculiar slang of a place he's never been and knows nothing about: the back streets of Hong Kong.

He also develops a lifelong disdain for pidgin English as spoken by a few smartass white guys who hang around the Elite.

"Hey, Yip, you makee chow mein! Two orders, chop chop!"

The boy wants to smash them in their fat, self-satisfied faces, but Yip won't let him.

"Better not," he counsels. "Just make more trouble. Man who seeks revenge digs two graves."

"Oh yeah? Who says?"

"Old Chinese proverb."

On weekends, he works in Yip's kitchen, washing dishes, running errands. He learns to cook. Without Serena's garden, the Chinese vegetables have to come from the Thousand Year Trading Company on 96th Street, and it's Freddy's job to pick them up and check the contents of the cardboard boxes with the Chinese writing to be sure nothing is rotten or too wilted to use. The vegetables come all the way from Vancouver, and Freddy quickly learns to call them by name: gai lan, gai choy, bok choy, een choy. He deals with problems in his limited Cantonese, trading insults with the stock boy but using terms of respect with old Mr. Sung, the wizened owner of the Thousand Year.

An ever-changing assortment of Chinese men have rooms above Yip's café. They're from Hong Kong or Vancouver, and he gets along well with the young ones. The others, old and locked within the silence of a different language, keep to themselves.

"Yip, why don't the old guys ever talk?"

"They're from Mainland. They don't understand us."

"Why not?"

"Some talk Mandarin. Some, Shanghainese. We talk Cantonese. Little bit different."

"But it's still Chinese, right?"

"Different sound. Same word, different sound. Maybe speak, maybe get it wrong. Better say nothing."

Freddy spent that cold Edmonton winter in the bright warmth of the Elite's kitchen, joking with the Chinese waiters who came and went, some staying a month or two, some a little longer, for they were a nomadic population.

He preferred the vast, steaming platters of stir-fried noodles Yip made for the kitchen to the greasy hamburgers they peddled out front. Sometimes Yip bought fresh pickerel from an Indian boy who came to the back door, and they steamed it whole with ginger and onions and a little soy sauce. Freddy was as careful as the rest of them about never turning the fish over.

There were no Chinese women in Yip's kitchen, and only one waitress, the pudding-faced Zena Klemchuk, a large, compliant girl of sixteen who occasionally accompanied Freddy upstairs after her shift. There on Freddy's narrow cot they shared a lusty hunger for each other's bodies. They giggled, wrestled, fell off the bed laughing, shushed each other for fear of rousing the old guys on the other side of the walls. Neither of them would have said they were in love, and beyond the definitive pleasure of burying himself in Zena's willing flesh, he knew nothing else about her.

He enjoyed the coarse humour of the Chinese men who came in the back door and sat smoking at the table late into the night. Freddy spent the Christmas Eve of his sixteenth birthday with them, gambling and getting drunk on Chinese wine, betting on anything and everything, including how long it would take a live soup turtle to make its way across the kitchen floor.

Happy birthday, kid, they said when he won the pot around 5:00 AM. May you live a thousand years, kid. Merry Christmas.

And so the winter passed.

▲　　▲　　▲

ONE APRIL NIGHT with a smell of spring in the air, Zena had news for Freddy.

"I'm pregnant."

"You're what?"

"Pregnant! I'm gonna have a kid! We have to get married, Fred. Or my dad will kill me. He'll definitely kill you!"

Freddy was dumbfounded. He looked around his little box of a room with its few treasures, a place he'd come to think of as home, and wondered where and how he was supposed to fit a pregnant Zena into his life, let alone a child.

On that day Freddy could have turned tail and run. Zena wouldn't have been surprised. She almost expected it. But there was something in Freddy McKee that wouldn't let him run. Bewildered though he was, he agreed that they should marry.

Zena's mother had finally extracted the truth when she could no longer ignore her daughter's expanding waistline. The woman had hidden her face in her apron and sobbed, fearing the unholy wrath that would be visited upon both their heads when her husband, big Mike Klemchuk, found out.

Freddy hadn't confided in Yip because he didn't know how to explain a thing like this to the Chinese man who had befriended him. Besides, nothing would really change, would it? Not right away. They'd have a few months to figure things out.

The wedding was set for four o'clock on a Friday at City Hall. Zena's pink dress, already a smidge too tight, matched a small pink hat from her sister's closet. She carried no flowers; hadn't thought of them, nor had Freddy. There were no guests, and as Freddy and Zena had nothing to talk about, they sat in silence, Zena chewing contentedly on a stick of Juicy Fruit gum, Freddy listening to the monotonous tick-tock of a big wall clock.

At ten minutes past four, a clerk waved them into the office, impatiently indicating where they were to stand. He would act as witness, and there was a secretary as second witness. It meant an extra dollar in her pocket.

The justice of the peace, shirtsleeves rolled above the elbows and glasses on his forehead, gave the couple a swift glance, no more than that. He adjusted his glasses, fumbled through the brief civil ceremony of marriage, and closed the book with a snap. He was a busy man.

In the brief silence that followed, he looked up and seemed surprised to see them still standing there—two wet-behind-the-ears kids, a boy who could barely count his own toes and a knocked-up girl, if he was any judge of these things. Really, what was the point? He looked at his watch.

It was Freddy who broke the silence.

"Is that it?"

"That's it. Just sign the register and you're done."

"So do I kiss the bride or what?"

"If you want. She's all yours now, you can do what you like."

The clerk stood by the door, hand on the light switch.

The whole thing had taken less than ten minutes.

▲　　▲　　▲

THE ALBERTA HOTEL was a turreted red brick building on the wrong end of Jasper Avenue. The bored clerk shoved a key across the desk without looking at them.

"Top of the stairs, third door on the right."

They stood awkwardly in the small, overheated room.

"Jeez, it's hot in here. I'll open the window."

Freddy struggled with it, but the lock had been painted shut.

Just as he turned to tell Zena he couldn't budge it, there was a noise in the hall: a man's voice, yelling. The door burst open. Freddy had a brief impression of the desk clerk, pale-faced and terrified, key in hand, as a huge bald man launched himself across the bed, howling in rage. Freddy, younger and leaner, sidestepped his initial lunge.

Mike the Mauler Klemchuk, whose wife had foolishly confided in Zena's older sister, who had immediately snitched to her father, was already half drunk when he heard the news of his second daughter's secret nuptials. Pausing only to punch his wife and knock her halfway across the kitchen, he headed for the Alberta Hotel.

Mike considered himself a fair-minded man, and when he was sober that might have been true. But as an immigrant who found himself on the low rung of society's ladder, he had discovered somebody even lower. It was the Chinese that held Mike's disdain. He'd been against Zena's working for those chinks in the first place. So what happened the minute his back was turned? She'd met some pasty-faced nobody, not even a Ukrainian, and got herself knocked up. Stupid cow!

A new possibility hit him. Christ, what if the baby turned out to be half chink? Mike's face purpled with rage.

"C'mere, you snotnose little pipsqueak! You're the little turd that hangs out with them chinks! I'm gonna beat the crap outta you!"

He lunged again, and once more Freddy sidestepped, but this time he tripped over Zena's suitcase. Sprawled full-length on the floor, he felt the breath leave his body as Mike landed on top of him. Zena screamed and continued letting out shrill squeals and squeaks as a crowd gathered in the hallway and two city policemen in blue uniforms, summoned by the terrified desk clerk, arrived on the scene.

With some difficulty they hauled the two apart, for by this time Freddy was defending himself and getting in the odd punch.

The cops told Freddy to shut up and let Mike's motor cool a little.

Finding that he had the floor and an attentive audience, Mike's oration took a self-righteous turn, reminiscent of a priest he'd once heard. Was he not the wronged father of this child? This innocent flower? God help him, she had brought disgrace on his family. Disgrace! His fists pummelled the air above his head for emphasis.

This marriage wasn't legal in the Church or before God, he bellowed. It would be ended. What was the word? Annulled. Zena would marry a good Ukrainian Catholic from the old country, a man who would keep his stupid cow of a daughter in line, just the way he, Mike Klemchuk, kept her mother.

Distracted by Mike's lengthy speech and the soap opera unfolding before him, the cop who had been restraining Freddy loosened his hold. Freddy looked at Zena, who gaped at her father.

"Zena?" Freddy touched her lightly on the arm.

She looked up at him and smiled.

"'Bye, Freddy," she said, and it didn't sound like she was heartbroken.

Freddy turned and walked out of the room, and nobody made a move to stop him. He trotted along the threadbare carpet, past a dusty brass spitoon, down the stairs two at a time, gathering speed as he headed out the door and into a street that was slushy with the melting snow of Edmonton's reluctant spring. Crossing Jasper Avenue, he began to run. He ran until his feet were soaked, his pant legs wet halfway up. Ran until his breath came in short gasps.

When he turned into the army recruiting office, open late on a Friday, it was partly because he was out of breath and couldn't run any farther.

"How old are you, son?"

"Eighteen," he lies.

On the application form, under next of kin, he writes Yip Lee.

The recruiting officer watches the skinny kid sign the document.

"Welcome to the Winnipeg Grenadiers, son."

"But this is Edmonton," protests Freddy.

"That's what trains are for," says the officer. "They move recruits around. You're a Grenadier. You're going to Camp Shilo, in Manitoba. Tonight."

Lights were coming on in the shops along Jasper Avenue, and the air smelled of melting snow and poplar sap. It was the hour when people headed into cafés for an early supper. Through the briefly opened door of a restaurant called The Silk Hat, he heard laughter and smelled meat cooking on a grill.

Freddy realized that he was hungry. Maybe Yip would make egg rolls, or fry a fish. He crossed the street again, heading north. When he passed a shop with a basket of yellow daffodils glowing in the window, a feeling washed over him, a lightness of spirit that comes with spring in such northern places. Private Freddy McKee felt terrific.

Two months later, Zena sent him some legal documents, care of Yip Lee, who had them forwarded to Freddy at Camp Shilo. With the cooperation of a priest and a well-greased palm, the marriage had been speedily annulled. She enclosed a note, telling him she had remarried, this time to her father's friend, Yaroslav Shepko. She hoped he, Freddy, would find someone else and have a happy life.

She didn't mention the baby.

He never heard from her, or of her, again.

FIVE: The Battalion
Camp Shilo, August 1941

THE BATTALION KNOWN AS the Winnipeg Grenadiers was an odd mixture. The men came from all over the prairies, and a lot of them didn't fit the usual military profile. Some were too young to be soldiers. Others were too old. Some were too short, or a little on the heavy side, or they wore glasses or had some other flaw, like flat feet or poor hearing. One man stuttered so badly nobody could understand him. Officially, the regiment was described as unfit for active duty. They would be shipped off to Jamaica for garrison duty, then shuttled back to Canada, under-equipped and ill-prepared to fight a war.

But army life suited Freddy. Although he was the youngest guy in his unit, he was nearly six feet tall, with broad shoulders and the dark good looks of his French-Canadian mother. He soon made two close friends.

One was Antonio Cecci, known as Tony. Born and raised in Winnipeg's north end, he was twenty-two, bright, single, the first Cecci ever to attend university, where he'd been studying law.

"The old man was so proud, he nearly popped his buttons," he told them.

Unfortunately for Papa Cecci, Tony majored in women and poker and had such a good time that he failed most of his exams. His father raged about his laziness, his ingratitude, his total lack of ambition, so one day Tony just dropped out and joined the army, mostly to get back at the old man. His law career could wait. It would have to, wouldn't it?

Meanwhile, the army was a good a place to hone his social skills. The uniform boosted his success with the ladies, and his escapades with women and cards were soon legendary in camp.

Freddy's other friend was Michael Keegan, who everybody called

Mick. What you noticed first about Mick were his eyes. They were so blue it was like they'd been painted. A quiet man of twenty-three, he admitted that he read a lot, a pastime Tony and Freddy found distinctly odd, but he was such a good guy that they forgave him his bookish habits.

Michael Keegan had come to the war by accident, through the simple need for a job and a paycheque. At nineteen, an apprentice carpenter, he'd married his childhood sweetheart. They ended up in northern Manitoba, in a place called Trout Creek, where he had a summer construction job in a lumber camp. By the time the job dried up, he had fallen in love with the great expanse of lakes and forest. He loved the solitary beauty of the long winters, the shining quality of the mornings, and there was a simplicity to his days that felt right. Mick often talked about his wife, Joanna, and the child he'd named Hope, and the house he'd built for them out of two old railcars and a caboose.

So Mick had stayed on in Trout Creek, doing freelance carpentry when he had a chance and guiding rich Americans who came north to hunt.

"They get off the train with these big fancy shotguns, but they can't hit the broad side of a barn."

Given a choice, Mick would have stayed in his northern woods with his wife and daughter, and the smell of spruce gum on his hands, but the army had been his route to a steady income. He never intended it to be more than that.

Of the three, Mick was the quietest, a situation the other two attributed to marriage and advanced age, but they were determined to reform him during their off-duty hours.

Most nights they sat in the servicemen's club run by a local ladies' auxiliary, where a clutch of motherly women kept them supplied with coffee, cake, and canasta partners.

"So what do you do for fun, up there in Fish River?" Tony asked Mick.

"Trout Creek," corrected Mick, but Tony had lost interest as a tall, gorgeous brunette in high-heeled sandals undulated across the empty dance floor, hips swaying, breasts bouncing under a too-tight sweater.

The cloud of Shalimar in her wake made Freddy wonder whether this is what jungle flowers smelled like.

"Jeez, where'd she come from?" Freddy asked, poking Tony in the ribs.

"Sweet Lord, a goddess! Pretty mama, come to Tony," and he was off like a bloodhound on a hot trail, falling into step beside her, slipping an arm around her waist, whispering in her ear. She giggled and swatted the hand that had quickly moved from her waist to her well-rounded bottom.

"Mercy," he cried, and they disappeared into the night.

One of the motherly women brought Freddy and Mick more coffee, and Mick took an envelope out of his pocket.

"These are my girls," he said. In the picture, a young woman stood beside a decorated Christmas tree, hugging a little girl. The woman had a mass of dark curly hair that overwhelmed her face. She was pretty in a fine-boned way, though Freddy thought she could have used a few more pounds. The snapshot was slightly out of focus, and the kid's eyes were squeezed shut, as though she hadn't wanted her picture taken.

"That's my Joanna, and that's Hope, our baby."

"Cute," he said. "Nice girls, Mick. You're a lucky guy."

Mick traced their outline with a gentle finger.

"Yeah, they're a sweet pair, and my little Hope, she's so . . . well, I miss her," he said. "I miss both of them. I thought . . ."

"Thought what?"

"I thought I'd be back home by now. I never expected it would get this far." His voice had gone hoarse, and he cleared his throat.

"You got anybody, Freddy? Some pretty girl stashed away in Edmonchuk?"

Freddy grinned and shook his head.

"Naw. Nobody special."

Briefly, an image of Zena flitted through his mind. It would have felt good to have somebody, somewhere, to miss him. Somebody to write to him and send him snapshots. Freddy wasn't exactly lonely, but it occurred to him that he was sure as hell alone.

SIX : Basic Training

A BALD MAN STANDS BY a London window, a cigar between his teeth. He watches the rain-slicked pavement and mutters, thinking out loud.

"I cannot ask the British people to commit one more man to Hong Kong. But the Japanese will invade it, and soon. Without reinforcements, the island is certain to fall."

Puffs on his cigar. Reflects, still muttering. Musing.

"Who in the Commonwealth would support a hopeless cause?"

"For the island will surely fall in any case."

A fog of smoke wreaths his bald head as he drums impatiently on the polished window casing. "What to do? Where to turn?"

"The Anzacs? No. They suffered such heavy losses in Crete, and now both New Zealand and Australia are under threat from the Japanese on the homefront."

Who else? The Canadians! Of course. Good people, but such a small population. Still, no possibility of invasion there. A battalion or two from Canada . . . He walks to the desk, rests the cigar in an overflowing ashtray, and reaches for the red telephone.

▲   ▲   ▲

FREDDY HATES BAYONET practice. It has a bizarre quality that bothers him on some deeper level he can't quite define.

They start by sticking hay bales, and move up to more realistic targets. The drill sergeant stuffs an old German uniform with hay and they charge the dummy, running at it with their rifles, stabbing awkwardly, struggling with the unfamiliar weight of the Lee-Enfields held at waist level. The sergeant is a leftover from the last war, an old soldier from the British army who considers humiliation of the young and vulnerable to be part of his duty, and bullying to be his most effective training tool. He refers to them as lads, or ladies, or pansies.

"You-lot are all pansies," he bellows. "It turns my stomach, just looking at you!" Big sigh, disgusted muttering.

"Well, ladies, let's see what you can do! Thrust, twist, withdraw," he bellows. "Thrust, twist, withdraw!"

There's a guy in their barracks named Walter Candas. Private Candas is a skinny farm boy from some place south of Brandon. Like Freddy, he's young, but he's also nearsighted and painfully shy, with a severe stutter. Inevitably and soon, he becomes Candyass, which evolves into C-c-c-candyass. In the eyes of the drill sergeant, he has no redeeming qualities.

"C'mon, C-c-c-candyass! Get your back into it!

"Thrust! Withdraw! Thrust! Withdraw! It's just like screwing. But you wouldn't know about that, would you, Candyass? Answer me when I speak to you! Would you know about that, Candyass? Or is it Pansy-ass?"

"N-n-no! I m-m-mean y-yes . . ."

The boy's face turns scarlet, and the stutter grows worse.

One night Candas goes AWOL. Days pass, he doesn't come back. A rumour makes the rounds: he's been found face down in a slough three miles from camp, but Candas was a loner and nobody knows for sure. The drill sergeant finds a new victim, and Freddy begins to wonder what it would be like if the stuffing in the uniform was a man instead of a hay bale.

"What do you figure it feels like to kill a man?" he asked Mick, who sat shirtless in the autumn sun, polishing the barrel of his Lee-Enfield.

"Just aim and squeeze that trigger," Mick told him, hoisting the rifle and sighting down the barrel. "No different than killing a moose," he said. "Just like when you get your moose in the fall."

He looked at Freddy.

"You've been hunting? You must have shot something, sometime?"

"Oh, sure," Freddy replied. "Mostly birds. Geese."

▲   ▲   ▲

AN OCTOBER MORNING of his tenth year, two days before Thanksgiving: Freddy's dad has taken him along on the only father-and-son outing of their lives, a goose shoot. It's still dark as they drive south of the city in the old Dodge, one of his father's pals in the front seat. When they get out of the car, his father thrusts a 12-gauge double-barrelled shotgun into his hands.

"It's loaded, boy. Don't trip over your feet. Try not to do anything stupid."

So he walks carefully across the stubble in the chilly pre-dawn, and he sits carefully in the muddy trench so as not to accidentally shoot himself and disgrace his father. For a long time he sits there, shivering, listening to the men tell jokes he's not sure he understands, watching them pass a bottle of rye back and forth.

"Here, boy, have a swig," his father says. His father never calls him by his name. Always "boy." Freddy accepts the bottle and sucks back a great gulp of raw liquor. It burns his throat and he chokes, so it comes back up his nose and he gags, and the men laugh like it's the funniest thing they've ever heard. Like hearing a kid gag is some kind of joke. For a minute he hates both of them. They don't offer it again.

And when the great army of honking birds suddenly rises from the field behind them and flies directly overhead, so low that he can hear the strange clicking-whirring sound of feather, sinew, and bone taking flight, Freddy stands up, overwhelmed with what is unfolding above him. The sombre beauty of the black and brown birds against the grey morning sky delights his soul, and he feels as though a hand is lifting him to his feet. How beautiful they are.

"Shoot, boy," his father yells. "What the hell you waitin' for?"

Without even aiming, he raises the shotgun, squeezes the trigger hard, and the recoil slams the butt into his jaw and knocks him flat on his arse. But it must be okay because the men shout their approval.

"You got one," his father bellows. "Lucky little bugger, your first shot too!"

And they all watch as the graceful silhouette of the bird in flight changes, loses its balance in the morning sky, tumbles toward earth.

Good-natured laughter from the men now. Although his jaw feels like it's broken, he's apparently done something right.

"Go get it, boy!"

And Freddy lopes across the frozen stubble like a trained bird dog to retrieve his trophy, the unaccustomed sound of fatherly praise ringing in his ears.

When he finds it, the big bird is still alive, one wing flapping feebly, its broad chest oozing blood. It fights for breath, its beak opens and closes as though trying to speak. Freddy sinks to his knees and gathers the big feathered body in his arms, rocking it back and forth.

His father looms over him.

"Dad, it's hurt. Can you make it better?"

He feels a sob rising in his throat. Wisely, he chokes it back.

"What's the matter with you, boy? Goddamn little sissy! Ring its goddamn neck!"

Then the sob escapes, and the man turns on his heel and stalks away in disgust.

Freddy never went hunting again. All those war games he'd played with Siggy and Bucky and the other guys had been just that. Games, part Keep Away, part Hide-and-Seek. But he'd never killed anything after the stubble field, and he wasn't sure he could.

▲   ▲   ▲

IN A BIG stone house in Ottawa, the sound of a ringing telephone disturbs a small dog, asleep in the lap of his master. It's the special phone, the overseas line to 10 Downing Street, in London.

"Down, Pat. Get down," and the stocky man pushes the dog onto the carpet, picks up the receiver.

"McKenzie King here."

The very British voice crackles over the line, distorted but still familiar enough to make him sit straighter in his chair.

"Good evening, Prime Minister. This is Winston Churchill, speaking to you from London. I'm afraid I must ask you, and the Canadian people, for a very great favour."

▲   ▲   ▲

THEY'D BE SHIPPING out within four days. Hasty passes are issued for men with families nearby. Those from Saskatchewan and Alberta get a seventy-two-hour pass and are told when and where to catch the appropriate troop trains. Their final destination is top secret, but the khaki shirts are lightweight. Tony held up a pair of walking shorts and khaki knee socks.

"Wherever the hell we're going, it's gonna be hot!"

▲   ▲   ▲

FREDDY GRABBED HIS pass and caught a train back to Edmonton to see Yip.

"We're like a bunch of school kids playing baseball, running, cheering, it doesn't seem like we're serious enough," he told Yip, who was scaling a fish, squinting through the smoke of his roll-your-own. "I mean, we're supposed to be killing the enemy, right? So why does it feel like a game?"

Yip slid a whole fish into hot oil. He was cooking Freddy's favourite meal, sweet and sour pickerel.

"We march around with empty rifles, we throw dummy grenades, we fire empty mortars. Some life, huh, Yip?"

"Maybe not so bad, kid. No ammo, nobody get hurt," said Yip, who was picking up military jargon and used words like *ammo* and *kraut* whenever he could.

"So anyway, we ship out on Friday. They told me I don't have to report back to camp, I can go straight to the station tonight."

They sat in the back booth to eat the fish, Yip smacking his lips appreciatively and picking his teeth after the last morsel of white flesh had been cleaned off the bones.

Freddy passed his hand over the familiar wooden bench, looked at the jukebox that nobody played, noted the fat happy Buddha in the window, the picture of Yip's family behind the cash register. His eyes followed the curve of the grey lunch counter with its random pattern of cigarette burns and the line of red and chrome stools, the ones he used to spin on when he came in with Serena. Around and around he'd go, with his eyes squished shut, until he'd get dizzy and nearly fall off.

It occurred to him that something was ending here, and he wasn't sure how to let go.

"I'll send you and the guys a postcard from wherever we end up," Freddy said, and remembered too late that Yip couldn't read English.

"Listen, Yip, could you do me a favour? Keep my stuff for me? I'll take the mandolin, but can I leave my books here?"

"Sure, kid. No problem."

Freddy decided to shake hands. Yip looked down at Freddy's outstretched hand and folded it in both of his, holding on for a long time.

"You come back soon, kid. Always a place for you here."

▲   ▲   ▲

FOR A FULL hour, regiment after regiment of khaki-clad men march onto the platform, carrying duffle bags and full packs, Lee-Enfields slung over their shoulders. Two long troop trains stand chuffing on the tracks, and the cool October evening smells of coal smoke and long-boiled coffee from a big aluminum urn being manned by a Red Cross volunteer.

"Coffee, soldier? Hot coffee, boys?"

Most of Freddy's unit has been on the train overnight and all day from Winnipeg; some of them, the ones in the Royal Rifles, have come all the way from Quebec City. Now there are hundreds of others milling around on the platform, guys he's never seen before. Many of them are surrounded, enfolded in the arms of wives or girlfriends.

Neither Freddy nor Mick has anybody on the platform. Mick said his goodbyes back in Trout Creek. It was easier that way. His departure, the one he'd promised Joanna would never happen, had been the most painful hour of his entire life.

Just in time Tony arrives, swaggering along the platform with a harem of three luscious-looking women, all of them hanging on to him, each one trying to kiss him. Guys lean out the windows, yelling encouragement.

"Hey, Fredo! Mick! These are my Edmonton cousins," he yells. "Maria, Maria, and Maria! Ain't they gorgeous?"

Sergeants herd in the last of the stragglers and the conductor slams the doors. *Board? All aboard!*

Then, through the sounds of imminent departure: "Freddy! Freddy McKee! Where's Freddy McKee?"

It's Yip, yelling, running as best he can on the crowded platform. He's waving a brown paper bag.

"Freddy McKee! Hey, you guys! Anybody know Freddy McKee?"

"Up here, Yip," Freddy shouts as the long train jerks to life.

Yip is already winded from running, and as he spots Freddy leaning out the window, the train begins to move.

"Wait! Egg roll! I make egg roll!"

The crush of people is holding Yip back, and Freddy leans out as far as he dares, holding the window frame with his left hand, his right arm outstretched until there are mere inches between his fingers and a paper bag full of egg rolls that he suddenly wants very much.

The departing train picks up speed, and the old man's arms are too short to reach the window but he continues to try, holding aloft his greasy package.

A soldier at the next window is watching Yip.

"Look at that little chink run! Anybody order flied lice?"

Mick gets to his feet.

"Hey, buddy, why don't you just shut the hell up?"

Hanging as far out the window as he can, Freddy waves until he can no longer distinguish the figure of one small Chinese man in the crowd.

▲   ▲   ▲

ON OCTOBER 27, the *Awatea* lies at anchor in Burrard Inlet, the grey waters of the evening tide lapping around her hull.

Rumours about the ship's origin vary, depending on who tells it. Some say the *Awatea* was once a luxurious floating playpen for vacationing Australians. Others say it was a cattle boat. Either way, she's been refitted as a troop ship, designed to hold no more than 560 people. Yet before she sails at sunset, 1,976 men will come aboard. Also on the *Awatea* should be 212 motor vehicles: motorcycles, trucks, jeeps, and fifty-seven universal troop carriers.

When a red sun slides below the horizon, the *Awatea* hauls anchor and heads out to sea, riding considerably higher than anyone aboard would have hoped. Somehow the motor transport, every cog and wheel of it, has gone astray. Not a single vehicle accompanies the departing battalions, and the Canadians are effectively reduced to an army of foot soldiers.

The ocean is choppy, supper is late, and the novelty of being at sea soon wears thin. The mood doesn't improve when the British cooks finally call them to dinner. Mick, Tony, and Freddy are first in line.

"What *is* this?" Mick demands as a cook ladles a grey stew onto his plate.

"Tripe and onions, mate," replies the cook, slopping the mess onto Tony's plate. "It'll put hair on your chest."

"Tripe? That's cow's guts," Tony yelps. Tripe was the one dish in his Italian mother's culinary repertoire he had always hated. He drops his voice and pushes his face close to the cook.

"Listen, my Limey friend, we're Canadian. We don't eat cow's guts!"

The cook folds a pair of tattooed arms across his chest.

"Then I guess you don't eat at all!"

At seventeen, Freddy is still growing. He's always hungry, and he'll eat almost anything as long as it's hot and filling, so he attempts the tripe, but by now the *Awatea* is slicing through a choppy sea. He pushes his plate away.

"I don't feel so good. Think I'll hit the hay."

Below deck, it's hot, airless, and noisy. Hammocks are slung four deep in long, tight rows with barely enough room to squeeze between them. The creaking of the ship and throbbing of the motors is soon joined by the sound of men throwing up their dinners. The place reeks of sweat and vomit. Around midnight, curled in his hammock with the shoulder of the man above him almost touching his face,

Freddy's stomach churns with every roll of the ship. He has a sudden terrifying feeling that he's going to suffocate. Half falling out of his hammock, he steps on an outstretched ankle, ignores the curses, and charges down the narrow passage, bumping into men who are trying to sleep.

"Hey, watch it, will ya?"

Freddy shoves a retching soldier aside and races hand-over-hand up the ladder to the main deck as though the devil himself is chasing him.

So begins his first sea voyage.

When the *Awatea* anchors briefly off Hawaii to take on supplies, the weather softens and the trade winds blow warm and sweet. Leaning beside Mick on the rail of the blacked-out ship, watching the moon reflected on the rolling ocean, a feeling of joy washes over Freddy. Being with Tony is fun, but being with Mick is like having a brother, one who cares about him, and can talk about more than women and hockey.

The stars seem so close and bright; he's never seen stars like these. Mick can name the constellations, and he shows Freddy the great bear and both dippers.

"Does it scare you?" Freddy asks, watching the foaming wake cut a silver path through black water.

"Does what scare me? The war?"

"No. This. The ocean. In daylight I don't mind it, but at night it seems so bloody big. It must be a mile to the bottom."

"Deeper. It's twenty-five miles deep in some spots. That's all the way from Trout Creek to Snow Lake, except it's straight down. Helluva lot of water, eh, Fredo?"

The word is out. They're heading for Hong Kong. Hong Kong is where Yip lived, before Canada, before Edmonton. How bad could it be?

During the three-week voyage, the men aboard the *Awatea* have daily lectures about what to expect from their time in Hong Kong. There will be no consorting with the Chinese except for official reasons. Relationships with Chinese women are out of the question. In the mess, there's much discussion about it, and about the fabled inferiority of the Japanese army.

"They're all shortsighted, you can walk right past them and they won't know you're there," says a sergeant with a red face and a Limey accent. He acts like they're a bunch of British schoolboys heading off on a summer holiday.

"Japs can't see. Especially in the dark. It's their slanty eyes, lads. After dark, not a clue where they're going! Japs are blind as bats."

"This guy's got bats in his brain," Freddy says, remembering the warm summer evenings in Serena's backyard, when the tiny winged creatures would flit through the dusk, swooping and diving, faster than birds. They ate mosquitoes, she said, and they slept all day, so they never bothered anybody. Serena had been a big fan of bats.

The talk turns to further well-known weaknesses of the Japanese.

"Japs get seasick." The Limey sergeant again. "Won't attack if the water's rough. Too busy upchucking to pick up a weapon!" Neither Freddy nor Mick join the appreciative chuckle, and Tony's snort of disbelief is audible.

Each day at sea they have target practice, and Freddy excels.

He hasn't shot at any living thing since that day in the stubble field, but he's pleased to find that the Lee-Enfield rifle feels as comfortable in his hands as a pool cue, and his eye is just as good, his aim just as accurate as it was in the old Jasper Avenue Billiards.

It's an older Lee-Enfield, a .303 with a short magazine. The rifle has a good reputation among soldiers who'd used it in France and Germany during the last war, but it's longer and heavier than the newer model they'd heard about.

"This weapon weighs eight pounds before loading," drones the drill sergeant. "The magazine clips into the chamber from underneath."

Freddy likes the metallic thunk as it snaps into the firing mechanism. He likes the feel of the bolt under his palm, and the sharp clink when he pulls it up and back as the next cartridge snaps into the chamber.

"This weapon requires .303 cartridges. You'll find it fast and efficient," intones the instructor. "Look after your weapon, lads. It's your best friend."

Mick groans, but Freddy doesn't care. He's good with the rifle, even if it's an old one. During his time at sea he learns to fire twenty-six rounds a minute; the record is thirty. He can put more than two-thirds of his bullets into a four-inch circle at two hundred yards, a score that impresses even the drill sergeant.

The only thing he doesn't like about the rifle is the bayonet. He finds it awkward to attach under the barrel, and when the order comes to fix bayonets, he feels clumsy. It slows him down, just as it did with the straw-filled dummy. He doesn't want to think about circumstances that would force him to use it on a human being.

SEVEN: Strange Place, Strange Time

Hong Kong, November 1941

ON NOVEMBER 16, WHEN FREDDY'S battalion stepped off the *Awatea* and marched up Nathan Road behind the skirling pipes of the Royal Scots, crowds cheered them all the way to their barracks at Sham Shui Po.

"Hey, they like us," Freddy yelled over the racket.

"Wait till they get to know us," Mick replied. "They'll change their minds fast!"

"I don't care whether they like us or not," said Tony. "Just as long as they play poker and their women are willing!"

During their first few days in Hong Kong Freddy felt more like a tourist than a soldier. The duty hours were easy, and the city was at once amazing and appalling. He walked the streets, avoiding the business district known as Central, criss-crossing the harbour on the Star Ferries, goggle-eyed at the milling crowds of Chinese, some of whom ignored him while others, like the miniature old women and the beautiful black-eyed too-thin children, peered curiously from the rubble of the sidewalks.

The poverty was eclipsed by the rattle and yammer of Chinese commerce, the frenetic early morning markets where a few live fowl and fish were still available. He marvelled at fruit and vegetables he didn't recognize, and stranger still were the dried whatsits, horn of this, sinew of that. The high-pitched haggling, the heady blend of flesh and blood, charcoal smoke, and incense opened a window on a world he'd never known.

Hong Kong thrummed like an orchestra with every instrument playing a different tune. No day was long enough for Freddy to absorb the sounds, the smells, the flavours that seemed, if not familiar, not

44

entirely foreign either. As he wandered the alleys, he often wondered if Yip had been here, seen this place, tasted it. He hated to go to sleep in case he missed some detail of the life that surged around him.

Together he and Mick poked among the temples and markets. They walked through Mong Kok and Wanchai, where crafty old women tried to sell them live fish, thousand-year eggs, and occasionally their daughters. For the first two evenings they went alone, but on the third evening Tony joined them, flush with poker winnings, and they prowled the alleys like three curious tomcats, carousing their way in and out of bars where ten cents bought a beer and a dollar bought a girl.

On their fourth night they crossed The Fragrant Harbour on a Star Ferry, watching the lights of Hong Kong reflected in the water. They tore through Wanchai, drinking prodigiously and brawling happily with anybody who would take them on.

All too soon they had to get back to the harbour or miss the last ferry. Piling into three rickshaws, they headed for the pier, urging their human steeds to go faster.

At first, the rickshaws had troubled Freddy. Something in him said that no man should have to pull another man around the streets as though he was no more than a horse with two legs. It seemed undignified. But as he watched the rickshaw men fighting for customers, he learned to pocket his western sensitivities.

"C'mon, Fredo! Time's a wastin'!"

From the beginning, Tony's driver, a scrawny old man with a wispy beard, lagged behind. It was a position Tony didn't enjoy.

"Stop, my good man! Halt, I say," he yelled. It was his drunken version of the pompous British officer they all despised. The other two managed to stop their rickshaws and join Tony, prepared to supervise this new phase of the journey.

"Haul your arse into this seat, old boy, there's a good chap!"

Ignoring his protests, the three of them pushed and prodded until the ancient rickshaw puller was seated in his own rickshaw. Tony, by now wearing the old man's hat, yelled, "Wagons Ho!" and took off at a fast trot, with the onshore breeze blowing in his face and the other two drivers, bewildered but game, pelting along behind him.

At the point where the street began to slope down toward the harbour, the road had grown slippery with evening rain; by the time Tony and his passenger hit the pier, the rickshaw had gained so much momentum that it was running merrily along on its own.

The driver howled a rich torrent of Cantonese curses at Tony, who was too drunk to notice the slick footing, even when his feet started playing tricks on his brain. Still, they were all surprised when suddenly he sprawled face down on the pavement. His rickshaw, moving forward now by sheer inertia, bowled right over him and kept going. As it reached the end of the pier, passengers on the departing ferry watched in amazement while the rickshaw rose momentarily, executing a graceful arc above the water, the old man also rising, but travelling slightly above his vehicle as it began to descend. Spindly legs flailed, curses soared into a shriek as the rickshaw hit the waves with a mighty splash and sank below the water of The Fragrant Harbour.

For a split second the old man continued his frantic pedalling in midair, then plunged into the water behind his cherished rickshaw. A sailor on the ferry tossed him a life preserver, which he caught with surprising agility and clung to as he was hauled in, shaking his fist and screeching at the guilty trio on the dock.

They agreed that it had been a night to remember and hailed a woman in a motorized sampan to take them across the harbour.

"Gotta get back to the base," Freddy announced. "There's a war on! Gotta go whip some Japs!"

He'd never had this much fun in his life.

EIGHT : Lucky to Be Alive
December 18, 1941

BY TEN O'CLOCK THE MOON, usually so bright on the harbour, was hidden behind a heavy cloudbank. In a back-alley room in the blacked-out city, a few Chinese men changed western business suits for the ragged garments worn by coolies.

They had no interest in their fellow Chinese, who they didn't care about, nor in the British, whom they had reason to hate, but in the Japanese, who were paying them well for this little job. It was just business.

Silently they made their way uphill to Sai Wan Battery, manned by a handful of local volunteers, white men too old and soft for army service but fit enough to watch for an approaching enemy. Half asleep over too much after-dinner port, they saw nothing, heard nothing. For Chinese guerillas dressed as coolies, it was the work of a minute to creep through the unguarded gate, slit their fat white throats, and let them bleed to death.

They missed only one occupant of the battery, a young Chinese servant who slipped out a window. He ran along a scrubby path, stumbling in the darkness, literally falling into an encampment of Royal Rifles, the second Canadian battalion from C Force.

As the terrified boy blurted out his story, the Canadian major called the command post to demand immediate artillery support. He groaned as he heard the plums-in-the-mouth accent on the other end of the line.

"Major, you must be mistaken. Sai Wan Battery is fully manned by volunteers. They're the friendly ones, old boy. Remember?"

"They sure as hell aren't friendly now," barked the major, slamming the receiver down. Patronizing ass! Talking to the British brass was like banging your head against a brick wall; you could almost enjoy it because it felt so good when you stopped.

▲   ▲   ▲

NOW IN THE moonless dark, a coolie carries a basket along the water's edge. Inside is a large garoupa, a fish he'd bargained for in the dwindling wet market. Thinking of fried garoupa, his mouth waters, but he's suddenly distracted by a noise. Across the harbour? From Kowloon side? Sound carries far over water, and he stops to listen. Peers into the dark void.

Not fishermen, not at this hour. Ghosts? He shivers because now he sees them, all the little boats. So many, moving so fast. Ghost boats on The Fragrant Harbour! As the first one draws closer, he hears voices, but he can't understand this ghost gibberish. Not Chinese. Not English either.

Japanese! The boats are full of Japanese! Dropping his fish basket, he races for the British artillery post half a mile away, running as fast as he can.

"Japanese come," he cries. "Japanese!"

A sentry passes the coolie's breathless message to an officer, who is not impressed.

"Not a chance. That water's rough, and Japs get seasick. You wouldn't get them near Victoria Harbour tonight."

"But, sir, the coolie? He's sure he saw something."

"Troublesome little blighter—send him packing!"

The first contingent of Japanese crossed the rough water at Lye Mun Passage, the narrowest part of Victoria Harbour. Behind them were nearly eight thousand more, well trained, well armed. Before midnight the invasion was complete, and Hong Kong Island was swarming with Japanese.

Inside the artillery post, except for the sentry and his sergeant, the men were fast asleep. The first Japanese soldier smashed through the door with a dozen more behind him, bayonets fixed.

"Surrender!" The Japanese officer barked in English. "No harm will come to you."

In groups of ten, the men were tied with their hands behind their backs and taken outside, where their ankles were also tied.

"Good! Now none of you naughty boys will run away home."

The Japanese officer, whose spoken English had a faintly British intonation, smiled at his own joke. Then he gave the order.

"Kill them!"

The bodies were thrown over the wall. The invasion of the island had begun, a week before Christmas.

▲   ▲   ▲

FOR THE JAPANESE, these first few skirmishes barely mattered. The critical battle would be farther south, at a place called Wong Nai Chung Gap.

The Gap was the only road across Hong Kong Island, effectively dividing it in half, and General Sakai reasoned that once he controlled the Gap, he would quickly take the freshwater reservoirs. At the same time he would divide the defending army down the middle. Supply line? Gone. No food, no water, no ammunition. Surrender was inevitable, and it would be soon.

If they'd been Japanese troops, or even Chinese, his challenge would have been greater. Japanese fought to the death. But these inferior British and their Colonials were strangely unwilling to die in battle. They lacked any proper sense of honour.

General Sakai was a student of military history. His heroes were Napoleon and Sun Su, and this was textbook warfare. He allowed himself a thin smile of satisfaction.

▲   ▲   ▲

FREDDY'S WAR HAD lost its charm.

For days, they'd been hunkered down on this hill on Hong Kong Island, cold, wet, bored out of their minds with the waiting. The Japs had easily taken Kowloon, across Victoria Harbour, yet the British brass kept insisting the major invasion would come from the south side of this island.

"Mick, the Japs already have Kowloon. They're bombing us from our own airport. Why would they traipse all the way around the island

49

to hit us from the south? What's stopping them from just crossing that puddle of a harbour and walking right over us?"

"I don't know, Freddy. And I don't much care. All I want to do is get off this godforsaken island and go home."

Wong Nai Chung Gap was the lifeline for the Winnipeg Grenadiers, and Tony's squad had occupied a pillbox about a mile south. They were supposed to stockpile munitions, and for hours now, the lieutenant had been trying to contact them to have more ammunition brought forward, but he couldn't raise anybody. How was he supposed to direct traffic when the bloody radios didn't even work? He was running low on everything, and he didn't know how long they'd be able to hold out once the Japs got a bead on them.

"I can't get anybody on this damn thing. McKee, Keegan, I need that ammo forward, and fast. You two head back. Get some help and bring whatever you can."

"Yes sir," said Freddy, muttering under his breath about another trip in the rain. He and Mick took off down the Gap, moving as fast as they could, watchful, worried about snipers and Jap patrols.

When Tony's squad had finally reached the pillbox early that morning, they'd cursed the rain and mud. A trip that should have taken forty minutes cost them two bloody hours. A makeshift stairway had been cut into the hill, and men carrying heavy boxes of ammunition swore as they slithered and stumbled, stacking cases outside while they checked the place for rats and snakes.

The entrance was through a concrete tunnel that lead directly into a small room with two narrow slits high up in the wall. Tony had always hated enclosed spaces. What did the army think they were, a bunch of goddamn moles? He was the last man into the tunnel, and he hung back. Too many bodies, the pervasive damp, the lack of ventilation, it was enough to make you upchuck.

Nobody saw the lone Japanese soldier, struggling up the other side of the hill. Steep as it was, he'd managed to climb on top of the pillbox, where he quickly pulled the pins on two grenades and lobbed them through the ventilator.

Tony, the last man into the pillbox, heard the first one drop like a stone on the concrete floor. Small, lethal, it looked like a miniature black pineapple. He didn't even have time to yell a warning, and nobody saw the second grenade, the one that rolled and stopped six inches from Tony's feet. The explosions shook the hill, and the fact that the ammunition cases were stacked outside, and Tony was still crouched partway into the tunnel, saved his life.

Less than a mile away, Freddy and Mick heard the explosions. When they saw the sky light up, they started to run. By the time they reached the pillbox, two medics were in the midst of the carnage. Davey Wills, a rifleman from Transcona who played pretty good piano, was lying on a stretcher, making a high, keening noise. Freddy had never heard a sound like that in his life. Davey was shaking violently, his teeth chattering, a staccato *clack-clack* like a typewriter. A medic injected something into his arm while the second one tried to apply bandages, but half of Davey's chest had been peeled away, and in the mess of splintered rib and blood, Freddy could see something pulsing sporadically. On one of his prowls through the wet markets, he'd seen a fish like that, one of its sides sliced off, leaving its organs exposed and throbbing.

The noise Davey was making changed to a gurgling rattle, and then he was quiet. The medic stood up.

"I just wasted that shot of morphine," he said wearily.

Freddy could hear Mick's voice. Thick, like he was talking through a wadded-up towel.

"There should have been more guys in the pillbox. Where are the rest of them?"

The medic gestured at fragments of uniforms and bodies strewn about their feet, the orderly row of three anonymous corpses, faces covered, and now one more with Davey Wills.

"You blind or what? Three over there, and we just lost this one," he said, pulling the blanket over Wills's face.

"There's one more." He pointed at a stretcher near the entrance. "Tough bastard, that one. He's the only one left."

Tony's head was swathed in bandages. A blanket had been pulled up to his chin, and his eyes were closed. Freddy swallowed hard.

"Is he . . . ?"

"He's alive," the medic said. "Concussion, busted vertebrae, among other things."

Shit. That meant he could be paralyzed, maybe never walk again. Wills and three others dead, the rest of them blown all to hell, now Tony. Freddy felt his stomach convulse. He was afraid he was going to puke. He heard Mick questioning the medic.

"Will he be able to walk?"

"Not until they fit him with some new legs."

Freddy found his voice.

"What? What did you say?"

The medic looked blankly at Freddy.

"The explosion blew his legs off. This man is lucky to be alive."

NINE: Mick and Freddy

"MICK, DO YOU THINK TONY'LL be okay?"

"He'll be okay."

Freddy didn't know how to phrase his next question, but asking Mick was easier than asking anybody else. Mick had a serious side. He always gave a guy respect.

"What about . . . I mean, with women? Will women still go for a guy with no legs? And what about the rest of him? He looked pretty bad, Mick. We don't even know if he was all there."

He swallowed hard, needing to ask the question, scared of the answer.

"His balls, I mean! What about it, Mick?"

"I don't know, Freddy. There's just a helluva lot I don't know."

▲　　▲　　▲

THEY'VE BEEN MOVED to Mount Butler, a height of land northeast of Wong Nai Chung Gap. It's raining hard now, and Freddy eases out of his backpack and tries to light a cigarette, but the package is sodden. He tosses the cigarette away in disgust.

"Doesn't it scare you, Mick? Those guys in the pillbox, all blown to crap. All dead, except Tony. Even the sergeant."

"Sergeants die too, Freddy."

"But did you know it would be like this? So totally shitty? Wasn't it supposed to be different?"

"You mean like a big adventure? Like some kind of a hunting trip where a bunch of guys go out and shoot something that can't shoot back and then get drunk and brag about it?"

"I don't know. Something like that, I guess."

Mick was quiet for so long that Freddy thought he'd dozed off. The only sound was the steady patter of rain on their helmets, until Mick's voice came, soft and slow in the darkness.

"There was this guy who said there's only two kinds of soldiers: the quick and the dead."

Mick was always quoting somebody or other. Sometimes it was a big yawn, but other times, well, Mick could make a lot of sense.

"Yeah," Freddy replied. "Pretty funny, eh? Some sick joke."

"Not very original, though. He stole it."

"Oh yeah? Who from?"

"A guy named Simon Peter. You know, the guy in the bible."

They played a few hands of gin rummy, but Freddy wasn't in the mood. His stomach rumbled. He wondered why the mess tins hadn't arrived. They hadn't had anything hot to eat or drink for eighteen hours. Even a cup of that ungodly boiled tea would taste good right now. He almost jumped up and kissed the only other human being they'd seen lately—a private, crouching behind another rock, who moved over to bum a cigarette.

He'd come up later than they had, and he'd heard a rumour from a dispatch rider about some Japs crossing Lye Mun Passage.

The Royal Rifles were stuck back in the city, he said, and they'd be keeping those slant-eyes busy. Even if the Japs had crossed Lye Mun, they'd be wiped out before they got to this hill.

"Even if they made it this far, we'd pick 'em off fast," he said.

Shivering, Freddy sneezed.

"Jeez, I'll likely get pneumonia first."

The private laughed.

"Yeah? So you can spend the rest of the war in bed with some little nurse?"

"Not me," Freddy replied, and beside him he heard Mick chuckle quietly.

Freddy closed his eyes. Su Li. His sweet, lovely Su Li. If she'd made it into some hiding place with the old girl, the woman she called her amah, maybe she'd be okay. He dozed, dreaming of a big white bed and a slowly turning fan.

TEN : Something for Joanna

MICK WOKE HIM UP.

"Freddy, listen. I have something I want you to keep for me. A letter. It's for Joanna, just in case."

"In case what?"

"Oh, you know. In case something happens."

Freddy sat up, fully awake now.

"Like what? What are you talking about?"

"Oh, like I get bit by a snake or fall out of a goddamn tree! What do you think I'm talking about? In case I don't make it back!"

"Christ, Mick, why say a thing like that? Don't even think it! Besides, if you don't make it, I sure as hell won't."

"Freddy, don't be such an old woman. It's like insurance, see? You buy it even though you'll never use it."

"Why me, Mick? What makes you think I'd get back, if you didn't?"

"Because you're a lucky man, Freddy. One of God's chosen people. A bullet with your name on it would be a waste. It'd bounce right off that thick skull of yours. Here, take it! Dammit, Freddy, will you just take it?"

Reluctantly, Freddy took the flimsy blue envelope from Mick. He stuffed it inside his shirt.

▲　　▲　　▲

LOOKING EAST, FREDDY can barely see where the island ends, giving way to the gunmetal grey of the South China Sea. These hills are almost treeless, and trees that do survive here grow in deep gullies that run downward before broadening into the Gap.

The Gap is just spit-distance on his left, but then nothing is more than spit-distance here. What a crappy, good-for-nothing little island this is. Back home in Alberta, he knew people with ranches as big as this. Bigger. You could drop the whole damn island into Slave Lake and it would disappear without a ripple. Such a piddling little scrap of land sure as hell wasn't worth dying for.

Freddy looks at his watch. Eight hours they've been on this bloody hill, with no trenches, nothing to protect them but a few scattered boulders. He crawls toward a jutting rock and finds a hollow on the south side, big enough to hold two men.

"Mick, over here!"

They drop their packs and sit, propping their backs against the sandstone. Hugging his knees, shivering, Freddy tips his helmet low, covering his eyes. He's hungry, and thinking about food just makes his guts growl.

The rain has been alternately pouring and piddling, dribbling off his helmet. He feels water trickle down his neck.

I hate this place. I hate everything about it.

He could make a list, if anybody asked. The pervasive damp, the mouldy clothes, his stinking boots that leak, the constant drizzle, the sudden gales that sweep across the island in sideways-slanting sheets that blind him and leave him soaked to the skin. God, how he hates being wet. He hates every inch of fissured terrain and knobbly hillside, every bush that could hide a sniper, every rock that could trip him in the dark. He hates what has become of Hong Kong, the piles of refuse, the smells of garbage and human dung, the corpses. The stench of dead flesh. He hates the locals they call fifth columnists, the ones who spy for the Japs and will cut your throat the first chance they get. He hates the British officers, sitting on their aristocratic asses, issuing orders that make no sense while the dumb Canadians do the fighting.

He hates the rats and roaches and the possibility of snakes. He hates the Japanese, who are better at war. He hates losing people. Tony, with his legs shot off. His beautiful Su Li, the woman he'd known for such a sweet, unbearably short time, gone. The stupid bloody war has hidden her away, maybe killed her.

And for what? This useless scrap of an island, last holdout of a few snotty Brits who should have gotten the hell out a long time ago. For this, he was supposed to fight? To die?

A great rage begins to build in his heart.

An hour passes, then another, and his head drops on his chest. He dozes fitfully.

When Freddy wakes, the rain has stopped and layers of fog trail raggedly across the hills and into the valley below. He can see huddled figures all around him, crouching under their ponchos like so many rocks. In the woolly light it's hard to tell which is which.

The ragged fog begins to lift. Freddy's legs are stiff, and as he stands up to stretch, a shot whizzes past his ear.

▲ ▲ ▲

"JESUS H. CHRIST! Where did that come from?"

To their right, a mortar shell exploded, showering them with dirt and rocks. The firing was coming from the ravine below. Immediately, the ominous hum and screech of another mortar, and all hell broke loose around them.

"Japs! The Japs are down there!"

Below them, still shrouded in fog, the Japanese were setting up mortars, firing, charging blindly up the hill. These little bowlegged men in canvas running shoes, tough, determined, happy to die for the emperor, just kept coming. They'd reload, fire, and charge again, climbing steadily, their advance always covered by mortars.

Too often Freddy heard a human cry, a man screaming in pain. Canadian or Japanese, who could tell?

As they crouched behind their rock, the whine of bullets was constant. Mortar shells gouged holes in the earth, sending chunks of turf into the sky, raining debris on their heads.

The order came along the hill: Fix bayonets.

Freddy tried to snap the blade into place, but his hands were shaking so much that he couldn't do it.

Men ran past him and ahead of him. Bullets flew like hailstones, whined past his ears so close he could almost feel their heat. He saw bodies falling around him, heard a dull thud beside him, saw that it was an entire human arm, hand outstretched. No body attached.

"Let's go, Freddy!"

It was Mick's voice, but Freddy was crouched over, frozen. His feet wouldn't move. They felt like they were stuck in cement. Like in a nightmare.

"Jesus, Mick! I can't move my feet!" He heard his own voice crack.

"Sure you can!"

"No, Mick, I can't move!"

In the middle of a bloodier battle than he could have imagined, he felt the weight of Mick's arm across his back, the pressure of Mick's hand on his shoulder.

"We'll be okay. I'll wait at the bottom. Goddammit, Freddy, move your feet! C'mon, let's go!"

Mick started down the hill, his tall form bent double, running a zigzag pattern against the incoming fire.

He was about one hundred yards ahead when Freddy saw him raise his rifle to fire, then crumple and pitch forward.

Fear evaporated as he headed for Mick, running. And none of this seemed real. None of it. By the time he managed to get to Mick, the firing had slowed, the Japanese had backed off to regroup. When they came back, there'd be no hope of holding the hill.

Behind him, his sergeant shouted the order.

"We're moving south to Company A."

Mick was groaning, writhing on the ground, but he was fully conscious. "Jesus, Freddy, they got my leg!"

He'd been hit in the right thigh, inside and above the knee.

"Medic!" Freddy yelled the magic word, the one that would bring help for Mick.

"Medic," he screamed.

There was no medic. Freddy applied a gauze pack from the field dressings in his kit, felt his sergeant drop beside them, checking casualties. Mick was groaning, but it was just a leg wound; if he could get the bleeding stopped it would be okay.

"Sarge, let me get him to the aid station. It's gotta be close, sir. Maybe a mile."

"Okay, son, but leave him there. Get back as soon as you can. The Japs are clobbering us. I need every man."

The aid station is much farther than a mile.

The terrain is rocky now, and Mick is conscious, so at first the two men try a sort of three-legged run, with Mick's bandaged leg in an improvised sling and Freddy supporting as much of his weight as he can. Mick groans every time he lands on his left foot. It must be jarring the wounded leg.

Freddy keeps talking. He can't let Mick collapse or he'll never get him up again. He hears artillery behind them, sees the arcs trace across the sky. The Japs have regrouped, the battle is on again. After an eternity they stumble onto a path of the sort farmers use to herd animals, narrow, barely defined, slippery after the rain.

"This road is okay, Mick, no Japs. Could be any road. Safe as houses here. Just like that alley behind Yip's café." Freddy speaks in short bursts, breathing hard under the weight of the taller man.

"Freddy, stop a minute." Mick's voice comes in shallow gasps now, the words no more than a groan. They struggle into a shallow ditch and Mick collapses, his head lolling backward. Freddy checks the wound. The pant leg is soaked, sticky with Mick's blood.

"Christ, Mick! You're bleeding like a stuck pig!"

He puts his hand over the wound and presses, but Mick groans at his touch, and he feels warm blood gushing through his fingers every time Mick's heart beats.

Damn bullet must've nicked an artery, gotta get it stopped.

He opens his pack, applies another field dressing, tears the sling off, and wraps it tightly around the top of Mick's thigh, above the wound, trying desperately to remember the first aid lecture on how to stop a bleeding artery.

He's losing too much blood. What'll I do? What the hell do I do?

Freddy senses a change coming over the wounded man, and it terrifies him.

"C'mon Mick, we gotta get out of here. The Japs are breathing down our necks, I can feel it."

They try again, and they crawl now, their progress measurable in mere feet as Freddy half drags the larger man along the muddy track. They manage only a short distance when Mick slips from his grasp, collapses beside the trail where he lies on his belly, inert.

"Mick? Mick, c'mon, buddy! Jeez, Mick, don't quit on me now!"

Mick is trying to tell him something, and Freddy leans close so he can hear.

"Leave me."

"What?"

Slurred words, from far away.

"Leave me. I'm . . . finished."

"Shut up, you dumb bastard, you owe me poker money, you're not gonna die on me! Please, Mickey, you gotta stay with me."

But Mick is unconscious now. Freddy opens his canteen, turns Mick's head sideways, tries to get him to swallow water. Watches as it runs out the sides of his mouth.

"It's okay, Mick, we'll rest for a while. It's okay. I'm right beside you, Mickey. You rest a little, then we'll go again."

He waits as long as he can, but the sounds of battle echo through the hills, bouncing back and forth so it's hard to decide which direction the noise is coming from, except that it's closer. Freddy manages to lift the unconscious man. With Mick's body across his shoulders, he forces himself to one knee, struggles to his feet. Bent double under the weight, he moves as fast as he can, floundering down the trail and into a shallow ravine, afraid he could be heading in the wrong direction.

Please, God, let me just this once know where the hell I'm going.

The dressing station can't be much farther. The ravine is thick with scrub, nearly shoulder height. He trips on a root, stumbles, almost falls under the dead weight of the larger man.

"Hold on to me, Mick. You gotta help me a little, just try to hold on. I'll get us out of here."

He spots the stone hut. It sits at the end of the ravine, where the scrubby path levels into a clearing. At one side is a thick stand of pampas grass, fluffy white plumes bending toward the hut. He's lost all sense of time, but daylight is fading fast. High in the wall there's a small window, and in the lowering dusk he can make out a red cross painted on the wooden door.

The aid station. Thank God, there'll be a medic, maybe some food. They haven't eaten for so long, hot food will do Mick good.

Behind the hut stands a smaller structure, some sort of barn maybe, and on the west side, more pampas grass, tall enough to hide a man. He watches the feathery tops moving gently in the breeze, steps out of the scrub, slowly though, wary of the open space where they'd be easy targets. Scanning the clearing around the buildings, he looks for some sign. Anything.

Something doesn't feel right. He takes a step back, and as gently as he can, lowers Mick's body, sliding him off his shoulders onto the ground. Mick isn't moving at all now, and Freddy collapses beside him, exhausted, trying to catch his breath, trying to think about his next move. There's grass here, thick and soft, and it has a sweet smell, sweet and green as a summer night. How good it would be to forget everything, to stay here on this pillow of grass beside Mick and just sleep, maybe for the rest of his life.

On his knees now. Feels the side of Mick's throat, praying for a pulse. Finds it. Just barely. Can't wait any longer. Leans down, whispers in Mick's ear.

"Wait here, okay? Mick? We made it, Mickey. You're gonna be fine. We'll get a medic. Oh Christ, Mick, hang on! I'll be right back, soon as I get the medic!"

He gets to his feet and moves warily across the clearing, hunkered over now, both hands on his rifle. Like a coyote, his nerves are attuned for anything that doesn't make sense in the gathering darkness, the wrong smell, a sound he can't identify. There's no light showing in the hut's small window, but they'd have it blacked out anyway, he knows that.

Still the coyote in him wonders, watches, sniffs the air for signs of something wrong.

"Anybody home? I got a wounded man out here."

Rifle in his right hand, he places the flat of his left hand on the red cross and pushes.

The door swings open with a creak.

The bayonet is pointed directly at his belt. That's all he sees. The damned bayonet. He doesn't see the bodies crumpled on the floor, or the Japanese uniforms standing in the dim room, doesn't even see the other Jap's face as the stock of a rifle swings upward, the butt coming so fast that he hears the crack when it meets his skull.

His knees buckle and he falls backward, still conscious as a machine gun begins to stutter from the pampas grass. For the second time in a few hours, all hell breaks loose. The Japs are busy returning fire. It's his only chance. He rolls over and starts a frantic belly-crawl, back across the clearing toward Mick.

Two kinds of soldiers: the quick and the dead.

Bullets sing past his ears as he dives into the scrub. Where the hell is Mick? They can't stay here, the Japs will come after him and get Mick too. His eyes aren't focusing. He touches his forehead, feels the stickiness of his own blood.

At that moment the storm that has been threatening since morning bursts through the clouds, and the rain comes down in a solid sheet.

"Mick, where are you? The Japs, we gotta get outta here, Mick. Mick?"

Shit. I must have gone wide.

"Mick? Can you hear me, buddy? Mick, it's Freddy. Answer me, please, Mick!"

The cut over his eye bleeds, and he gropes his way along, feeling for the soft grass where he knows he left Mick, but the earth here seems hard and slick. He reaches blindly, doesn't even see the edge of the outcrop until he plunges over it, tumbling arse over teakettle fifteen feet off a cliff and rolling to a stop at the boots of a surprised Canadian soldier. Six guys are on their feet. One more, barely visible in the rain and near-darkness, is sprawled in the ragdoll posture of a dead man whose neck is broken.

"Where the hell did you come from, soldier?"

Freddy can barely make out a lieutenant's stripes, but the French-Canadian accent is unmistakable. He's fallen into what's left of a company of Royal Rifles.

"Up there, sir. I was taking a buddy to that aid station. He's still up there, somewhere in the trees."

"Not anymore, he isn't. The Japs are all over."

"All over where, sir?"

"All over us, you dumb ass. C'mon, we're getting out of here. South, along this ravine."

"Sir? I can't leave him, sir. He's waiting for me! Up there!"

The twenty-four-year-old lieutenant from Montreal looks at Freddy's distraught face.

Merde! He's younger than I am. Just a kid.

"He's gone, soldier. And we're moving out. That's an order."

"Sir, I don't have a weapon. I must have dropped it when the Jap hit me."

The lieutenant picks up the rifle lying beside the dead man and hands it to Freddy.

"Here. He won't need it anymore."

ELEVEN: Freddy Alone

DURING THE MONSOONS THE RAVINE had been a shallow river, and where it opened into a slough bottom it was mud, with sudden deep holes as though a herd of elephants had been dancing. On the other side, a rare stand of trees. Tall reeds grew in the slough, providing minimal cover. The rain had stopped, and the moving clouds revealed a full white moon.

"Down," the lieutenant ordered, and they dropped to their bellies in the mud.

"You hear anything, Pepin?"

"No, sir. Not a sound."

"I could swear I heard something out there."

"Want me to have a look, sir?"

"Maybe you better. I'll cover you. Go left."

Private Étienne Pepin moved cautiously to the left, crouching, skirting the edge of the slough bottom before he stood up. He got about ten feet before they heard the stuttering of a machine gun as bullets sprayed the clearing. Pepin didn't have a chance. The Canadians returned fire, poured everything they had back at the trees, but a machine gun has a deadly efficiency that even the best riflemen could never match. The last time Freddy squeezed the trigger, he heard the sickening click of the empty chamber.

The firing stopped on both sides.

They lay on their bellies waiting, and before long a voice came from somewhere across the clearing.

"You, Canadian. You surrender now. No harm will come to you."

The lieutenant waited, maybe thirty seconds. Then, incredibly, he pulled a neatly folded white handkerchief out of his pocket. In the moonlight its whiteness was astonishing. It took on a light of its own, like a second moon.

"Can you believe that?" whispered the guy beside Freddy. "Where the hell does he think he's going? To mass?"

The lieutenant stood up slowly, almost painfully. He waved his white flag tentatively at first, as though he wasn't sure, but then he began flapping it high above his head. Eternity passed during the three or four seconds in which he stood there, the young officer with his tidy white handkerchief aloft, pale and fluttering in the moonlight.

They heard the crack of a rifle, saw him go down, the handkerchief still clutched in his hand.

"Bastards," he heard the man beside him say. The body lay twitching where it fell. One of the men started to crawl toward him, but bullets sprayed the ground around him. He cried out once as the second round hit him, then he, too, lay still.

Four remaining men stood up together and threw their empty rifles into the clearing. Slowly, as though they were too tired to care anymore, they raised their hands above their heads.

"Step forward," came the voice again, sounding oddly friendly, as though inviting people who'd been waiting in line to approach a bank teller.

Three of the men obeyed the order because something in them accepted that their remaining time on Earth was being measured in a few heartbeats.

The fourth man had a different message playing in his head.

Two kinds of soldiers: the quick and the dead.

Freddy didn't act with any conscious strategy. He simply dropped to the ground, a split second before the Japanese bullet would have entered his brain. Instead, it merely grazed his skull.

He heard the other three fall, knowing by the silence that they were all dead, knowing by the deep, thudding pain in his head that he was not.

If the Japs checked, if they did a body count, they'd finish off anybody who was still alive. He held his breath and waited, listening to the sound of feet squishing toward him in the muddy slough bottom.

One of them stopped beside his head, stooped over and picked up his empty Lee-Enfield, then dropped it. They'd already collected their quota of souvenirs, and in any case, Canadian soldiers had nothing worth stealing. Their weapons were inferior, their boots were too big for Japanese feet. And the rain was starting again.

Playing dead, face down in the mud of that empty slough, Freddy felt profound relief that he was still alive; profound guilt that he was alive when the others are not.

During the last few days before Christmas in 1941, Allied soldiers wandered the hills near Wong Nai Chung Gap. Their commanding officers were dead, and they had no replacements. Freddy had become part of a motley army: Canadians, Scots, Punjabis, remnants of Churchill's token force on a doomed island.

For the next forty-eight hours, he was lost. He had no weapon until he stumbled across a dead soldier in a ditch whose still-loaded rifle lay where it had fallen. He'd lost count of the days since he'd last eaten or had anything to drink. Hunger had begun to weaken him, thirst was dehydrating his body. In daylight he hid, crouched behind rocks, in ditches, in patches of scrub. At night he stumbled around in the darkness, falling often in the unfamiliar terrain, dodging Japanese patrols, hoping he might find one living soul who didn't have a rifle aimed at his head.

The hills all looked alike, and he didn't have Mick's usual trail of mental breadcrumbs to guide him.

"See this rock?" Mick used to say. "Looks like a rabbit. Remember it on the way back. Keep your eyes and ears open and you won't need a map. You can always find your way home."

"Like those two kids in the fairy tale. Right, Mick? Handle and Gristle?"

Now Mick was gone, and even the sky betrayed him. No longer a red sunset to turn his face westward and give him his bearings. Only the false twilight of smoke, the lightning of artillery tracing flashy arcs across the dark sky, the thunder of bombs exploding, heaving up the ground around him.

He needed Mick, whose map was always in his own head, marked with the shape of a rock, the smell of a certain field, the sound of water running over stones.

"Now that's a sweet sound," Mick had said when they came across a burbling stream. "Did you know that the Indians bring their crazy people to the edge of a creek and leave them there so they can listen to it? Water music. It makes them feel better, hearing that sound."

Freddy is alone and so scared he can taste fear, like iron filings in his mouth. His breath comes in short gasps, as though he's been running. If there are Japs nearby, they'll hear his heart crashing in his chest.

Moving in what he hopes is a northerly direction, he rounds a sharp bend in the trail. There in front of him stands a Japanese soldier, fumbling with his rifle in the moonlight.

Freddy raises his own rifle and fires, but his aim is too low, and he knows by the scream the man has been gut-shot and will take a long time to die. Instinctively, he drops to one knee beside the wounded Jap.

Now a flare goes up, and for the first time he sees the face of his enemy, young, scared, contorted with pain. He's no older than Freddy. (And what had he been in real life? A poet, a cook, a fisherman?) The boy's eyes are wide open, and when he coughs, a dark trickle of blood appears at the corner of his mouth. Freddy knows with a terrible certainty that this Japanese boy, fumbling with his rifle on a dark road, would not have shot him. Not him or any other human being.

"Wait," Freddy cries, but the boy will die anyway.

The past two weeks have taken the last of Freddy's youth. He has seen death, caused it, run from it. He's been in battles that were an accumulation of bungling. He's been shot at by his own people when the Japs tapped into their communications system and faked an order.

Throwing his head back, Freddy gulps hungrily at the night air. Is he the only man who feels such despair? Mick had told him it was normal to feel weird about killing, but he didn't know it would be this bad.

He's heard about soldiers who deliberately aim high so they won't hit anything. Of others who never pull the trigger, go through entire battles without firing a shot. Or they go AWOL, or deliberately shoot themselves in the toe, or fake some kind of craziness.

Maybe that's the answer. Maybe he really is crazy because he sure as hell doesn't understand what he's doing in this bad joke of a life. What's the bloody point?

A second flare turns the road noon-bright, so bright that he sees his own shadow, and the answer to his question is standing no more than ten feet away, aiming a gun at his chest. He hears the double click of the bolt as the cartridge falls into place, sees the Jap's shiny white teeth grinning at him as he pulls the trigger. *I'm dead, oh God, I'm dead*, and then the Jap's gun jams and he shouts something in Japanese, a sound of sheer frustration as Freddy aims high and squeezes off two shots. The man's face explodes like a squashed tomato.

An instant later the whole world lights up in a flash so bright it blinds him. He feels all the air leave his body, as though something landed on his chest and pushed out every atom of oxygen. He's flying then, lighter than a feather, lighter than air, flying, flying. Tremendous pressure on every bone when he hits the ground, but no pain, none at all. He hears the pitter-patter of lesser debris landing all around him, gravel, small broken branches, clumps of sod dislodged by the blast.

After that, nothing.

He wakes in darkness. The wind whispers through the scarred stems of a clump of mature bamboo, rare in this part of Hong Kong Island, hand-planted by some optimistic Chinese gardener in a time of peace. A strange sound, this, the sighing and singing, the hollow tapping of stem against stem; unique to bamboo, like a lot of old bones clacking together.

Maybe I'm dead, he thinks for the second time that day. *I must be dead.*

He's lying on his back, his right arm hurts like hell. Tries to move the arm. A blinding pain shoots through his shoulder and chest. Then, oblivion.

Once, he wakes, feels wind on his face. So thirsty. Funny, how the whole world can shrink, become entirely focused on one simple need. If only he could have a drink of water, his problems would all disappear.

He can see a million stars. So beautiful. So cold-white and clean, close enough to touch. Like ice cubes, just out of reach, if his arm wasn't so heavy.

He knows he should move, but his body isn't listening to his brain. Maybe he'll just wait for the stars to go out, then he'll move.

The next time he wakes, shadowy figures are moving above him in the grey dawn. Japs? He moves, groans involuntarily, and one of the shadows pauses, stops, turns, looming over him. It seems to be trying to pick him up. Not a Jap, then. Japs shoot you or stick you with a bayonet. They don't take prisoners. Not wounded ones anyway.

And then, again, nothing.

TWELVE: The Quick and the Dead
Hong Kong, December 24, 1941

HE WAKES IN A WHITE room with a fan turning overhead. Slowly, slowly. A woman's face swims into view. Dark hair. Dark eyes. A woman's smell, like some kind of flower.

"Su Li? Oh thank Christ, Su Li, I thought you were dead. I was dead too."

"No chance, soldier. You're very much alive."

Not Su Li. Not her voice, not her eyes. Freddy tries to focus.

"Where am I?"

"You're in St. Stephen's College. It's an emergency hospital."

The two-storey building sprawls into four wings in the shape of an H, with a library in the middle and tall, arched windows along each side. Originally a boy's boarding school, it stands alone on a rocky hill above the market village of Stanley. For the past week, it's been a field hospital.

Nearly a hundred wounded men are lying on cots in the classrooms and library on the main floor, with more upstairs in the long gallery.

"What day is it?" he croaks.

"It's Christmas Eve!"

The woman has a British accent and the relentlessly cheerful manner of her profession.

Christmas Eve? Tomorrow would be his birthday. Eighteen. It sounded so old! Practically a geezer, and he was still alive!

"Nurse?" Again, the croaking. "How'd I get here?"

"Two Rifles found you and brought you in. You must have been separated from your platoon—so far you're the only Grenadier to join us."

The only one! He feels unaccountably happy, like he's been singled out for the honour. Visions flit through his brain, a parade of people and places so crystal clear that they have to be real, yet somehow he can't seem to hold on to them, the images keep going out of focus, fading in and out, fluttering like the pages of a book caught in the wind.

He's in the kitchen of Elite Eats, and there's Yip, frying up one of his noodle platters, yelling at the guys to wipe the snow off their feet. Jimmy Soo is there, with a wine bottle sticking out of his coat pocket. The old boys are sitting around the table, Kenny Wong and Lucky Lee, smoking and clacking the tiles in a hot game of mah jong. Freddy laughs out loud.

"Yip! It's me, Freddy!"

The image fades, the page flutters. He's running, looking for somebody. An empty street, alleys with no names. Su Li! She's here someplace, he knows she's here, but he can't find the right door. She's waiting for him, in a room with a slowly turning fan. Somewhere. An infinite sadness wells up in him.

"Su Li!" He tries to call her name, but his voice isn't working. She can't hear him. There are soldiers, Japanese, he can feel them coming closer and she's just sitting there, his beautiful Su Li, waiting.

Sobs shake his shoulders, and he tries to stifle the sound in his pillow.

A woman's voice, low, near his face.

"It's all right to cry, soldier. Just let go. You've lost a lot of blood, and you're weak."

Su Li, gazing down at him. She looks worried, so he smiles and lifts his hand to touch her hair, but she's wearing some kind of veil, and anyway, his hand is too heavy to lift, it weighs a tonne. Her face is fading. The hand falls back on the bed, useless. He can't move the other one at all, it's strapped down somehow. He watches the lazy revolutions of the fan blades, waiting for her face to come back.

"Stay with me, Su Li, don't leave me," he cries, and this time his voice works.

"I love you, Su Li."

"I'll bet you say that to all the girls."

The nurse swabbed his arm with something cold, and he felt the needle prick his flesh.

"You have a broken arm, four broken ribs, a broken collarbone, and we've taken a bullet out of your shoulder. You also have a severe concussion. That's why your head aches. Who is this Su Li you keep on about?"

"She's my . . ." His voice trailed off. His tongue was suddenly too thick to talk.

She patted his hand.

"Never mind. Treats tomorrow! Doc has a case of whisky, and we'll crack it for Christmas lunch. Now, sleep."

"Wait, don't leave me! Stay with me, please."

Freddy heard his own voice whimpering, close to tears again. She pulled a chair near and took his hand.

He focused hard on her face. She was a pretty woman, older than Su Li but pretty. Her dark hair was almost covered with a white veil that nearly reached her shoulders.

"Are you a nun?"

She smiled.

"No. I'm a nursing sister. Don't let the veil fool you."

"Oh yeah, I forgot . . . hospital . . ."

"You should sleep now."

She stood up to leave, but he clutched at her hand. Mick! He tried to sit up.

"Nurse, my shirt, I had a letter . . ."

"Don't worry," she said. "I have it right here."

She had wrapped Mick's letter in gauze dressing and made it into a little package, pinned shut at the top.

"Would you feel better if you kept it with you?"

She leaned over and pinned it inside his T-shirt.

"Thanks, nurse. It's not my letter. It belongs to a friend. I have to deliver it . . ."

His voice broke. Hot tears rolled down his cheeks.

"Mick. I lost Mick. I left him. I should never have left him."

He reached for her hand again, and she took it, holding it in both of hers, patting it as she might have patted a child who needed comfort.

"Don't worry, I'm here. I won't leave you."

He slept again, and Su Li floated past wearing a white veil and speaking with a British accent.

"Please, Freddy, take me to Canada?"

▲　　▲　　▲

CHRISTMAS DAY 1941 is grey and drizzling. Doctor Graham Kaspar, owner of a comfortable practice in Harley Street, London, has been on the phone for at least fifteen minutes pleading with the brass at general headquarters. His improvised hospital overflows: he has British and Rajputs and Canadians, some with severe head wounds, some with chest wounds, most of them requiring surgery. None of them can walk on their own. Now he's playing a trump card, calling a general who happens to be an old school chum.

"Listen, James, we need more nurses and at least one more doctor. A surgeon. I know, I know, but if we don't get some help soon we'll start losing some of your boys."

He sips a mug of tea.

"Damn, it's stone cold. Sorry, I'm just complaining about the tea. Haven't had a cup of hot tea since I left England. Hello? Hello? Damn!"

He hears the telltale buzz and then silence. The line is dead.

Can't this bloody army ever get anything right? A simple landline for a simple phone call? Damn Churchill, swanning around London in his flying suit, making speeches! Damn all of it!

He's still glowering at the receiver when something at the window catches his eye. A slight movement, a minor change of light and shadow that makes him look up.

A Japanese soldier, nose pressed flat against the glass, looks back at him. The face is like a mask, some kind of goblin, with the squashed nose and the grinning lips.

He stands up slowly, replacing the receiver, and for a few seconds he and his enemy look each other in the eye.

The Jap isn't alone. Behind him there are at least a hundred more, moving in a giant U-shape around the building, toward the door. They're drunk. Some are staggering.

Without taking his eyes off the face at the window, he raises his voice just enough so those who are awake will hear him.

"Listen to me. There are Japs outside, but we're flying a red cross, so we're all right. Stay quiet, everybody."

He opens the door quickly, so they'll have no excuse to break it down.

"Hospital," he calls out to the advancing Japanese. "This is a hospital! No weapons here!"

The Jap looking in the window moves to the door, raises his rifle, aims it at Graham Kaspar's face; he hears the double click as it's cocked.

"Hospital," he says again, and the drunken soldier grins and squeezes the trigger.

Five or six Japanese clamber through the door at once, yelling, repeatedly plunging bayonets into the fallen doctor as though this is some kind of ritual hazing by a sadistic fraternity. They start on the wounded, some still unconscious, others simply sleeping, but the Japanese shout their war cries as they go about the killing, and their drunken hollering wakes those who are on the second floor.

Freddy's cot is up there, in a classroom with a dozen injured men. School desks have been piled against the wall to make room for the cots, and somebody has scrawled *Happy Christmas* on the blackboard in coloured chalk, red, green, yellow.

Through a fog of morphine Freddy hears the door being kicked open. The room is suddenly full of yelling Japanese soldiers, plunging bayonets into wounded men.

Freddy's cot is the farthest away from the door, against the end wall. In the confusion he manages to wedge himself between the cot and the wall, just enough so he can roll off and wriggle underneath. When the soldier in the next bed tries to stand up, he is stabbed in the stomach with a bayonet and falls backward across Freddy's hiding place.

He has no idea how long he lies hidden under the flimsy shelter of a cot and a corpse, listening to the horror unfolding around him, but the next thing that registers in his befuddled brain is a man's voice, speaking English with a slight British accent. The voice sounds faintly bored.

"Hiding, are we? Come out. I insist."

From under the cot Freddy can see shiny leather boots, but he says nothing. Colonel Tanaka isn't accustomed to waiting. The cot is kicked away, and one of the shiny boots smashes into Freddy's side, landing squarely in his broken ribs. The pain takes his breath away.

When he can focus again, he sees Tanaka's white teeth smiling down at him.

"I'm afraid you think my men overzealous."

Tanaka is proud of his faultless English and his Oxford accent, acquired during three years reading history at All Souls. In fact he has little taste for mindless violence such as this. His days at Oxford, sherry in the Don's rooms, rare roast beef at high table—those were good times. English life had a measured civility that appeals to him. After this is over, he'll go back. Possibly he'll teach, become a Don himself, at All Souls. They have quite the best cellar.

"Get on your feet," he says cheerfully, yanking Freddy up by one arm, sending fresh waves of pain crashing through his broken body, so he cries out. Disgusted, Tanaka drops him in a heap.

"What a tiresome lot you English are! Take him away."

Freddy is dragged down a hallway and flung through a door into a dark storeroom where he lies crumpled, gasping for breath.

When the pain recedes far enough for his eyes to focus, he sees that he isn't alone. The room is crowded with men. The faint light from a high, narrow window is just enough to distinguish faces and features.

Most of them have their heads down. Propped against the walls, seated or standing, they stare at the floor or keep their eyes closed. He knows why. If they refuse to look, it might all go away.

But nothing goes away. The door opens and a man is dragged into the corridor. One Jap guards the door, but this time he keeps it open, so the prisoners are forced to hear and, God help them, to see.

They can't shut out the young corporal's frantic pleading as he begs for mercy or his terrified scream as three men hold him down and a fourth slices off his left ear and dangles it in front of his eyes, waves it around for all to see. They toss it, hand to hand to hand, this detached bit of flesh and bone that bleeds surprisingly little.

He screams at them, screams his pain and rage, so now it takes four of them to hold him down while the fifth forces his jaws apart and cuts out his tongue. The only sound after that is a kind of bubbling, snorting rattle as they continue to hold him on his back while he chokes to death on his own blood. It takes a long time.

The door slams shut. In the sweltering room, some men pray, silently or in whispers. Freddy hears the muttered words "Our Father, who art in heaven . . ." but most are silent, each man alone with his own fear.

In half an hour or so, it starts again.

At seventeen, a young man doesn't think about dying. Death is still an abstract concept, something that happens to other people, old and sick, or stupidly careless, or just unlucky. At seventeen, even when the dying begins, a young man doesn't really get it.

But fear is another matter. Fear has no respect for youth, and in that room Freddy comes to understand fear in new ways.

His conscious mind rebels. This is not happening. This is not possible among human beings. *Please, God, let me wake up now. Please, let this nightmare end. Please, God, let me die now . . .*

A man retches. A door is jerked open, then slammed shut. In a corner, someone sobs. Suddenly, involuntarily, Freddy's bowels let go.

"Oh, Jesus, I think . . . I think I shit myself . . ."

"It's all right, son."

The gruff voice belongs to the older man beside him. Freddy has begun to shake so hard that his teeth are chattering.

"I have a boy about your age," says the voice. "He's in France. How old are you, son?"

"Seventeen," Freddy tells him, his voice shaking more now because of the chattering teeth. "No, I mean eighteen. Today's my birthday." And to his shame, he begins to laugh, a high, hysterical giggle.

▲   ▲   ▲

THEY BEGAN RAPING the nurses.

Part of the spoils of war, this ritual destruction of the enemy's women. A recognized perk of man-the-conqueror. They stripped the nurses, threw them naked across the bodies already there. Held down by three or four men while their attackers hooted, they were repeatedly raped before their throats were slit.

Freddy, too near the door, closed his eyes to shut out the horror, opened them just once, saw the woman. The nurse who had saved Mick's letter for him.

At that moment a kind of numbness settled over Freddy, but his subconscious brain took it all in, every evil sound, every evil smell and evil act, and stored it away for later, when he would have to pay. For having been to hell and survived, there would be a price: his personal collection of nightmares, the ones that would haunt him every night for the rest of his life.

At 3:15 on the afternoon of Christmas 1941, a British general sat in a room in the Peninsula Hotel and signed the surrender of Hong Kong, sealing the fate of every human being on the island.

Freddy's war had turned a corner. On his eighteenth birthday, he became a prisoner of the Japanese.

THIRTEEN : The Homecoming
Japan, August 1946

ON AUGUST 8 AND 9, 1946, two atomic bombs are dropped on Japan. Freddy's war is over. He'll be going home.

▲　　▲　　▲

THE MAN WHO steps off the train in Edmonton has been gone five years, but spring smells the same as it always had. Poplar sap. Fresh. Green. He breathes deeply, shaking off the coal smoke from the train. He hates the smell of coal smoke.

The months in a Vancouver veterans' hospital have put forty pounds back on the near-skeleton who walked out of the Japanese prison camp the previous August, but he's still thin, especially his face.

There are deep lines around his mouth that weren't there when he left and scars under his shirt that nobody sees. His eyes are different too. During conversation people sometimes notice the blank look, as though a blind comes down somewhere in his brain.

He takes a cab from the CPR station across the river to the address on 97th Street. In the window of Elite Eats, the porcelain Buddha grins at him through dusty foliage where the familiar begonia still sprawls across the ledge. Through the window, he sees the red and chrome stools along the counter, the wooden booths, the picture of Yip's family hanging by the cash register. He remembers it all as though it were yesterday, but it's been a lifetime.

Pushing through the swinging doors from the kitchen, Yip Lee sees the thin man in the uniform.

"Freddy? *Freddy McKee?*"

Face alight with recognition, he pumps Freddy's hand, slaps his shoulder.

"Hey, kid, you come back!" he cries. "That's good! That's good, kid!"
He leans into the kitchen, yelling.

"Boys, see who we got here! Freddy McKee is home!"

Home. After five years. Home.

Freddy hears Yip's voice from a distance, and with difficulty he drags his brain into the moment, trying hard to concentrate. Goes through the motions, receives Yip's welcome, greets the guys in the kitchen like long-lost brothers.

"Yeah, it's great to be back, Yip," he says. "It's great!"

Yip yells a general announcement to his customers.

"Hey, you guys, we got a war hero here! Freddy McKee! He jes' back from Japan. Right, Freddy?"

Customers turn toward the skinny guy in the uniform. The red shoulder patch of the Winnipeg Grenadiers, and the other one, the stylized gold HK embroidered on a red background, aren't familiar. This is not Edmonton's regiment. Some of them grin at him, others just stare but not for long. These days, everybody's a hero. They go back to their hamburgers.

Yip installs Freddy in the back booth and sits across from him, watching his face. One of the boys brings coffee in thick white mugs.

"You okay, kid? Nobody shoot you or anything?"

"I'm okay, Yip. I had a couple of scratches. Nothing much."

"You been a POW, Freddy? In Japan, ha?"

"Yeah."

"How long in Japan?"

"Nearly four years. Seemed like a long time."

Seemed like a goddamn lifetime.

A silence now with Yip looking for words because this is not the Freddy he remembers.

"They feed you okay in the army?"

"Army food isn't great, Yip. Nothing like yours."

Yip grins, blows smoke through his nostrils, and gives him an approving nod before the blinds come down in Freddy's eyes.

Yip, I stole food from a dead guy. Took it off a dead body. I was lost for days, didn't know where the hell I was. Got so hungry. There was this dead guy in a ditch. He had a mouldy sandwich in his pack. Rotten meat. I ate it.

The Japs, Yip. They hunt you like an animal, eh? Like a deer or a moose. They stalk you, just for the fun of it. Nothing in your stomach for days, you do crazy things. You eat a dead man's rotten food. Drink a dead man's canteen dry. Steal his ammunition and keep running.

"What happen over there, kid?"

"Not much, Yip."

Why do they ask that question? It's like they're reading from a script. The army doctors. The shrink in Vancouver. Even the hooker, that night in Chinatown.

I shouldn't have gone down there anyway. I have to stop looking.

"You don't want to talk about it?"

"Not really, Yip. Nothing much to say, I guess."

I went to hell, Yip. Lost my lovely Su Li. Lost Mick, my best friend. Left him when he was wounded. Spent four years in Jap hell. Now I can't even remember the names of the guys who were with me. How do I explain that, Yip?

Yip knows something isn't right with the kid. Goddamn Japs, goddamn turnip-heads. They hurt this boy. Yip senses the pain but feels helpless.

"Hey, kid! You hungry? I cook something for you! Very special!"

Yip disappears through the swinging doors and minutes later he's back with a plate of fried egg rolls and a dish of yellow plum sauce.

"Long time ago, you come here with Mrs. Serena. Remember? Jus' a skinny little kid. But you always like Yip's egg roll. Now you skinny again! Gotta fatten you up, ha!"

Yip laughs at his own joke, beams as Freddy devours the egg rolls. Skinny as he is, he's always hungry now, as though he never gets enough to eat, like he's storing up for hibernation.

On that ship coming back, they gave us steak, fried potatoes, chocolate cake, food we dreamed about. I puked it all up. See, Yip, I got used to the rice. Rice gruel, once a day. No salt. Grit, though. Lots of grit. And maggots. I ate the maggots. We all did, after a while. Maggots for protein. Christ, Yip, how could I ever tell you about that? How could I tell anybody?

After the egg rolls, Freddy lights a Players. He looks at the picture hanging behind the cash register. Yip's family.

They'd have been on the Kowloon side. A woman with three little girls? No chance they'd survive the Japs.

Unless they made it to the island. Holed up somewhere in Hong Kong. Su Li could be there too. Could still be there. Except she'd be starving. Unless the Japs got her? This is crazy, gotta stop thinking about her.

"What you do now, kid? You stay here awhile? Rest. Maybe work for Yip again. Okay, kid? Maybe you be a cook."

"Thanks, Yip. Maybe I will."

I'm home. I'm alive. I should feel great. So why do I feel like such a piece of shit? I've gotta get out of here. Need some air.

He tells Yip he's going for a walk. Yip looks at him long and hard, pats his shoulder gently, like he'd pat a child.

"Sure, kid. You come back later. Come tonight. The boys will all be here. Everybody want to see Freddy. We have a party!"

He walks fast, up one street, down another, no particular destination in mind. Walks away from Chinatown, past the familiar landmarks, The Bay, Eaton's, Woolworth's, the old City Hall. Scenes from another life.

On Jasper Avenue he doubles back, catches a trolley north across the CN railway tracks, toward the old neighbourhood. Familiar sounds, trains switching in the rail yards.

The vacant lot where the guys used to hang out among the poplars is no longer vacant. A three-storey walk-up sits where he and Siggy and the others once played at war. Such innocents, he thought. Kids who play war.

He gets off at the next stop and turns on to Dieppe Road, walks toward the end of the short street, past the vacant lot that once was Serena's garden, to the last house. Two little boys in the yard shoot at each other with wooden sticks. A chubby blonde woman steps out the front door, hand on hip, watching him where he stands by the gate.

81

"Looking for somebody, mister?"

"I was wondering if the McKee family still lived around here."

"McKee? Nope, never heard of any McKees. Not in this neighbourhood." She pauses, squinting at the stranger in the uniform. "You a relative or something?"

"No. It's not important. Sorry I bothered you."

He turns up his collar and starts the long walk back.

▲   ▲   ▲

ON THIS NIGHT, Yip Lee does something he usually reserves for Chinese New Year. He closes his restaurant early.

The kitchen fills with men. Familiar faces, every one. Jimmy Soon, Lucky Wu, Frank and Denny Toy. Mr. Wong from the Thousand Year Trading Company. Even the old guys from upstairs come shuffling down, taking Freddy's hand, shaking it limply between their soft palms, grinning at him with their withered-leaf faces, murmuring greetings in high, quavering voices.

He looks around the room.

"Where's Willy Lo?"

"Willy join up. Government finally let our boys do that, you know. Last year of war, they need guys with yellow skin and slanted eyes. They figure we can pass for Japs. We all look alike, eh?"

Yip smiles and lights another cigarette.

"They can drop Chinese guys behind enemy lines. Spy on Japs! Sabotage! BOOM! All that stuff! So, they let our boys in."

The room is quiet while Yip talks.

"Lots of our boys join up. Bing Mah, Tommy Wu. Some don't come back. They give Willy a parachute. Drop him into Burma."

Yip smokes busily for a minute. Stubs it out in a saucer.

"We don't hear from him since."

Shit. They used these people. Just like they used the rest of us. We were all disposable.

For a while the only sound is the sizzling in Yip's wok, but then the back door bursts open and two young guys come flying into the

82

kitchen. It's the Ho boys, twin brothers, Kenny and Benny. They were just little kids when Freddy left, but look at them now, two young men, sixteen last birthday.

"Hey, Freddy, welcome home!"

Freddy's face breaks into a grin and he gets to his feet, extending his hand to these suddenly grown-up boys who were once like little brothers. Benny strikes a match, lights a short fuse, and tosses a double string of small red firecrackers into the middle of the kitchen floor by way of celebration. It's a good string with no duds, so the banging and popping and the smell of cordite that accompanies every important Chinese occasion suddenly fills the kitchen of Elite Eats.

"Down!" Freddy yells. "Get down!"

He dives under the table, and by the time the banging and popping of the firecrackers has fizzled out at the end of the last fuse, he's curled up in a ball with his hands over his head, rocking back and forth on his knees, whimpering words the astonished men can't understand.

Yip helps Freddy up the stairs, half carries him along the hall to his old room. He helps him out of his sweat-soaked shirt. Freddy shivers uncontrollably, his teeth chattering.

"You sick, kid? You need a doctor?"

"I'm okay, Yip. I'm okay."

Goddamn malaria . . .

He passes out. Yip covers him with a blanket, then another. The shaking doesn't stop, and Yip pulls a chair beside Freddy's cot, waiting. Shortly after four o'clock in the morning, Freddy wakes up, shouting, crying out words Yip doesn't understand but somehow knows: he's pleading for mercy, in Japanese. The yelling stops, reduced to whimpers. When the old boys come shuffling in to see who's being murdered, Yip sends them away.

"No problem. Jus' bad dream."

The old boys nod and shuffle back to their rooms, each one with his own ghosts hovering nearby.

Several weeks later, and only this once, Yip indulges his curiosity.

"You got any medals, kid?"

"Yeah, I guess. A couple."

"You ever wear them?"

"No."

▲ ▲ ▲

IN FACT HE'D shoved them into a shoebox. Everything. Medals, documents, all the visible debris of his war. He didn't want to open it. Didn't want to see it, ever again.

The box held the following items: the Canadian War Medal; the Pacific Star; the Defence Medal; and the Canadian Volunteer Service Medal with clasp. Each medal was attached to a striped ribbon, different colours, different widths of stripe.

Also in the box were his discharge papers, noting that Private Frederick Alphonse McKee had joined the Canadian Armed Forces April 15, 1941, and served on active duty in Hong Kong from November 16 to December 25, 1941.

His medical documents said he'd been wounded in action some time in late December 1941, and on December 25 had been recovering from surgery at St. Stephen's Academy, a temporary field hospital, when he'd been taken prisoner.

It was mentioned that he had been in a prisoner of war camp at Sham Shui Po and then at North Point in Hong Kong for fourteen months before being transferred by ship to Japan, where he had spent the remainder of the war at forced labour, first in the shipyards in Tokyo, then in a Japanese coal mine. The documents noted that he'd been liberated August 26, 1945.

The same documents mentioned that Freddy had at varying times suffered from yellow fever, malaria, and dry beriberi; had suffered multiple broken ribs and a severe skull fracture with involvement of hearing loss in both ears that was likely to be progressive. He also showed some permanent lung damage.

His weight during his enlistment medical was 167 pounds. His weight on the day he checked into Shaughnessy Veterans' Hospital in Vancouver was 98 pounds.

All of this was a matter of record, written on various documents, white, pink, yellow. All consigned for the moment to Freddy's shoebox.

The documents said nothing about the nightmares.

They said nothing about his terrifying claustrophobia, from years of crawling through cramped underground passages on hands and knees, or doing repeated time in the coffin, an ingenious wooden box in which a man could neither stand up nor lie down; in which, when the sun was at its highest and a man was about to suffocate he sometimes lost consciousness; and from which Freddy emerged each time unable to walk so he was forced to crawl back to his cell block on his hands and knees.

Neither did they mention the barrel with the wooden lid. The drowning barrel.

They said nothing about how he has come to love the sound of a bottle clinking against a tumbler, the *glug-glug* as the rye is poured (the rye, the rum, the gin, he's not fussy, not anymore), and the blessed oblivion that comes when he finally passes out.

They said nothing about his uncontrollable rages.

BOOK TWO
The Homefront

ONE: Stan and Hope

STAN NOVAK WILL NOT GO to war in Japan. Unlike Mick and Freddy, unlike Tony, Stan's war will be spent in Canada; essential service, they call it. A corporal in the RCMP, he's stationed in northern Manitoba, in tiny Trout Creek, a two-trains-a-week settlement near a phantom airbase called Dogrib.

"Phantom because it doesn't exist," he's been told by air force brass. "Top secret. The minute we clean up the mess in Europe, Dogrib disappears."

Stan's position in Trout Creek is odd. As the sole enforcer of law and order, he's respected, even liked, but he's not one of the boys.

Except with Mick Keegan. Mick is a friend. With Mick and his wife, Joanna, Stan can be himself. Have a few beers, tell a joke, express an opinion. He loves listening to Joanna play the piano. His affection for them grows out of his own solitude, and the arrival of their baby girl, Hope, strengthens the bond.

From the beginning, Stan showers the baby with presents, and when she begins to talk he teaches her to call him Uncle Stan. If she develops a sniffle he fusses over her like an old hen and wonders out loud if Trout Creek is any place to be raising a child. The baby grins and gurgles at him, pats his face with small sticky hands, gives him damp kisses at arrivals and departures. He brings her so many stuffed animals that her room begins to look like a toy store. Joanna accuses him of spoiling the baby, but Mick just laughs.

"Relax, Jo. When Stan has a tribe of his own kids, it'll be our turn to spoil them. All ten of them!"

For Hope's second Christmas, Stan lugs an awkward package through the door. She squeals with delight at the beautiful wooden rocking horse he's made for her. Painted shiny black with a bright red saddle, the horse has a shaggy mane and luxuriant tail made of thick multicoloured yarn he bought in Winnipeg.

"I told the woman in Woolworth's I was learning to knit," he tells Joanna, who strokes the wonderful Christmas horse and says not a word about spoiling the baby.

▲   ▲   ▲

IT WAS IRONIC that just as the economy began to turn around down south, things got worse in Trout Creek. By 1941, Mick's savings, never very large, had dribbled away until he could barely pay for the weekly grocery order. He suspected Jo's sister, Marg, had been subsidizing it.

Hope's third birthday fell on a Tuesday, the day the train went south through Trout Creek, heading for Winnipeg. Early that morning, while Joanna was mixing pink icing for the cake, Mick gave Joanna the bad news. He was going to miss the party.

"I have to go to Winnipeg today."

"On Hope's birthday? That's ridiculous! Why, for heaven's sake?"

He took a deep breath.

"I'm going to join up," he said, trying hard to keep his tone casual.

"Join up? Join what? What are you joining?"

In the small silence that followed, the look on his face told her everything.

"You're joining the army." She slammed the bowl on the table. The spoon bounced, landed on the floor, pink icing everywhere.

"You're joining the bloody army!"

"I have to do it, Jo."

"Why? Why would you do this to us? To me and our daughter?"

Joanna was furious. She couldn't remember being so angry before, never. She yelled at Mick, shrieked like a fishwife, demanded that he change his mind, accused him of not loving her, not loving Hope, of being a selfish bastard who didn't care about either of them. Then the anger ran out and she began to cry. Mick wrapped his arms around her, rocking her back and forth, murmuring into her hair.

"Joey, I can't make a living here anymore. I've been kidding myself, but I can't support us. We have to think of Hope."

"I *am* thinking of Hope," she told him between sobs. "I'm thinking of what her life will be like without a father! And what about me? What about my life without a husband? I don't want to be your widow!"

Mick held her away from him, looked down at her, and grinned.

"Jo, now you're being silly. I'll come back on leave at least once a month. Likely every weekend. The army will only be for a couple of years, and then I'll be home for good, and we won't be poor anymore."

"But there's a war! Canadians are getting killed in Europe! What if they send you overseas? To France or some other awful place? Poland, maybe!"

She cried harder, but he knew the worst of the storm was over. The third stage of Joanna's wrath, when she tried to make up for having made him miserable, would come next.

"They'll never send me overseas, Jo. I have you two. You're my good luck charms. I'll be tucked away in Camp Shilo, safe as a baby in a cradle, and I'll come home whenever I can wrangle a pass." He kissed the top of her head. "Jo, we just can't live on love anymore. I have to make a living."

When Stan walked in the door, the tension in the kitchen was palpable. Joanna had her back to him, stiff as a ramrod, and she sniffled loud enough for him to hear.

Mick had always been a peace-loving man. He had no desire to become a soldier and he certainly didn't want to fight in anybody's war, but army pay was good and recruiting offices were begging for men.

Stan had done some checking for him, and he figured with Mick's wife and child, two dependents, he'd easily be kept in Manitoba, likely given a desk job. Maybe he could even move Jo and Hope south, scrape up a down payment on a little house after a few cheques. The army was a reasonable option.

"Where's my girl?"

Stan stood in Hope's bedroom door, wearing his big buffalo coat and fur hat. To Hope he looked like a bigger version of one of the many stuffed bears he'd given her. He scooped her into his arms, feeling her small face warm against his cheek.

"Uncle Stan, you're too cold!"

They went through their ritual of bear hugs and growls, then she placed a hand on each side of his face, looked into his eyes, and came right to the point.

"Uncle Stan! It's my birthday! Any presents?"

He laughed out loud.

"That's my girl, Hope. Check the pocket."

Hope made a dive for the big outside pocket where she'd often found treats.

"Careful, it might bite!"

Her hand touched something soft and furry, like a stuffed toy, but it moved, and she jerked her hand away. Stan, fearing tears, brought his latest present out of his pocket and placed it gently in her lap.

"A kitty," she squealed. "Mom, Dad! My own kitty!"

When her parents appeared in the doorway, Hope was cuddling a loudly purring kitten.

"She's beautiful," Hope breathed. "She's my best birthday present ever!"

Stan beamed, and Joanna took the birthday cat and turned it upside down.

"She's a he, Stan. You brought us a tomcat?"

"Goody, goody," Hope yelled, beside herself with delight. "Tom Cat!"

"I guess we'll just have to find Tom Cat a litter box," Mick said, loving their four-legged guest for diverting Joanna's attention.

Tom Cat was orange and white striped, with a white belly and a fluffy orange tail, evidence of his mother's brief fling with a handsome Persian. For Hope and her cat, the affection was instant and mutual. When her dad climbed on the noon train, Hope waved goodbye without shedding a tear. All afternoon she and the kitten were inseparable, and at bedtime he hopped onto her bed and curled up at her feet.

"Be sure that cat doesn't get on your pillow," Joanna warned, and as soon as the door closed, up he went. Tom Cat wriggled a little, by way of adjusting himself to his half of the pillow, and Hope fell asleep with the comforting vibrations of a purring kitten.

TWO : Piano Nights

MY MOM SAYS TROUT CREEK is just a godforsaken wide spot in the bush, and no civilized woman should have to live here. I don't think she means it.

I guess I should tell you about Trout Creek. It has one street and six houses, with the lumber camp on the other side of the railway tracks. My mom and I live at the Trout Creek Inn. It's two boxcars with windows and a caboose stuck in the middle. My dad built it for us. If you could look down on it, you'd see an H. At least that's what my dad told me.

Partly our house is just one big room. We cook and eat at one end, and the other end is the sitting part of the house. That's where Mom's piano is, in the sitting end, beside the window.

Our bedrooms are in the caboose. Mom and Dad's room is the biggest, except now it's just Mom's. It has a ladder up to the crow's nest and window seats. That's my favourite place in the whole world. I go up there with Tom Cat, especially if Georgie Leski, my enemy, is hanging around, which he usually is. I can't stand Georgie, but I get stuck playing with him because there are no other kids in Trout Creek and my mom says I have to learn to socialize with people my own age.

The last part of our house has four bunkbeds. If you're stuck in Trout Creek, you won't mind a couple of roommates. That's what my dad used to say. Dumas the Trapper stays with us when he's off his trap lines, and Tubby Clarkson from the Steeprock Mine. There's a secret Yankee airstrip up at Dogrib, and sometimes we get pilots and soldiers from there.

Uncle Stan says they come for my mom's good cooking and Mary

Leski's goodwill. He says Mary's not too good but she sure is willing, and don't tell my mom he said so. He didn't say why.

We used to have hunters, but they stopped coming since my dad isn't here to guide them. One of them tried to guide himself last year, and he got so lost it took the whole town two days to find him. He was in the muskeg, and Mom says the mosquitoes and no-see-ums just about ate him alive. Uncle Stan said he was lucky a bear didn't get him, but my mom said no self-respecting bear would eat anybody stupid enough to get lost in the muskeg.

The next house to ours belongs to George Leski, the section foreman. He works on the CNR tracks, and has his own gas-car to run up and down, as long as there are no trains in the way. Sometimes he gives me a ride, but then his horrid son, Georgie, has to go too. Mary is his wife, and my mother's best friend. Mary wears a lot of perfume, but not Evening in Paris, like my mom.

Next is Baba and Steve Popovich. Steve works on the tracks with George. Baba always wears an apron and lace-up moccasins with felt liners, even in summer, and nobody has ever seen her without her babushka.

Uncle Stan boards with Baba and Steve. He's not really my uncle, but I call him that. His real name is Corporal Stan Novak, and he was my dad's friend, before Dad went away. He's in the RCMP, and he has an office beside Baba and Steve's house, but there aren't enough bad guys in Trout Creek for him to get his own jail. Mom says you can't have everything.

Next is the railway station. Chris Stinson is the agent, and he and his wife, Kay, live behind the office. Mrs. Stinson (Mom says that's what I have to call her) makes the best raisin cookies in Trout Creek.

The log house next to the station belongs to Bertha Yellowquill. She's there in winter, for the electric lights, but in summer she packs up her canoe and moves across the Steeprock River so she can live in her tent.

The last house belongs to Dahlia Rempel and Deaf Gilbert. Dahlia (I have to call her Mrs. Rempel) has the post office in her front room.

She and Gilbert aren't exactly married, but it doesn't matter because nobody else would have either one of them as a holy gift. That's what Mary Leski says.

That's all there is on the town side of the tracks. The bush comes right up behind our houses, and Mom gets mad when the bears eat her raspberries. We saw one! Mom got out the .410 shotgun my dad left for her and shot at the bear but she missed. Uncle Stan put the gun away in his office and told her to call him whenever there was a bear in the berries.

Across the tracks is McLaughlin's lumber camp. He always has seven or eight guys living in his bunkhouse, and there's a cookshack where they'd eat if they could find a cook.

McLaughlin has his own streetlight. It stays on every night until nine o'clock. That's when he turns off the generator. He blinks the lights twice so we can get the wick lamps going. Mom always lights three wick lamps and the whole house turns soft and yellow, like melted butter. I like it that way.

On Thursday at five o'clock the train comes through from Winnipeg, heading north to Churchill. That's the best train because it has our grocery box from Aunt Marg, who works in Eaton's Groceteria. Every Thursday, she packs everything on Mom's list into a big cardboard box and drives it down to the station where her friend Al the brakeman looks after it. She always puts a comic book and an all-day sucker in a bag marked *For Hope, Private, Keep Out*. Thursday is my favourite day.

Tuesday the train comes back the other way. Anybody going to Winnipeg has to be ready by noon because the Tuesday train never stops for long.

Every week I dust my mom's piano. The keys remind me of Dumas the Trapper when he grins. Some teeth are long and yellowish white, some are short and black.

Mom used to play the piano almost every night before Dad went away. Sometimes the whole town would be in our house, and she'd play so they could sing. I loved those piano nights.

My dad sang too. He taught me a song, "Froggie Went a Courting," about a handsome frog who fell in love with a mouse. Most frogs are ugly, but not this one.

Mom stopped playing her piano after we got the telegram about my dad. It makes her sad to remember our piano nights.

We talked about the sad stuff when I was still a little kid, after the night I went looking for Dad and everybody thought I was lost in the woods. I saw him that night. He was behind our house, looking at my bedroom window. Mom says it was just my imagination, but I know he was there.

THREE: Lost in the Woods

Trout Creek, September 1943

ON THAT NIGHT IN EARLY September, Hope had been trying to sleep. The house was quiet, and it seemed like she'd been in bed forever.

Hope is a big girl now, or so her mother keeps telling her. Five years old, which means Tom Cat is two, or fourteen in cat years.

Her mother is asleep in the next room, but her father isn't there. He's been gone for a long time.

Sometimes when she can't sleep Hope remembers the nights before her dad left. There were people in the living room, talking, laughing, her mother playing the piano, Mary Leski singing. Mary had a pretty good voice, loud anyway, and Hope could still hear the music, *"Pack up all my care and woe, here we go, singing low . . ."*

Hope climbs out of bed and pads barefoot to the window. There are animals out there in the forest. She can see their eyes, twin points of light glowing in the darkness.

Baba Popovich says her dad has gone to heaven and turned into an angel. She says he watches over Hope all the time, day and night, so even though she can't see Dad-the-angel, he's really there.

Hope checks the window again. Sure enough, the lights are still there. Two small lights, close together, like two eyes.

Maybe she should go out there. Maybe she can find him. There's nothing to be afraid of because he's an angel, and as soon as he sees her he'll pick her up in his arms and carry her, the way he used to, on those nights when her mom played the piano.

A tear runs down her cheek, and she sticks out her tongue and tastes salt. She presses her face against the window, feeling the coolness against her forehead.

There! There it is again. Two lights. Two eyes, looking at the house. He's out there!

She puts on the fuzzy bear slippers Uncle Stan gave her and ties a bow in the belt of her housecoat, the way her mom taught her.

"You have to stay here, Tom," she tells the cat. "You'd be scared in the dark."

The cat sleeps on.

The house is quiet as Hope slips into the hallway. Carefully, carefully she tiptoes through the living room, past the closed piano, past her father's chair that hasn't been moved an inch since he left, carefully between the stove and the kitchen table, and slowly now, slowly, she opens the back door, taking care that it doesn't squeak or slam as she steps out into the night and looks up.

So many stars. Her dad taught her about stars, so she knows how to find the lady in the chair, and the big bear, and both dippers.

"Dad?" she whispers as loud as she can without the possibility of rousing her mother, who can hear through walls.

"Dad? It's me, Hope. Where are you, Dad?"

She heads toward the forest.

▲   ▲   ▲

JOANNA WAKES WITH a start. Hope's cat is on the bed, purring noisily.

"Tom? What are you doing here, you silly cat?"

The clock on her bedside table says it's past 2:00 AM. Once again, she's fallen asleep with the lamp burning. McLaughlin shuts the generator off at nine o'clock, but a coal oil lamp will burn for hours. Joanna gets out of bed and picks up the purring cat, snuggling him in her arms.

"This isn't your bed, Tom. Let's go back to Hope."

Hope's bed is empty.

Dropping the cat, she searches, panic rising. She grabs the lamp, looks under the bed, in the closet, down the hall, the bathroom, the living room, the kitchen. Under the table, behind the stove. Inside the big woodbox. All the places Hope likes to hide.

"Hope! Are you hiding from Mommy?"

Joanna's heart thuds in her chest. She grabs the lamp, races through the house, checks the guest room, the other closets, the bunkhouse.

"Hope! Hope, this isn't funny! Where are you?"

Please, let her be hiding.

Stan! It's Thursday, he'd have been on the night train. Stan will find her. Abandoning the coal oil lamp on the kitchen table, Joanna runs barefoot along the familiar path to Baba's door and pounds on it, yelling his name.

"Stan!" *Oh God, let him be here, please.*

"Stan! Wake up, Stan!" *Please, please, be here.*

Steve Popovich appears in the doorway, half asleep, holding a flashlight to her face.

"Something is wrong, Joanna? You need Stan?"

"Steve, Hope is gone! Please, wake him up! Now!"

Stan was dreaming. He and Joanna, swimming together in the Steeprock River. Joanna nude, even lovelier than he'd imagined. He wants to make love to her, there on the mossy bank, but she disappears. He can hear her voice, and she's calling his name, but he can't see her.

"Stan! Help me!"

Where the hell is she?

Abruptly he's awake. Years of training kick in fast. It takes him three minutes to get the relevant information out of a nearly hysterical Joanna, ten minutes and five phone calls to get the word out, ten more to organize the search party in Joanna's kitchen. George Leski, Steve Popovich, Chris Stinson. Five men from McLaughlin's camp. Dumas the Trapper materializes from somewhere. They all have lanterns or flashlights, and they carry the odd assortment of hunting rifles and shotguns that are routine in a place where having the right weapon in your hand at the right time can save your own skin or somebody else's.

The men are huddled around a forestry map when Bertha Yellowquill strides into the room.

"I take the Steeprock path," she tells Stan, shouldering George aside, leaning over the map as though she could read it.

Stan clears his throat.

"Uh, Bertha, I just thought, well, maybe you'd want to stay here with the others. With the women, I mean."

Bertha makes a noise that's half snort.

"You want to find her, eh? Or not? I know the bush better than all you white boys put together!"

Stan hands her a flashlight. Then he holds up a flare gun.

"We'll fan out. When we find her, I'll shoot off a red flare to bring you in. She can't have gone far, she hasn't had time. If we get into daylight, you'll see red smoke. I called the airbase at Dogrib, and they'll start a search at first light."

He and George Leski exchanged glances. They both knew how futile a search plane would be if they hadn't found her by daylight. A five-year-old in the forest, concealed under the canopy of spruce and pine? Not a hope.

"Okay, let's go."

That night, McLaughlin turned the generator back on, and Trout Creek's only streetlight shone from the camp north of the tracks.

"She might get lucky and see it," he said. "She'd come toward the light."

Except for Bertha Yellowquill, the women had gathered in Joanna's kitchen. Kay Stinson in curlers, Baba Popovich wearing her babushka, Dahlia Rempel and Mary Leski with chenille housecoats over pyjamas. Smoke from their cigarettes floated upward, into Hope's playroom in the crow's nest. That's where Mary found Joanna, holding the baby picture she had taken the year Mick went away. Hope, perched on the knee of an Eaton's Department Store Santa.

"Jo?"

Mary's head appeared above the ladder. She balanced two mugs of coffee in one hand, a lit cigarette in the other.

"Jo? I thought you might need some company."

Joanna was clutching the photograph to her chest, and she rocked back and forth as though she was in pain.

"She didn't cry when she sat on Santa's knee. Did I ever tell you that? Did I tell you she was the only baby who didn't cry?"

"Right, Jo. Hope's a brave little kid."

"Mary, she's alive. I know she's alive. I can feel it."

But they have to find her soon or she won't be. Oh please, God, please, you've got Mick, don't take my baby . . .

"The boys will find her, Jo. They found that asshole American hunter, didn't they? They'll find her."

All night long the women kept their vigil, taking such comfort as they could in one another's company. They all had kids of their own, and though they'd never have said it out loud, each one knew their truth: more than husbands and lovers, more than the whole world, was the fierce and painful love they felt for their children.

At daybreak they heard the drone of a small Cessna, the search plane heading south.

"That'll be the boys from Dogrib," said Mary. "Jo, why don't you come down for a while? Maybe try to sleep?"

"I can't sleep. Not until they find her."

The first rays of the rising sun slipped over the treetops and through the east windows. Kay Stinson looked at her watch.

"It's been six hours. Nearly seven."

"There's time yet." Dahlia Rempel got up stiffly and started a fresh pot of coffee. "Still lots of time."

"At least it's daylight," said Kay. "That'll be a help."

"At least it isn't cold," said Mary. "Not for September. She could be curled up under a tree somewhere, sleeping."

Baba Popovich just shook her head.

"Oi, yoi," she muttered, fingering her rosary. She'd been praying all night, counting on her direct pipeline to the Holy Mother to bring the child home safely. "She be so small," moaned Baba to her favourite saint. "So small, alone in bush."

Nobody spoke of the muskeg. The algae-covered sloughs that looked deceptively like grassy meadows, even in daylight. The open sinkholes, black and bottomless. The Steeprock River, purling gently past Trout Creek but gathering speed in the rapids, crashing over the falls. Bears, wolves, the possibility of hypothermia after all these hours of exposure, even though September had been warm. The bush was so thick that man, wolf, or bear standing ten feet away would be invisible. How much harder would it be to find a child, curled up under a tree?

Lost in their own thoughts, the women didn't hear the kitchen door open, the small slippered feet cross the floor. Hope, rubbing sleep out of her eyes, looked around the room at the astonished gathering.

"Where's my mom?"

It was Mary who scooped the shivering child into her arms and ran to the foot of the crow's nest.

"Joanna! She's here! Hope is here, and she's okay!"

The search party took almost two hours to reassemble in the Keegans' kitchen, straggling in one by one to devour platters of pancakes and eggs, drink cup after cup of coffee. Each one had his own tale to tell of where he searched and what he saw, or thought he saw, for it was true, there were strange lights now and then, the phosphorescent glow from a rotting log, or even (this from Dumas the Trapper) ghost lights, a pale light emanating from an old but shallow grave of some long forgotten trapper.

"I don't know how we missed her," said Stan. "I walked right by that tree."

Hope had fallen asleep no more than twenty feet beyond the end of Joanna's garden, at the edge of the thick forest. Now, wrapped in a quilt in Stan's arms, surrounded by the assembled adults, she pointed to the tree, a big old poplar, somehow managing to thrive where conifers ruled.

"That's Dad's tree," she said with the confidence only a truthful four-year-old could have. "He's an angel now. This is his tree, and he was here."

Hope had seen no need to travel further. She had plunked herself down in the fallen leaves, wrapped her bathrobe more firmly around her small body, and leaned her back against the familiar trunk. She'd often sat under it with her dad, looking back at their house.

From here she could see the light in her mother's bedroom. This, she reasoned, would be the very spot where her father would be sure to find her. Waiting, she had dozed off and had slept a dreamless sleep through the commotion of the search party.

Hope had been hugged, cried over, checked for scratches and bites, lectured and fed. All day long, she did exactly as she was told, with no arguments.

That night when she went to bed, Joanna stretched out beside her and took Hope's small, warm hand in her own.

"Hope, you must never leave our house again without telling Mommy. Especially not at night."

"Were you scared, Mommy?"

"Yes, Mommy was scared. Even Uncle Stan was scared. If you'd been lost in the forest, we might never, ever have found you. Promise me, Hope."

"But I wasn't lost. I was just waiting."

"What were you waiting for?"

"Dad! He was there, Mom. I saw his eyes!"

"Hope, whatever you think you saw, it wasn't your daddy. Darling, Daddy is gone. I just haven't been able to accept it, and I'm sorry. But he's not coming back."

"But Baba said he turned into an angel, and he's always with us!"

"Yes, and that may be true, but she didn't mean the angel on her calendar with big shiny wings and a white dress. Angels are invisible. You can't see an angel, Hope."

"But, Mom . . ."

"Hope. I know you miss your daddy terribly. So do I. But we can't bring him back."

She got up and kissed the child on her forehead. The cat wriggled deeper into the pillow and began to purr.

"Goodnight, now. And you stay in bed!"

"G'night, Mom."

Joanna went out and closed the door.

Hope yawned and smiled at the window, where twin points of light winked deep in the forest.

"Night, Dad."

FOUR : The Phone Call

Trout Creek, March 1946

JOANNA WALKS ALONG THE SNOWY path with a big orange cat marching ahead. They're both trailing a little girl, hop-skipping in front of them. She watches the child disappear behind a grove of snow-laden spruce and calls to her, worrying out loud.

"Hope, not too far. Mommy can't see you."

Look at her, Mick. She's fearless.

You gave Hope her name, remember? The night she was born in that godawful storm. "She's our Hope," *you said. I was afraid the other kids would call her Hopeless. But you told me hope was a magic word, the best word in the world.*

Ahead of her, Joanna heard the child giggle.

"Hope, come back here, stop hiding on Mommy."

Where have they taken you, Mick? Are you alive somewhere, trying to find your way home? Sometimes you seem so close, I can feel your breath against my throat. Your warm breath. At night, when I can't sleep.

"Mommy, are you sad again?"

"What makes you think I'm sad? "

"Because your eyes are all watery."

"No, darling. I'm not sad." She scoops up the cat, brushing snow off his feet. "I think we'll have to put Tom on a diet. He's getting fat."

For a long time, Joanna's face in the mirror had not been her own. Since Mick had disappeared, a haunted-looking woman stared back at her.

She had his letters, written before Christmas in 1941, numbered one, two, three, four, six.

Often she sat on their bed, unfolding each letter, smoothing it on her knee the way she had done so many times over the years of his absence. The paper was beginning to crack along the folds, and once again she noticed how Mick had written in such small, economical script, with only a pen-slash between paragraphs, so he could squeeze in more words.

My Darling Joanna/This is my first letter from this strange Chinese city. I've never seen so many people! We NEVER see NOBODY, and that's NOT a double negative, Jo, this place is amazing./We live in barracks, like our bunkhouse at the Inn. The food is terrible, thanks to the Limey cooks, so we've been eating in a local place called The Fortunate Noodle House. A big bowl of noodles with half a chicken costs about five cents! No kidding!/My two best buddies, Freddy McKee and Tony Cecci, are still with me. Tony is a handsome guy who has a million girls on his tail every night, so it's a good thing I have Freddy to keep me company. Freddy's not much of a girl chaser, and we hang around together./So far it doesn't seem like there's a war on. Mostly we line up and wait. Some guy at a table who's supposed to hand out supplies says "No more blankets today." And the next guy tells us they're out of socks or helmets, and so it goes./I love you my darling girls. Mick.

Letter #2:

Dearest Joanna,/Freddy and I just came back from a night market. I don't even know where to begin. There are hawkers in every street, offering the strangest things. One old woman was selling dried pigs' heads. They'd been squashed flat, as though they'd been run over with a tank. Actually they were kind of cute. Looked like they were grinning. Some day we'll come here together. Have a second honeymoon./Not much time to write more. Freddy and Tony are yelling at me to hurry, they want to go out for noodles. We have a late pass, and I'm hungry too. Army food is awful. Kiss my little Hope for me, tell her Daddy loves her very much. Freddy says Hi. You'll meet him when we get home. All my love, Mick

Letter number three was a love letter. When she unfolded the envelope the first time, a dried flower had fallen out. The petals scattered like pink confetti, and she'd carefully gathered each one and put it back. Every time she opened the letter, a few more fell out, until now they'd been reduced to pink dust, sheer and delicate as face powder.

Joanna, I never knew how much I needed you until I no longer have you with me. At night when I reach for you and you aren't there, I ache for you. When I can't sleep my mind wanders through our house, room by room, and you're in every one. I see you in our bedroom, darling Joanna. You sit by the mirror, naked, brushing your hair. You come to bed, and we make love. The way we used to, remember? Afterwards, you fall asleep in my arms./This pressed flower is for you, my darling girl, until I can bring you a fresh one. I love you so much. Mick.

Letter number four was sweet.

Dear Jo and Hope, My dearest girls, this is the strangest experience! Sometimes in the morning, when the sun is just coming up and things are still quiet, I can hear birds singing, and it seems like the war isn't happening. Yesterday, when we were on patrol in the country, we passed an old lady hoeing her cabbages, just like Baba Popovich. A dog came running out to bark at us, and the old lady waved. It doesn't feel much like a war. I'm enclosing a leaf from a kind of herb that grows in the ditches here. It smells good when I pinch it. Wish I could just reach out and pinch you, my gorgeous girl. Just wait 'til I get home! Hugs, kisses, pinches, Your loving Mick.

Letter number five had not arrived.
Letter number six frightened her.

Dearest Joanna, It seems we may see action soon, though I can't say more or the censor will black it out. We're all fine, Tony and Freddy send love. Freddy feels like he knows you and Hope and Tom Cat, because I talk about you so much./No news this time, at least none I can say, so I made a list of what I miss most. (Not in order.) The smell of fresh coffee in the morning, YOUR coffee, not the muddy dish water they make here. (I wonder if they'll censor that?) The way your hair smells when you've dried it in the sun. The way your face looks after we've made love. Miss you, miss you, miss you./Which reminds me, Freddy has a girlfriend. Says it's serious./Might not be able to write for a while. Don't worry. Love, Mick

After number six, nothing.

Except the fear. Fear of the radio, with its censored news that nobody believed anymore. Fear of the dark without Mick's warm body beside her. Fear of going crazy, for she'd begun sleeping with his old blue sweater against her face because it still had his smell.

Fear of the telegram.

▲   ▲   ▲

THAT DAY IN January 1942, she watched Chris Stinson slog through the swirling snow, head bent against a rising blizzard. She'd flung the door open before he knocked, before he handed her that damned telegram with her name in the cellophane window.

Mrs. Michael Keegan.

Chris had delivered a lot of telegrams in his time but never one he disliked as much as this one. As he listened to the urgent *tap-tap-tap* of the telegraph, it was as though he held Mick Keegan's life at the end of his fingers. Briefly he wondered: what if he didn't respond? What if he just got up from his desk and went into the house, as though he hadn't heard the persistent clicking? Had a nap, maybe. If Joanna Keegan kept her husband for another few hours, would it really make any difference?

He waited until after lunch, when he saw young Hope go skipping through the snow with that big orange cat behind her, heading for Leski's.

It was time.

> Regret to inform you Private Michael Keegan missing in action.
> Presumed killed.

He handed her the envelope. Heard her sharp exhalation as the breath left her body, saw her shoulders slump, stepped forward to catch her if she should fall, but she raised a hand, took the envelope, and, without a word, closed the door.

Chris told his wife, Kay, who told Mary Leski. Both women rushed over, but they found Joanna oddly calm, almost detached. Mary made a pot of tea, and the women huddled together at the kitchen table, mostly silent.

Daylight began to fade. Mary went to turn on a light, but Joanna said no, no lights. Not yet.

She didn't cry. Hardly spoke. Sat there dry-eyed and silent until Mary mentioned a memorial service.

"No!" Joanna's protest exploded into the darkening room. "You mean a funeral? DO NOT SAY THAT WORD, Mary. Don't even think it!"

She stood up, started pacing the kitchen, table to cupboard to stove, back and forth.

"Mick is alive. He *could* be alive somewhere! They said *presumed*, so they don't know. Do they? But I know. Mick is alive!"

Joanna lowered her voice, spoke in a calmer tone. Quietly hoped they'd go away.

"I'm sorry. I need to be alone for a while. Mary, would you keep Hope for me? Just until later?"

▲   ▲   ▲

JOANNA SITS IN the living room, staring at the opposite wall. The pattern on the wallpaper disappears as daylight leaves and night settles over the room

Presumed killed.

How did they know? Who presumed? She would know if Mick was dead. She would know! The very second Mick's life was snuffed out, surely her own heart would have stopped beating.

Two weeks went by, and she hadn't broken the news to Hope. She couldn't. Then one night, when she was listening to Hope say her prayers, the little girl didn't mention Mick.

"Hope, aren't you forgetting somebody?"

"Nope."

"What about Daddy?"

"Daddy's dead. Georgie Leski said so."

Joanna's hand shot out, and she heard the sharp sound of the slap as it met the child's cheek.

The imprint of Joanna's hand was outlined on Hope's skin, and as her small face crumpled, Joanna fell to her knees and wrapped the sobbing child in her arms.

"Hope! Oh, baby, I'm so sorry! Mommy didn't mean to hurt you, darling."

Hope's frantic sobbing trailed off to a few hiccups.

"But where is Daddy? If he isn't dead, where is he?"

"Hope, I don't know where your daddy is. Maybe he's just lost. Maybe they'll find him. But we can't leave him out of our prayers, Hope. Now, we have to pray even harder."

Word that Joanna would not acknowledge Mick's death spread through Trout Creek. She refused to hold any kind of memorial service, and everybody had something to say about it.

Chris Stinson said she couldn't look at him when he handed her the telegram, just turned away and closed the door, but he'd seen her eyes. Terrified. It was a bloody shame.

Baba Popovich clucked her tongue. No funeral service? No prayers for Mick's immortal soul? She would say prayers.

Stan Novak said there was no law that she had to have a memorial service, and anyway, there was no body. The Japanese had taken a lot of prisoners in Hong Kong, maybe Mick was among them. Maybe they were rushing things.

Mary Leski said okay, who needed it anyway? Memorial service was just a fancy name for funeral, and funerals were goddamn depressing, unless you had a good wake. Mick was gone, and there was no bringing him back. Well, not likely, not with Japs running all over Hong Kong, and Mick right there in the middle of everything. Nope, Mick wasn't coming back. Mary leaned back and blew a smoke ring, looking thoughtfully at the ceiling.

"What Joanna should do is circulate," she declared. "Soon as possible. Start meeting other guys."

George Leski said if it'd been him out there in Hong Kong, and Mary got that telegram, she'd already be spending his insurance on a replacement.

"Stan, she'd be on your doorstep with a pie before my bones were cold."

"Uh-huh. What kind of pie, George?"

▲   ▲   ▲

JOANNA COULDN'T CRY. For months, she was numb. She'd be sitting in a chair, eyes focused on some insignificant thing, a picture on the wall maybe, and suddenly it would come to her that most of the morning had gone. Once, she found Hope standing at her knee, patting her arm and looking up into her face.

"Mommy? Are you sad again?"

On the surface, her life looked much as it always had. She opened the inn whenever a customer showed up between trains, and after a while she resumed a sort of social life, having coffee with Mary and even with Stan, who had waited a couple of months and then helped her through the military red tape of applying for her widow's pension. He seemed to find business in Trout Creek more often than before, and he'd always drop in to see if she needed anything before heading to the Popoviches' for the night.

But Joanna no longer took pleasure in reading to Hope, or cooking a meal, or watching the light change on winter afternoons. She'd always loved those early twilights when the snow turned pearly blue and she knew Mick would soon be coming through the door, his face so cold, his hands so warm.

Now the waning of the day depressed her. She'd closed the piano. Stopped listening to music. The Glen Miller album Mick had bought her gathered dust. As time passed, a kind of numbness replaced the pain, and a reluctant acceptance crept into Joanna's life. She stopped thinking of herself as Mick's wife and became his widow.

What an awful word you've left for me, Mick. Widow. What a lonely, sad, bitter word.

▲   ▲   ▲

WHEN THE PHONE rang one March night in 1946, she thought it would be Mary, suggesting canasta.

"Hello, is this Joanna?"

A man's voice.

"Are you Joanna Keegan? Mick's wife?"

Joanna felt her heart crash against her ribs. She couldn't breathe, couldn't get a word out of her mouth.

"Hello? I'm looking for Michael Keegan's wife. Would you know . . ."

"Yes! I'm Mick's wife!"

For a split second she felt a wild, joyful surge of hope, but then it was gone. "I mean, I'm his widow. Mick was killed overseas."

Freddy thumped his forehead against the payphone. *Dammit! How can I be so stupid?*

"I know. Mrs. Keegan, Joanna, I'm sorry, this isn't coming out right. I'm a friend of Mick's. Freddy McKee. Maybe he mentioned me?"

More silence, then her voice again, so soft he could hardly hear her.

"Freddy? I remember your name. You were with Mick in Hong Kong."

Thank Christ for that. At least I've got that to go on.

"Listen, I'm in Winnipeg. I have something for you. From Mick. It's a letter."

Oh God, that sounded like Mick was still alive. Like that other guy from C Force, the one who'd been a POW *for four years and all the time his family thought he was dead, but then he showed up. Dammit!*

"I mean, he gave me this letter. Before he died. For you. So if he didn't make it and I did . . ."

He ran out of words.

Then she was talking. Rescuing him. Telling him which train to catch.

▲   ▲   ▲

THE WOMAN AND the kid were on the platform as the train pulled in. She was even thinner than she'd looked in Mick's picture, with the same unruly mop of dark hair, and she was holding a little girl by the hand. That must be Hope, the kid Mick was always talking about.

He smiled at Joanna and looked down at Hope, who was looking up at him.

"She looks just like . . ."

"I know. Just like Mick."

FIVE : The Letter

JOANNA MADE TEA WHILE FREDDY sat at the kitchen table with Hope across from him holding a big orange cat with a loud, persistent purr.

"Sounds like his motor needs oil," he said to the child. "Is he a good mouser?"

She didn't reply but looked solemnly back at him out of Mick's blue eyes.

It seemed to Joanna that every sound in the room was magnified, the purring of the cat, the ticking of the clock, the glug-glug of tea into cups.

Freddy cleared his throat.

"I guess you want to see this."

He took a brown envelope out of his jacket. His fingers trembled as he handed it to her, and when he picked up his teacup to hide the shaking, it rattled against the saucer.

"Freddy, would you excuse me?"

Joanna went into the bedroom she and Mick had shared. She'd kept his letters in a Black Magic chocolates box, thinking there'd be many more to come. The telegram was in a small cedar jewellery chest, Mick's wedding present to Joanna. It had become a sort of urn, and she ran her hands over it slowly, for as much as she hated that telegram, it had been her last contact with anyone who knew anything about Mick.

Until now.

Inside the brown envelope was another, a familiar blue onion-skin paper, but wrinkled, smudged, worn. Soft as cheesecloth. Her name, barely legible. Address completely worn off. Flap never glued.

Mick's handwriting, still clear enough to read.

My Dearest Joanna/This is one letter I hope you will never have to see. If someone else delivers it, it's because I've had to leave you without saying goodbye./My will is filed with Drexler Law in Winnipeg. Everything is looked after. You'll have my army pension and my accumulated wages. Stan will explain everything, and he'll get you through the red tape./The Inn is yours, free and clear. When Hope leaves to go to school, sell it for what you can get and go with her so she'll have her mother near./I want you to start a new life, Jo. You're young. You'll need somebody./I can't tell you how much it hurts to write this. I know it isn't the way we planned. It's not the way it should have been, darling Jo. I always thought we'd have time. Years and years./I love you more than my life. Forever, Mick.

When Joanna came out of the bedroom, Freddy and Hope were playing Snakes and Ladders at the kitchen table. They both looked up at her.

"Hope, time to get ready for bed. I need to talk to Mr. McKee."

Reluctantly, the little girl left. She was beginning to enjoy Freddy's company and decided to stay in the hallway so she wouldn't miss anything.

"I have to ask you something, Freddy. Nobody told me what happened. Were you with him?" She takes a deep breath. "Do you know how my husband died?"

Freddy takes so long to answer that she wonders if he heard the question.

He's listening to another voice. Serena, talking to an eleven-year-old boy.

I was his wife. I had a right to know.

"Freddy, please. I need to know!"

Why? Why do they insist on asking these questions? What difference could it make to know things like that?

He tries to light a cigarette. Hands shaking. Ashamed to hear his own voice tremble as he fumbles for words.

"There was a battle, on a hill. A place called Mount Butler. We had the hill, see. Held it all night. But all of a sudden there were Japs everywhere. It happened so fast. Mick was running downhill, right at the Japs. I was behind him."

Truth sits in Freddy's throat like a hot stone. His tongue feels thick. Useless. He closes his eyes.

I thought I knew where I left him. I tried to find him, so help me God, I tried.

What to tell her? Not truth, for that would be too cruel for both of them.

Just lie to her. Give this woman some peace.

"I was with him. He'd been wounded in the leg. It caught an artery. He just lost too much blood, too fast. He didn't suffer. I'm sorry, Joanna. I know he loved you very much. He talked about you all the time. Both of you."

I should have been the one, not Mick.

"The letter, Freddy. Mick's letter. You kept it all those years. Even in the prison camp. How did you manage to hang on to it?"

"I taped it to my skin."

▲   ▲   ▲

FREDDY PLANNED TO stay one night, catch a train back the next day. But the next train wasn't until Tuesday, and of course he must stay with them. Joanna insisted.

He stayed in the bunkhouse, and their conversations were careful, cautious, like two strangers on a journey who find that by coincidence they have something, or somebody, in common.

On the third evening, after Hope had gone to bed, they sat together at the kitchen table, the coffee pot between them. He began to talk about the Mick he knew, and she began to tell him about her Mick, and after that it wasn't so bad anymore. When he told her about Mick and Tony and the rickshaw race, he finally heard her laugh.

Tuesday morning he was packing to leave when she knocked at the bunkhouse door.

113

"I thought you might want to know. They need a cook at McLaughlin's. I mean, if you don't have another job waiting. Can you cook?"

"Can I cook? Hell, yes. That's what I did in Edmonton before the army. Cooked in a restaurant. I was going back to Yip's place, but he has a cook now. He won't miss me if I don't show up."

Hope escorted Freddy to the station. He wrote out the telegram and asked Chris to send it to Yip Lee at Elite Eats in Edmonton.

"Staying Trout Creek awhile. Everything fine here."

Chris Stinson smiled.

That summer, they became a threesome: Joanna, Freddy, and Hope. Freddy drank a bit, mostly on Saturday nights when the boys from McLaughlin's camp ended up at Mary's, or less often at Joanna's, but it seemed that everybody drank a bit. One of the boys had a guitar, and on a night when Joanna's living room was full of people and they'd all started singing, Freddy asked Joanna if she'd play something.

"Play what?"

"The piano. Mick told me you used to play." He grinned at Hope, who clapped her hands and said yes, Mommy, you can play.

Mary nudged George in the ribs, and Baba Popovich muttered something that sounded like "Oi yoi," but Joanna opened the piano.

"It hasn't been played in a long time," she said. "It's likely out of tune." But as her hands ran up and down the keys Hope slipped onto the bench beside her.

Freddy picked up the guitar. It wasn't that different from a mandolin. He strummed a couple of chords and began to play.

"Hope, this song is just for you," and he began to sing.

"'Froggie went a courtin' and he did ride, Uhuh . . .'"

"It's the froggie song," she squealed. "Mom, Freddy knows the froggie song!"

Hope sang along, and when the duet ended more or less in tune, they got a round of applause.

"Where did you learn that song?"

"My dad taught me!"

Hope was allowed to stay up later on these musical nights, and as she watched Freddy standing with one foot on the piano bench beside Joanna, strumming "Roll Out the Barrel" on a borrowed guitar while everybody sang, the little girl could feel her mother getting better.

For Joanna, it was as though she was recovering from a long, wasting illness.

Only one thing about this new arrangement bothered Hope. Stan didn't come by as often as he had. He'd still pick her up in a bear hug when she met him getting off the Thursday train, and he'd ruffle Tom Cat's fur, but they no longer spent long evenings together at the kitchen table, playing Snakes and Ladders.

Hope wondered why.

As the weeks passed, Freddy grew more comfortable with his new life in Trout Creek. Joanna and Hope were like family, and they brought him closer to Mick. But the nights were hard. He hated falling asleep. He'd wake up terrified, sweating, and he was afraid he'd been talking in his sleep, maybe even yelling.

His ghosts. They wouldn't leave him alone.

six: Hope and Freddy

I TURNED EIGHT THIS YEAR, but everybody says I'm old for my age.

Freddy McKee is one of my best friends, after Tom Cat and before Georgie, who I hardly even like. Georgie calls me Hopeless, but he's a little creep and nobody ever listens to him.

The best time for Freddy and me is between the noon rush and the supper rush, when things are quiet. Freddy always puts on a clean white T-shirt and turns his apron around to the un-messy side, so he looks neat. He'll have a cigarette while Tom Cat and I work on the pies.

Sometimes he rolls smokes with a little machine. He pushes the paper in one side and turns the handle 'til a cigarette rolls out the other side. I wanted to help, but he won't let me.

"It's a bad habit. Your mom wouldn't like it if I taught you to roll your own smokes."

He's right about my mom. She's the only woman in Trout Creek who doesn't smoke, except for Baba, who's so old she doesn't really count.

Sometimes I ask Freddy stuff about my dad, and he tells me funny stories, like about the time he and Dad and this other guy named Tony were racing some two-wheeled wagons called rickshaws. He must like that story, because he tells it a lot. He always explains first about the rickshaws, and the guys who pull them because it's the only way they can make any money. I guess he forgets that he already told me.

I wanted to hear more about my dad. I showed Freddy my heart-shaped locket, and I told him Dad gave it to me, but it was a fib. Stan gave me the locket on my last birthday. I just wanted it to be from my dad. It makes me feel good, talking about him. It makes him real again.

One day I told Freddy my worst secret: sometimes I can't remember what Dad looked like.

"Yeah, kid, I know. You were so little when he went away." Freddy stopped rolling his pastry and sat down across from me, so I'd be sure to listen.

"Hope, your dad was the best man I ever met. Like a brother, only better. He was good, and kind, and he was smart. He taught me a lot."

"Like what?"

"Oh, things he knew that I didn't. Stuff about books, stars, rocks. Plants. He was always picking some weed or other and pressing it."

"I guess he loved us a lot, huh?"

"He loved you more than anything. More than his own life."

While the pies bake, we drink tea with canned milk and three sugar lumps. Four if I want them. My mother won't let me drink tea at home because it might stunt my growth, and I'm supposed to drink powdered milk, but I hate it. She says there are starving kids in China who'd be glad to have a nice glass of powdered milk, but if they ever tasted it they wouldn't say that.

"This powdered crap tastes like horse pee," Freddy says. "But don't tell your mom I said so."

I wonder how he knows? Maybe it's something from the war.

I guess a lot of bad stuff happened to Freddy in the war. Sometimes things scare him while he's sleeping, so he wakes up yelling. The guys in the bunkhouse heard him. They told George Leski, and he told Mary. Mary told everybody. Uncle Stan says Mary has the biggest mouth in Trout Creek.

My mother says his nightmares are worse than ordinary bad dreams because they really happened. After Freddy has one of his nightmares, he drinks a lot and does all kinds of silly things, like picking a fight with the McLaughlin boys, but they go easy on him.

He's always sorry.

When Freddy's sober, I love him almost as much as Tom Cat.

Last week Freddy told us he had to go to Winnipeg and he'd be leaving on the Tuesday train. Mom was having coffee at the Leskis' the afternoon he left, and I was under the table with Tom, doing my spelling. Mary asked Mom why Freddy had to go to Winnipeg.

"He had something to look after at Veterans' Affairs," Mom said, and Mary laughed like Mom had told a good joke.

"That's not the kind of affairs he's looking after," Mary said. "That horny little bugger's gonna get his ashes hauled."

"Mary, don't be so crude!"

Mom had her shocked voice on, the one she gets when people use bathroom words in our house.

"Why would you say that? You don't know anything about him."

"The hell I don't. He's a healthy, young guy, and he's not getting any action at your house, is he? You're a sweet girl, Jo, but really, you're such a prude! Freddy's no priest. What do you expect him to do?"

I came up from under the table to get more information.

"What's 'ashes hauled' mean, Mary?"

Mary started laughing again, and Mom sent me outside to play. I always get sent outside just when I hear something interesting.

Freddy stayed away a whole week and a half. When he came back, he brought Tom a present, a red leather collar with a bell on it, because Baba Popovich didn't like him catching birds. The collar had a special snap that would let go if he got hung up somewhere, falling out of a tree or something. After that, whenever we went to the cookshack, Tom wore his fancy collar.

Lots of nights Freddy would drop into our house after supper, and we'd play Snakes and Ladders. I had to go to bed at eight o'clock every single night, even though I was never sleepy and would be awake for the longest time, listening to Mom and Freddy talking in our kitchen.

Sometimes, I'd pretend. Pretend that Georgie Leski got stolen by a witch and never came home. Or that he got lost and a bear ate him.

Or that I got lost and Freddy found me, and carried me home to my sobbing mother. Everybody in Trout Creek came to cry over my lifeless body, and my mother cried loudest of all because she made me go to bed too early, which is why I ran away in the first place.

Freddy told her to leave me alone because she hadn't been nice to me until I was dead. Then he kissed me, and I woke up. Freddy and Tom Cat and I lived happily ever after.

SEVEN: Mary's Party
June 21, 1946

IN MID-JUNE, DAYLIGHT IN TROUT Creek lasts until nearly midnight. Afterwards, a few hours of lingering twilight are followed by sunrise around 4:00 AM.

By tradition, on the longest day of the year, Mary Leski throws a party. She calls it her Summer Solstice Supper, and the regulars call it Mary's Big Booze-Up. Either way, they wouldn't miss it for a million bucks.

During the run-up to the event, Mary has a keg of beer shipped in from Winnipeg, and she'll personally decant an entire batch of Chris Stinson's homebrew, code-named Matilda, into gallon jugs. By party day, she'll have stockpiled enough liquor to float a barge.

Early in the morning, she'll badger George into setting up sawhorse tables outside, even though nobody will sit down to eat until almost midnight.

The midnight seating is Mary's rule.

"I don't want them sobering up too soon," she declares. "Why waste good booze?"

Around five o'clock, guests will start rolling in. They'll arrive by train, foot, canoe, lake barge, and one US military track vehicle via the forestry trail from Dogrib, and they'll have worked up a major thirst. For people like Dumas the Trapper, who prefer their liquor hard with a certain edge, there'll be shots of straight Matilda.

"Any man still on his feet by midnight will be pie-eyed drunk and hungry enough to eat a horse," Mary predicts, with confidence born of experience.

You had to admit, Mary really knew how to roll out the red carpet for her friends. Her parties lasted all night and into the early dawn, when Bertha Yellowquill would get busy baking bannock while Dahlia Rempel and Kay Stinson heated up a cauldron of venison soup laced with Chris's homebrew ("Hair of the dog," Mary said.) They'd ladle out big bowls of it for anybody who was still up and walking.

By midnight there'd have been be at least one fight, usually just a couple of the boys from McLaughlin's mixing it up a little. As Mary explained it, a bit of blood might be spilled: nosebleed, split lip, that sort of thing, but it was just fists. Nobody ever pulled a knife, and Stan declared that all guns had to be locked up in his office twelve hours ahead of Mary's big soiree, just in case. They stayed locked up until the collective hangovers had worn off.

Mary figured the odd skirmish lent entertainment value. As she remarked to Joanna over coffee in her kitchen, you could never be sure whose bed your shoes might be under in the morning.

"Mary, you got a dirty mouth," said George, who happened to be passing through the room, so she threw her arms around his neck.

"Yeah, George, and you got a big dick," she said, grinding her hips into his and laughing at his shocked expression. He clamped his hand over her mouth before she could get any worse.

"Jeez, Mary! The kids!" His ears got red, but then he gave her a smack on the bottom and headed outside to put up her tables. "Grinning like the cat that ate the canary," Mary pointed out to Joanna.

Joanna hadn't been to a real party for such a long time. Not since Mick had gone away. She'd avoided Mary's Solstice parties, hadn't even dressed up, not really, not in years. There'd been no reason.

Maybe that's why she decided to wear the red shoes to Mary's party. Maybe it was time.

They were ridiculous shoes, she'd known that when she bought them. Red patent pumps with platform soles, dangerously high heels and a perky little bow just above the open toes.

"We call these our peek-a-boo toes," the clerk in the Winnipeg shoe store had said, cradling her ankle a little longer than necessary as he slipped the second shoe onto her foot. On a whim, she decided to take them, and they'd reposed in their fancy shoebox ever since, waiting for the right occasion, like Mick's homecoming. Waiting for nothing, as it turned out. He'd never had the chance to see her wear them.

The night of the party, dithering over the shoes took longer than it should have. Twice she tried them on with her only black dress, a slinky low-necked sheath, almost too big now. She'd lost weight since Mick left. Twice she changed back to sensible sandals, white, with low heels. Maybe she wasn't ready for a party. Maybe she shouldn't go at all.

Then the phone rang, and it was Mary.

"Jo, where the hell are you? This crowd of baboons is getting out of hand! We need your sobering presence, sister, get yourself over here!"

Joanna could hear the party in the background, music blaring, Mary giggling.

"*Stop* that, you *awful* man! Oooh!"

And she hung up.

Joanna took a deep breath, slipped her feet into the red shoes, and headed for Leski's. George had the record player cranked up to full volume, and music poured through the open windows. Glen Miller, "In the Mood." Her favourite song. Hers and Mick's. They'd danced to it the year it became a hit, and it had stayed popular through the war years and after, but she'd stopped listening.

She could see people dancing in Mary's living room now. How long since she'd danced? Six years? Maybe she should just go home.

Too late. She'd been seen. Some of McLaughlin's boys were outside, gathered around the beer keg, and one of them whistled at her.

"Hey, Jo, those are some fancy-lookin' booties you got there, girl!"

The house was wall-to-wall people. George handed her a glass of Stinson's homebrewed Matilda, and she sipped at it automatically, surprised at how smooth it tasted.

She wondered where Stan was. If she could just find him, she'd be okay. He'd get her a ginger ale and talk to her, and it would look like she was having fun. She moved through the crowd, inching her way toward the kitchen where Stan was slicing the mammoth ham. She saw Freddy standing at the loaded kitchen table in his white apron, carving the moose roast. Mary, supervising activities in the tones of a drill sergeant, yelled at her.

"Well, it's about time you got here . . ." she stopped in mid-sentence, her eyes taking in the new, improved Joanna.

"Mother of God, will you look at this," she shrieked. "She has legs! Freddy, would you look at our Joanna? The woman is gorgeous!"

"I'm looking!" He grinned at Joanna and handed her the platter. "Here, Jo, make your gorgeous self useful."

Just before midnight George lit his kerosene lanterns while Mary and Baba Popovich laid out the feast: cabbage rolls and perogies, coleslaw and homemade buns, a giant hip roast of moose, and Mary's famous once-a-year venison burgers served with a horseradish mustard so hot it made George's eyes water. He began urging people to grab a seat and dig in before it got cold.

Joanna couldn't find Stan, so she sat beside a woman she didn't know, some friend of Mary's who'd come up on the Winnipeg train especially for the party. Freddy took the chair on Joanna's left, and Mary squeezed in beside him. Finally, when all the chairs, upended nail kegs, and borrowed benches from Freddy's cookshack were occupied, forty-six pairs of eyes turned toward the head of the table where George, after many cups of Matilda, was about to bellow his traditional blessing.

"Knives and forks and lottsa dishes,
Now let's eat, you sons-a-bitches!"

▲ ▲ ▲

LATER, JOANNA WILL try to remember how it started. She'll try to recall the smallest detail.

Freddy had seemed completely absorbed in Mary, who was telling a long joke about a priest, a rabbi, and a bartender. Accents were involved, and the punch line cracked Freddy up. He laughed out loud.

Maybe that was the moment she'd become aware of his arm, draped casually over the back of her chair. He wasn't exactly touching her, more like brushing her shoulder with his fingers, but suddenly it felt as though an electric charge was jumping between them, and the sensation was so real, so powerful. She turned and looked at him. At his shoulder, at the back of his head, at his hairline, where the tanned skin of his neck was so dark.

Joanna shivered.

What's the matter with me? Why do I want to touch him? Just touch his neck. It must have been that last drink, that sneaky Matilda. I better be careful.

As though he'd read her mind, Freddy turned toward her.

"Everything okay, Jo? Having a good time?"

"Yes. I'm fine. Thanks."

He leaned close to her ear, voice too low for the others to hear.

"By the way, I do like your shoes."

When she didn't respond, Freddy took his arm off her chair and turned back to Mary. Joanna felt disappointed. She thought he'd been joking about the shoes. Teasing her. She hasn't been teased by a man in so long, her social skills are so rusty, she's forgotten how to have fun at a party. Lost the knack of small talk, forgotten how to flirt.

She shouldn't have come. She should just go home. Instead, she closes her eyes, willing him to put his arm back.

Mary is into another joke, something about a travelling salesman and a farmer's daughter, when under the table Joanna feels a hand close around her heel. Freddy's hand.

A flock of butterflies takes off in her stomach.

Gently, deliberately, he slides the red shoe off her foot. She swivels toward him, opening her mouth to say something. But what? When a man starts undressing you under a table with forty-six people sitting around, what do you say?

He isn't looking at her. He's apparently absorbed in Mary's silly story, one they've all heard a hundred times.

While under the table, there is his hand.

Joanna holds her breath and wonders if anybody hears the soft thud as her shoe hits the ground and he slides his palm under her instep, cradling it, his fingers encircling her bare foot, his palm under her heel now, thumb and forefinger lightly massaging. Pinching a little. His whole hand encircling her ankle.

How long do they sit like that, with his hand locked around her ankle?

She's certain the whole table can hear her heart thumping.

Slowly, deliberately, he tightens his grip, and still he doesn't look at her.

For the first time in years she feels the slow fire building, the delicious burn rising in her belly.

The world could stop turning right now and it wouldn't matter because all she cares about is this moment, this man.

She closes her eyes and hears his voice close to her ear.

"Joanna. Open your eyes. Look at me, Joanna."

When she does, his face is very near hers. He leans closer, his breath warm on her cheek.

"Joanna, I'm not Mick. You understand? I can't sleep three in a bed."

"I know. I don't care anymore. I'm so tired of waiting."

He stands up and pulls out her chair.

EIGHT : Loving Freddy

THEY'RE BOTH A LITTLE DRUNK, just enough to let them forget the awkwardness of first-time lovers, and they get no farther than Joanna's living room. They sink to the floor and make love quickly, hungrily. No words.

Afterwards, his question.

"Hope?"

"At Baba's."

She hears him laugh. Asks him, "Do you think we'll be missed?"

"Not a snowball's chance in hell."

They retrieve scattered clothing, move to the guest bedroom. It's new to her, the strange need, this hunger for a man's body. If she ever felt it before, she has forgotten.

Her boldness surprises both of them. Delights Freddy, makes him laugh again, holding her beneath him. She can't let herself remember anything else, not now, not with Freddy. Afterwards they fall asleep, exhausted.

When Joanna wakes up, she stretches both arms over her head, flexing her toes, enjoying the unaccustomed soreness of muscles long neglected. She smiles, turns her face to the other pillow, but he's gone.

She puts on her robe and pads barefoot into the living room, to the north window. White smoke from the cookshack curls straight up into the bright dawn.

△ △ △

JOANNA WRAPS THIS secret around herself, wears it over her life like an invisible coat. Wakes up thinking of him. Waits for him, hoping he'll come. Feels disappointed when he doesn't. When he does, oh it is wonderful.

He always comes to her late at night, when he's sure Hope is asleep. They never go to Mick's bed (even now that's how she thinks of it, as

Mick's bed) but to the guest room. It's because they'll be farther away from Hope's room, she tells herself. One door farther down the short hallway.

She makes love to Freddy almost silently, as she always had to Mick, because she doesn't want to risk waking the sleeping child. There's a fierceness about their lovemaking, a desperate edge to it, as though they're stealing something, and part of her likes the secrecy, the faintly scandalous possibility of being discovered. (What would Mary say?) But in the morning, no matter how early Joanna wakes up, he's always gone, and she feels sad, in a slow, heavy way she won't examine too closely.

Don't let this go to your head, Freddy. It's not just the sex I need from you, although, God help me, that's a big part of it.

It's that you loved Mick too.

After he falls asleep, after his breathing is slow and regular, she raises herself on one elbow and watches the rise and fall of his chest, traces the cleft in his chin with her eyes, the outline of his jaw. His hair, rumpled now, so it curls against his forehead. She takes silent inventory. The crooked nose that must once have been broken, the scar on his left cheek, near his eye, the raised, jagged scars on his chest. Sometimes in his sleep he mumbles words she can't understand, or he cries out, and the muscles in his face twitch, or a nerve at the base of his eye jumps, and she wonders what he sees in those strange dreams of his.

I'll stay awake and watch you, until you wake up and look at me. Maybe then I'll ask.

But she falls asleep, and in the morning he's gone.

The next time she watches him sleep, she bends her head over the raised scar on his chest and touches it with her lips, but gently, as gently as a butterfly might land on a leaf, so she won't disturb him.

In a fraction of a second he's on top of her and his hands are around her throat, choking her. Choking the life out of her.

Something stops him, and he lets go, jerking his hands away, holding them above his head like a thief caught in the act, and he's looking down at her as though he's never seen her before. As though she's a stranger. This, while she fights to breathe again, gasping for air.

They are both shaking. His body is drenched with sweat.

"Oh God! Jo, I'm so sorry. I'd never hurt you on purpose."

He holds her gently now, wipes the tears off her cheeks with the side of his hand.

"Jo, listen to me. Please, listen. Don't ever touch me when I'm asleep."

"But why?" Her voice is hoarse, her throat already sore.

"Just don't."

So all that day and for several more she wears a turtleneck sweater, even though it's July. The bruises stay for a week.

One morning before sunrise as he crosses the tracks, he's caught in the headlights of Stan's old army jeep.

Stan brakes, leans out. The motor idles, the only sound in the silent morning while the two men eye each other. Like a couple of stags in heat, Freddy thinks later.

"You're out early, Freddy. Everything okay?"

"Yeah. Sure."

He pauses, searching for a reason that would explain his presence halfway between Joanna's house and his cookshack while the rest of Trout Creek is still fast asleep.

"Joanna thought she heard something outside," Freddy says.

"Oh yeah? And what would that be?"

"She thought it might be a bear. In the garden."

"A bear."

"Yes. So, uh . . . she called me."

"I'll bet she did."

Stan slams the jeep into gear and takes off, rear wheels spitting gravel.

▲　　▲　　▲

SOME DAYS FREDDY walks to the creek and sits beside it, listens to the water running over the stones in the shallows, hears it pick up speed downstream as it hits the short rapids before it churns into the gorge. These things comfort him in ways he can't explain or even understand, except that here, by the water, he feels close to Mick, and whatever guilt he feels about Joanna begins to fade.

The subarctic summer is always short, and as fall arrives Freddy finds small things oddly soothing. Stinson's pipe as it fumes away in the cool of early morning. The crackle of wood in his cookstove. The smell of fresh bread baking.

He likes the sound of the wind in the swaying pines that grow near the cookshack. He waits for the wind at night, and on a good night, one with no nightmares, it sings him to sleep.

Now it's October and he moves a small cast-iron stove into his room behind the cookshack, snakes the stovepipe up the wall to a spot near the ceiling, cuts a hole for it, installs the tin flashing. All of this he does himself, and it feels good to light a fire, open the two small doors, watch the flames lick at a piece of birch wood.

He will not have coal for his fire. He hates the smell of coal, it's a dirty, evil, painful thing, the smell of coal.

It's part of his nightmare.

▲   ▲   ▲

THE MINE SHAFT was so hot, the water always dripping. The stink of sulphur overcame the stench of unwashed bodies. Every day, he'd stand for hours, halfway to his knees in the yellow water that ate at his skin, left him with running sores, rotted the flesh, gave it the texture of an old sponge. Twelve hours at a time in the sulphurous pit. It was like being buried alive.

Every morning before sunrise they had dragged themselves into the mines. A two-hour march there, two hours back. After the first year it became a death march, and those who were too weak to walk any farther collapsed by the path. The guards beat them, finished them off where they had fallen.

Twelve hours later, the march back. Thin soup and saltless rice, if they were lucky. Before an hour or so of exhausted sleep. Before his shift on the bunk was up. He remembered thinking that one day he simply wouldn't wake up. He'd be dead, and that would be a good thing. Death would be a relief.

Yet something in Freddy makes him cling to life. He will endure the sulphur in the mine, the smothering fumes and the heat, eat the rotten food, pick the lice off his own body, see his wounds fester, pray for release, and even wish he was dead.

But he'll fight for his last breath.

He remembers now that there were women in the mine. Japanese women. So skinny, shoulder bones protruding, working shirtless and nearly naked like the men, battery belts slung around skinny hipbones, lights strapped to their heads. Nobody cared about the naked women. They were all too exhausted to care.

One day during the march from the pit-head they heard explosions. The Japs were dynamiting, but the last shift was still in the tunnel. They hadn't bothered to wait. Everybody still down there would be buried alive, too far into the earth for their cries to be heard on the surface.

He shut his eyes, wishing the images away, but they wouldn't go. They were among his personal ghosts, always hovering.

"I'll be catching the train on Thursday. Have to run down to Winnipeg again."

"For long?" Joanna feels her pulse thump, like a warning.

He doesn't answer.

He sits at her kitchen table, a coffee cup anchored in his left hand, his right index finger moving around the rim, down the handle, up again, as though memorizing the contours, the dimensions. He does this a lot. Tries to remember how objects feel, how they are shaped, where they're positioned in relation to other objects. There is no conscious purpose for this attention to the minutiae of a room or an object, yet he has this need to remember details, to draw maps in his own head.

"Freddy. Will you come back?"

These days he has begun to lean toward her when she speaks, as though he has trouble hearing her.

"I think so."

As soon as he says it, he sees the bewildered look, the fear behind her eyes, and he grins, pats her hand.

"Jo, I'm just kidding. Of course I'll be back. I'm not that easy to get rid of."

NINE: Big News in Trout Creek
September 1947

JUST AFTER DARK THE SNOW started to fall. I remember because the last week in September was too early for snow. We were on our way to meet the Thursday train, and I was catching the flakes on my tongue. My mom said I looked pretty silly with my tongue stuck out like that, and wasn't I afraid somebody might see me? She always worried about things like that.

The Thursday train brought our grocery order, and that night, I remember, it was running late. I guess I remember just about everything that happened that night.

When the engine came roaring in, I headed down to the express car to talk to Al the brakeman, but I saw the conductor leaning out of the passenger car, which meant somebody was getting off in Trout Creek.

The first person off the train was Uncle Stan.

I started yelling, "Uncle Stan, over here," but he acted like he hadn't heard me. He turned around and lifted a big suitcase off the train. Then he reached up both arms, like he was going to help somebody down the steps, but he decided to lift that person instead of letting her walk on two perfectly good feet like anybody else.

Stan was looking at her while he was busy setting her on the ground, and he kept on looking, talking to her. Then he took her elbow in his hand and steered her in our direction.

I'd never seen anybody quite like her before.

She was Chinese, and she was something to look at with her hair piled up on her head and the snowflakes settling on it and getting caught in her eyelashes. She wore earrings shaped like teardrops, and they were the exact colour of spring moss on a pine tree.

"Stan! We didn't know you were coming back tonight, did we? Or maybe we forgot? It's always so good to see you."

Mom was babbling, pretending she wasn't all unstrung at what Stan had brought with him.

"Jo, this is Miss Sue Lee. She's here to see Freddy," he said in a funny voice, still looking down at her. "She wrote to him. He's expecting her, at least we think he is, so where the hell—where is he?"

Uncle Stan sounded kind of edgy, if you know what I mean. He hardly ever swore. And his jaw looked kind of tight, like he was clenching his teeth real hard.

I knew exactly where Freddy was. Right now, he'd be dishing up roast beef and potatoes and yelling at the guys. That's likely why he wasn't here to meet this Miss Lee, whoever she was. I thought it was funny he hadn't told anybody she was coming. I guess he wanted to surprise us.

I must have been staring at her because Mom told me to close my mouth and stop gawking, it wasn't polite. I added gawking to my list of things not to do, but by that time Chris Stinson had come out to the platform with his wife, Kay, and they were gawking too.

We were all so busy staring that we forgot about Mom's groceries, until Al the brakeman hollered down the platform.

"Hey, Joanna, you folks on a diet? We got groceries here!"

Mom wasn't paying much attention. She was busy grilling Freddy's surprise visitor.

"So, Miss Lee, you're here to see Freddy? Will you be, uh, working for him? I mean, are you a cook, or a waitress, or . . ."

Mom's voice trailed off like she was embarrassed, and Stan opened his mouth as though he had something to say, and then he shut it again.

The Chinese woman stuck her hand out for Mom to shake, and said, "Very please to meet you. I am Su Li McKee.

It was Mom's turn to gawk.

"McKee? But Stan said your name was Lee . . ."

"Yes. Su Li McKee. I am . . . wife."

She smiled a beautiful smile. I noticed her small white teeth, like pearls.

"I am wife of Freddy McKee."

She spoke slowly, carefully, and her pronunciation wasn't that good, but there was no mistaking what she said.

I looked up at my mom, and I thought she was going to fall right over. I thought I might too.

▲　▲　▲

WE WERE ALL in our kitchen. Mom, the Chinese woman, and me.

When she took her coat off, I could smell perfume, and I knew my mom noticed too. It was light and flowery, like the ladyslipper orchids my dad used to find for us in the spring. It stayed in my head, in the same place where I stored the smell of wild strawberries. I wanted to lean closer and take a real deep breath.

Mom told me to make tea. She was sitting on a kitchen chair, just staring at the Chinese woman, who was looking down at her hands, not saying a word. We were all waiting for Freddy.

Stan was back in a few minutes with Freddy right behind him, wearing that big parka of his, which he hadn't even bothered to zip. His white apron flapped in the wind as he came through the door, and his hair was messy.

When Freddy saw the Chinese woman, his mouth started opening and closing just like a fish when it's lying on the bank of the creek, trying to figure out how to breathe out of water. Except that I always feel sorry for the fish, and for some reason I didn't feel sorry for Freddy.

He finally found his voice, and he said the woman's name, Su Li? Like a question. Like he didn't believe what he was seeing. She stood up then, and sort of fired herself at him like a cannonball, and he ended up with his arms around her.

I guess you could say that Freddy just melted, like snow turning to slush on a rug. His eyes were closed, and his arms were wrapped around the Chinese woman so hard I wondered if she'd have any trouble breathing.

Then he started to talk to her, in a language I couldn't understand. There were people in Trout Creek who spoke Ukrainian, like Baba and

Steve Popovich. Bertha Yellowquill spoke Cree to Dumas the Trapper, who spoke French to Deaf Gilbert, who could only understand when he was looking right at him because all Gilbert could do was read lips. Some of the boys at McLaughlin's spoke Swedish, and some of the Americans at the Dogrib airbase talked funny because they were from South Texas. But when we were together, all of us spoke English.

Nobody we knew used whatever language Freddy was speaking with this woman. She was talking back, and it sounded like she was pretty excited.

Then it was Stan's turn to talk to Freddy, and it was pretty interesting stuff, so I was glad he stuck with English.

"Freddy! This young lady says she wrote to you. Don't you read your mail anymore?"

"I didn't get a letter. Nothing. There's been no word, not since Hong Kong."

Freddy shook his head like he couldn't believe she was real.

"The Japs came. She was gone. I thought she was dead."

"She looks pretty lively to me. Freddy, she tells me you two are married. Is this true?"

Freddy seemed to be taking a deep breath. My mom looked kind of sick, like she had a bad headache or something.

"Well? Yes or no? We're waiting, Freddy."

"Short answer? Yes. We were married in Hong Kong. The day before the invasion."

My mom's face went really queer, and I started to ask if she wanted an aspirin or anything, but she shushed me.

Uncle Stan's voice was icy. The kitchen was so quiet you could almost hear the wheels turning in his head.

"So did you just forget to mention to anybody that you were a married man?"

Freddy looked at my mom, then back at Stan.

"I guess you didn't remember to tell Joanna either, did you?"

Freddy just shook his head, like he might be trying to wake himself up. Like it was some kind of a dream, or a nightmare or something.

The Chinese woman was still wrapped around him, and she wasn't letting go.

"I thought she was dead," he repeated. "She survived the Japs. I can hardly believe it myself! And she made it all the way to Vancouver!"

He put his hands on the woman's arms and pushed her away then, but nicely, gently, sitting her down on a chair like she was a little kid.

"It sounds like Yip found her there, working in her uncle's restaurant," Freddy said. "She thought I was dead. She pawned my mandolin, and Yip saw it. He told her I was still alive, and he sent her up here. She says there was a letter. But I didn't get any letter . . ."

The Chinese woman watched Freddy talk, and then Stan talk, and then Freddy again. I wondered if she knew what the heck they were talking about because I sure couldn't figure it out, and my mom looked really confused.

Freddy was still talking.

"Look, I know this must sound crazy. It's a long story. And it's complicated."

"Yeah? Well I've got all night," said Stan, folding his arms.

Freddy looked like that fish out of water again, but I still didn't feel sorry for him. Not even a little.

BOOK THREE

Eating Bitterness

ONE: A Place for Dragons

Hong Kong, November 1941

NOVEMBER 16, 1941, WAS GREY with fog. As far as anybody in Hong Kong could tell, the rolling green hills where the nine dragons lived might have disappeared overnight.

The amah had explained about the dragons four years ago, the day she and Su Li arrived in Hong Kong. On that day, the old woman and the small-for-her-age ten-year-old climbed the last hill of their journey from China and looked down on the city that was to be their new home. It sprawled all the way to the water's edge, across a broad harbour and onto an island.

"Tell me a story," whined the tired child when they sat down to rest, so the amah began:

"One day, long time ago, boy emperor tells his servant: eight hills here, home of eight dragons."

The amah raised her short arms and made a sweeping gesture that embraced the eight hills of Kowloon.

"But this servant is clever. He say, 'Majesty, you, too, are great dragon. You are ninth dragon!' Sweet words in small emperor's ear, you see. Kowloon. Means nine dragons."

It was a good thing to have dragons on your side, Ah Ming told the child. In spring their breath in the warm wind brought rain and turned the land green. When there was lightning you knew they were fighting, and their fiery breath would strike a tree or a house, or even a luckless human who got in their way, and whatever the dragons struck would be reduced to cinders. No more to be said.

This morning the dragon hills could not be seen at all, and the Peak, that lofty perch of the rich and privileged across The Fragrant Harbour on Hong Kong Island, might have evaporated overnight.

All that was left on this foggy morning was the chaotic sprawl of waterfront and the burgeoning slums of Kowloon.

They were a no man's land. Decrepit tenements. Open sewers. Walls thrown up from scraps of this and that, roofs of corrugated tin anchored by assorted garbage thrown from the windows of taller buildings.

This place existed outside the law, and the vast bureaucracy of Hong Kong ignored it as buildings rose higgledy-piggledy. Through poor construction and necessity of space, alleys and passageways narrowed until, in some places, they were no wider than the length of a woman's arm.

The city within a city began to close in on itself, shutting out the sun and the rest of the world. It became home to the homeless, the coolies, the beggars, the destitute, and the professional criminals. Then the refugees came, the first of the million or so who would eventually wash up on Hong Kong's shore like a great human river running south and east from the Japanese. The ones who made it that far burrowed in, living nine, ten, a dozen to a room, sleeping in shifts, sharing their lice and their diseases. Children were born, lived, and died here, their brief presence on Earth unremarked by any official document.

The enterprising Kowlooners learned to dig into the earth and latch on to such cables and pipes as were needed, siphoning off water and electricity. Wires frayed and sparked, pipes dripped, passageways snaked crookedly and dead-ended, stairways led nowhere, cellars and their entrances disappeared under well-placed piles of junk.

Business carried on. Fortune teller, bone setter, letter writer. Dentists and doctors plied unlicensed trades, goods of all kinds were bought and sold, and the traffic in opium and human beings became common currency.

As they settled into their new home, the amah puffed away on her small pipe and gave thanks to Kuan Yin, Goddess of Mercy. It would be a long time before any Japanese patrol stumbled on this inner sanctum. They had a roof. Walls. It was better than a patch of dirty pavement. They could be safe here, she and the child. Unless the Japanese burned it down. Then, nobody would survive. They would all go to their ancestors together. No more to be said.

And so it went, for the next four years.

Certain things had changed. There were no more stray animals competing for edible garbage—Su Li hadn't seen a dog or a cat in two years. The strays, too tasty for their own good, had long ago been eaten by the refugees who were scratching out an existence any way they could, and the rich folk, the ones on the Peak, wisely kept their domestic livestock under wraps.

Only the rats still flourished, and although impressive numbers were being trapped in Kowloon and salted down by frugal cooks, it seemed that no shortage would arise in the near future.

Su Li had been up early this morning, charting a careful path through the rotting garbage, avoiding the huddled figures scattered here and there. Dead or alive, they were bad news. An imploring whine rose from a pile of rags, and she sidestepped the wizened fingers that made a surprisingly energetic grab for her ankle.

The pervasive smell in the air, part decay, part smoke (singed feathers, fried garlic, sandalwood incense) was not unpleasant to Su Li. She picked her way among heaps of refuse and various life forms that littered the place, stepped lightly over the bloated carcass of a rat lying in a puddle, and scarcely noticed the bleakness around her.

Now she squatted on a rock by The Fragrant Harbour, scrubbing clothes in the amah's tin basin. The water was cold on her hands, and Hong Kong's humidity kept her chilled until the sun came out to burn off the fog. Even in summer, when the heat became terrible and the tiny room she shared with the amah was like an oven, the dampness lingered.

When the hoarse moan of a ship's horn sounded from the harbour she could see nothing in the enveloping murk, but as she watched, the hull gradually became visible. A couple of small military boats darted past, zigging and zagging around the bigger ship like flies around a pot of honey.

The horn sounded again; now she saw that the decks and even the portholes were jammed with men, all in khaki uniforms, all waving and whistling and yelling. Su Li didn't wave back. She knew instinctively that the amah wouldn't approve.

AWATEA, she spelled out the letters on the hull, said them slowly, tried the unfamiliar sounds on her tongue. During four years in British Hong Kong she had learned to speak some English, and although she couldn't yet write it, she could read the alphabet.

These must be the soldiers who came from the place the southern Chinese called Gold Mountain. For days the rumour mill had been trumpeting the arrival of a massive force of gweilo soldiers, Canadians, swooping in to replace the departing British. This was news for the amah!

She squeezed cold water out of her washing, dumped the basin, and started back to the small room where she and the amah lived. At first they had shared the space with five other refugees, an old couple and a young woman with two sick babies that howled all the time, but the old ones had conveniently died within a few days of each other and the mother took the babies out one morning and never came back.

"Gone," said the amah happily. "No more to be said."

Now instead of seven people in one small room, there were only two, and such privacy was a luxury. True, it was more closet than room. It had been been partitioned from a slightly larger space and lost the only window in the process, but the amah thought to herself that being windowless was a good thing. Better nobody see in.

Su Li ran up three dark flights of a narrow staircase, along an unlit hallway, and up another, narrower flight with the third step missing entirely, to the room where the amah had been coaxing a kettle to boil over a charcoal burner.

She could smell the still-smoking incense from Kuan Yin's shrine, so she knew Ah Ming must have been seeking divine guidance again.

"I saw a ship! The Canadians are in the harbour!"

The amah only nodded, slurping her tea in thoughtful silence, ignoring the girl's excitement. Today she had a mission, and when at last she spoke, it was about another matter.

"I go to Old Wong," she said. "Must not delay longer."

Su Li sighed, but she knew the amah was right. Old Wong was one of four uncles on her father's side, so she referred to him as Fourth

Uncle Wong, but he was no relation to her amah, who simply called him Old Wong.

By mid-morning she and Su Li were making their way along Nathan Road in the direction of the Fortunate Noodle House, Old Wong's place of business. In the distance they heard the squalling of a Scottish pipe band. To the amah it sounded like a pig killing in progress, but what else could one expect of such uncivilized people?

The crowd that came out to greet the Canadians was so dense that the amah's well-placed elbows had to clear a path. She had no time to watch this rabble of foreigners playing their silly noisemakers.

They had been lucky with Old Wong. Four years ago, when they'd arrived from China, the amah sought him out. By a stroke of good luck, he needed a girl child to help in his smoking rooms above the noodle house.

They were reached by a narrow staircase on the right side of the main door. In spite of continual traffic up and down the staircase, the Hong Kong police never questioned Old Wong's big lie about his wife's family living upstairs. As long as Old Wong paid them well, they would continue to believe his fable, transparent as it was, and the law wouldn't dip its greedy fingers into what had become a tidy little business.

Had anyone accused Old Wong of running an illegal opium den above his restaurant, he'd have been genuinely shocked. Illegal it may have been, but Chinese memories were long, and the dirt from the Opium Wars was on British hands. Foreign mud, the Chinese called it.

Su Li had gone to work, a tiny, silent figure preparing pipes for men who dreamed the hours away. Old Wong's parlour was better than most. His customers reclined in discrete cubicles, six on each side of the room, divided from one another by folding screens. Each cubicle held a wide wooden bench fitted with a thin mattress and a padded block where the customer could rest his head.

The room was always warm, and as the hours ticked by the air became thick with the heavy sweetness of opium. It was quiet except for the shuffling of slippered feet, and dark except for a single dim light at the table where sticky black pellets were rolled and spirit lamps were filled.

The only other light was the red glow of a shrine at the end of the room, for as careful as Old Wong was about his customers' comfort, he was equally vigilant about keeping the gods happy. You never knew when a deity might be needed to intercede, especially with the Japanese at Hong Kong's back door and the barbarian British not yet out the front. For his part, one was as bad as the other. May the gods preserve him from both.

It was easy work for Su Li, kneading the opium into a tiny black ball, warming it over a spirit lamp until it was soft and sticky, stirring it with a steel wire until it began to bubble, packing the thimble-sized bowl of the pipe, and waiting until the customer inhaled that first soothing breath through the mouthpiece. It never took long. The effect was almost immediate, and she could see their faces relax as the smoke worked its magic. She would smile shyly and move on. The men would each smoke five or six pipes, but if one of them wanted more, Su Li was paid a small bonus.

It wasn't so bad, the amah thought. Old Wong had been kind to the girl. At least she hadn't been sold as a slave, hadn't become a flower woman, selling her body on the street. Opium smokers didn't care about young girls. All they wanted was to lose themselves in their dreams.

But now Su Li was fourteen. Beautiful, like her mother, the amah reflected. Soon Ah Ming would be joining the ancestors, and what then of the girl? Without her amah to guard her, would Old Wong still look after this child? No. These were evil times.

In the underground economy of Kowloon's slums, everything was harder. Prostitutes and their pimps could no longer attract a reasonable trade. Go-betweens and fortune tellers lost their customers. For the pickpockets and thieves who made their living reselling whatever fell off the carts, business was also down, and the always-thin veneer of civilized behaviour was beginning to crumble.

The amah suffered sleepless nights over these matters. Kowloon was awash in desperate people who would as soon slit your throat as look at you. They were almost as bad as the Japanese, except nothing could be as bad as that. The Japanese would be in Hong Kong soon. Then it would be over for all of them. Finished, thought the amah. *No more to be said.*

Still, one more thing must be done: Old Wong must find a gun for her. The time ahead made it necessary.

T W O : Fire in the Sky
Pearl River Village, September 1937

SU LI REMEMBERED THE FIRE in the sky. It was just past her tenth birthday.

One night came a strange thrumming noise, the vibrations of the Japanese planes coming closer. Then the sky exploded, and their quiet market town on the bank of the Pearl River was on fire. They heard running feet, screaming, the staccato *rattattat* of artillery, the crack of rifle fire near their house on Pigeon Street.

There were four people living in the little house. Her mother and father, plus Su Li and her amah, Ah Ming. Ah Ming was a short, stout woman who pinned her greying hair back in a bun and wore the traditional black cotton samfoo, the tunic and trousers of her profession. Occasionally she puffed on a small pipe. She had been amah to Su Li's mother, the rather spoiled baby in a wealthy Shanghai family. When the baby grew up and married, her amah came with her, so Su Li was the second generation to be in Ah Ming's care.

Then had come their time of eating bitterness. As the Japanese rolled steadily southward, the family had moved too, leaving property and personal wealth behind them in the last move. During those years Ah Ming had become a de facto member of the family, and she would have given her life for any one of them.

Now, a long and terrifying night. Mother and Father at the window, watching. Town in flames, everything burning, evil wind coming closer.

In a far corner of the room the amah squatted, holding Su Li between her knees. Su Li was small for ten. Sometimes Ah Ming called her by a pet name, Butterfly, because she weighed so little and moved so fast.

Father speaking: "Don't you move. Be quiet, no matter what. No noise!"

In the corner, Mother piles quilts on top of Ah Ming and Su Li. All the bedding in the house, on top of them. Hard to breath. But Su Li can see through a space between two quilts.

She sees the Japanese soldiers come through the door, one, two, three Japanese with guns. Long knives sticking out the front.

Father dies quickly. A soldier shouts at him, smashes his head with a rifle butt, shoves his long knife into Father's stomach. Father doesn't fight back. Does nothing to stay alive longer. Mother, grabbed by her hair, thrown to the floor. Her tunic ripped. Mother screaming. She sounds far away, Su Li thinks. Maybe not Mother at all, this screaming. Maybe somebody else.

One soldier, kneeling on Mother's stomach. Maybe she hears Mother groan? Maybe not? Same soldier, punching Mother's face, banging her head on the stone floor, *thud, thud*, like the sound a green coconut makes before it breaks.

Tallest soldier now: sees the pile of bedding, raises his rifle in both hands, comes closer with his gun and long knife, so close she can smell his sweat.

(*Now we die*, the amah thinks, squeezing Su Li's tiny body between her knees. Ah Ming holds her breath, waiting for the first lunge, for the stabbing to begin. She will protect the child as long as she can.)

Mother, still conscious, fights for her life, summons the last of her strength. Opens her mouth, bites the soldier. Bites almost through his finger. Su Li will remember his scream, the pain and rage of it. The noise distracts the tall one, so he does not stab them just then. He turns his attention to Mother.

After that Mother dies quickly. Anyway, Su Li prefers to think so.

She must have been dead, even while the short one, the one she had bitten, raped her. Even before he pulled out his knife and sliced it across her throat. Dark blood runs fast, stains the floor. Su Li worries that it will stain Mother's blue tunic. The short soldier stands up, pants around his ankles. He does a barbaric thing. Makes water on Mother. Pisses on her face and laughs. Ah Ming's hand is so tight across Su Li's mouth that she can hardly breathe.

After that, soldiers smash everything. Chairs, table, the red wooden godhouse where Kuan Yin lives. Her mother loved the little goddess, always kept oranges and incense there. Often at night, rolled in a quilt and just at the edge of sleep, Su Li would drift away to the comforting drone of adult voices and the smell of sandalwood incense that Kuan Yin preferred. Now her little godhouse is gone.

The soldiers tear the pictures off the wall, pointing and laughing at the sepia portraits of Grandmother and Grandfather who are with the ancestors, of Father and Mother on their wedding day, of Third Uncle Wong who has gone to Gold Mountain, the place called Vancouver, to make money. They smash the glass and grind it under their heels.

It seems they will leave now, but the taller one hangs back, pausing to light a cigarette, and his gaze returns to the corner. To the pile of bedding. He walks toward it, three steps, four steps, bends low, holds the match to one of the quilts. Squats on his heels, waiting until the flame catches the silk cover. Blows his sour breath on the flame, this tall soldier. Helps it to burn. He draws once more on his cigarette, watching the tiny flame play at the silk before he stands up. Walks toward the door, three steps, fours steps.

Out of the house.

Su Li can smell the smouldering of the silk, feel the heat against her face, but the soldiers are still talking.

Trapped underneath the burning quilts, the amah decides they must wait until the flames engulf them.

Help us, Kuan Yin, Goddess of Mercy, who sees the pain of all women.

Smoke fills the corner now. Hard to breathe.

Better to die this way. Better to die than let the Japanese find the child.

But it was the rainy season, and though the fire burned away most of the silk coverlet, it could only smoulder in the damp wadding of the heavy quilt.

Thank you, Kuan Yin, thank you for your mercy.

In the whole length of Pigeon Street, only Su Li and the amah survived the Japanese that day.

Even when the soldiers had gone, they didn't dare move. For most of that night they waited, cowering under the smoky bedding, terrified that the soldiers would return. All that night they listened to the distant agonies of the dying town.

In the darkest hour before dawn the amah got stiffly to her feet. Peeked out the door, carefully, carefully. Made Su Li stay under the quilts.

"Quiet. Soldiers maybe come back."

Su Li was hungry, but the amah was too busy to feed her.

"You be good girl now. You wait."

One thing remained unbroken in the room. Somehow, neither of them could imagine how, the small statue of the goddess, Kuan Yin, had survived the stomping feet and the rifle butts. The amah found her in the rubble of smashed furniture, for by now Ah Ming was rummaging to see what could be salvaged in the few moments that remained.

While they'd waited under the quilt, the amah had been considering their options, and she had a plan. Quickly she gathered those things she had listed in her head: rice bowls, chopsticks, chopper. Her pipe. A small sack of rice, some tea, and a few dried fish, no more than a handful. Her beloved charcoal burner she could not take, but they would find a new one when the time came. All of these things she packed carefully together, so it took little space inside her bundle. She felt the hem of her padded cotton jacket, just to be sure the gold rings, the earrings, and the fine gold bracelets were still where she and Su Li's mother had sewn them days ago.

Then she told Su Li to come out and gave her some dried fish to chew on while she carefully, tenderly salvaged the portraits from the smashed frames: Su Li's parents and grandparents, now with the ancestors, and Third Uncle, safe in Gold Mountain. Along with the ancestral scroll and the little statue of Kuan Yin, she rolled them tightly in a smaller bundle.

Gave it to Su Li to carry. Made her wear two tunics under her padded jacket. Closed the door on Pigeon Street. Left Mother and Father.

"Don't you look," the amah said. "Walk fast."

In the darkness, they made their silent way through alleys and narrow passages between buildings, avoiding fires that were still burning, backtracking whenever they heard voices. Soldiers had looted the wine shops, and drunken bands roamed the streets, killing any dog or human who was still alive. Once, they rounded a corner and almost ran into a Japanese sentry, but he was lighting a cigarette and didn't see them.

The woman towed the child along until they reached the bank of the great Pearl River. Su Li had come here often with her mother and the amah to buy vegetables and fish from the women who kept their stalls along the water. She had loved the fishing junks with their giant brown batwing sails, and she envied little girls her own age who lived on the boats, sailing who knew where, down the river into the green water of the China Sea.

"Lucky, no moon," the amah muttered as it began to rain, hard cold rain beating down like small pellets, but even in the dark the amah found what she was looking for. The boat was already crowded when they climbed aboard.

"Be quiet," they said. "No noise."

In the darkness, her face pressed into the amah's jacket, Su Li thought they were alone on the water, but a sheet of lightning turned the river white and in the sudden flash she saw that there were boats all around them. One was a Japanese patrol, and they were caught in the glare of searchlights. There was a burst of gunfire, but their boat roared, its engine smoked and flamed like a dragon, and they slipped away while the patrol boat pounced on the others. She heard a groan. A woman beside her had been wounded, and would soon die, so was pushed overboard.

It was well past noon when they drew close to shore in the place called Deep Bay, in the New Territories of Hong Kong. A hopeful murmur went through the crowd. No sign of sentries. No dock, so everybody had to jump in. Su Li could swim, but she choked and spluttered as the water closed over her head. Then many people joined hands. Soon she felt the mud beneath her feet and she could stand up.

When they reached the shore the amah wasted no time on good-byes. She set off purposefully across the green hills, dragging Su Li with her. The hills were high, but they followed the zigzag paths used by farmers in the New Territories, and the walking was soon easier. They passed fields and gardens and brown ponds with flocks of white ducks. They walked a long time without stopping, and Su Li whimpered because her feet hurt and her stomach growled for food.

In the early evening of the second day, they topped a high hill, and there below them were the lights of a great city winking in the dusk.

"Hong Kong," said the amah, and it sounded like a prayer.

They sat down for a moment's rest, while the amah told Su Li the story about the nine dragons. Su Li leaned against the old woman and would happily have slept, but Ah Ming pulled her to her feet.

"No time to waste. Must find my friend."

In those days the outskirts of Hong Kong were a series of villages that had evolved from the nearby farms, and the sprawl of the city was not welcomed by these agricultural people who valued arable land above all else. When the amah stopped to ask directions they stared at her, defiant in their silence. She pressed on, into the rapidly darkening streets, past teahouses with lighted windows, past food carts with delicious smells where women steamed dumplings and fried noodles, past huddled bodies curled up on the pavement, and the little girl was astonished by everything she saw.

It was dark by the time they found the place where Ah Ming's friend lived, in a small, airless room already crowded with too many people. She made them move over so Su Li could lie down, her head in the amah's lap.

"We stay here now," she told the little girl. "We are home."

And so it had been, for nearly four years.

THREE : China Girl

Hong Kong, December 5, 1941

THE RICKSHAW RACE HAD BEEN a blast. Considering that they'd already missed their curfew and would have to sneak in anyway, Mick, Freddy, and Tony reasoned that one more beer and some food would put the right spin on the evening.

"How 'bout thish 'plashe?" Tony suggested, and they stumbled happily into the Fortunate Noodle House.

It was only moments, maybe less than that, before one of the three apparently jostled the arm, and the drink, of a tall Scottish soldier wearing a regimental tam and kilt. As the beer soaked into the front of the Scot's khaki shirt, Freddy opened the conversation with a solicitous inquiry about his headgear.

"Hey, buddy, where'd you get that hat?"

"Something wrong with my hat, laddie?"

The Scot was in a belligerent mood, and a perceived insult was as good a reason as any to fight, but it got better.

"Looks like a pansy-type hat to me," Freddy observed.

"He's wearing a skirt," yelped Mick. "Look, Freddy. This guy is wearing a cute little skirt!"

From Tony: "Ahhh, isn't that sweet?"

"Looks pretty damn stupid if you ask me," Freddy announced.

The Scot looked down at him and smiled.

"I don't think I asked you, now did I?"

"Well, I'm telling you anyway!"

So Freddy got thrown out of one more pub.

Landing on his rear end on the wet pavement, he heard an ear-splitting shriek, and just as he was trying to stand up something solid hit him in the chest, knocking him flat again.

149

"Hey, watch it, fella . . ."

But this was no fella.

To his surprise, the missile was a Chinese woman, and she was upright in an instant. She yelled a stream of Cantonese, shook her fists, and stomped her small feet in fury. The door she'd just been tossed out of slammed shut, the sound of female laughter ringing behind it.

She looked down at him, and he saw that she was hardly old enough to be called a woman, but oh, she was lovely.

Su Li was just about as mad as she'd ever been in her almost-fifteen years. In recent months her clientele had changed. Her old customers, addicted to opium, were indifferent to sex and never bothered her. But there were new clients, men not yet so eager for the sweet lulling smoke that took away desire. Some of them had made remarks, upstairs in the darkened smoking room. Even Old Wong, her venerable uncle, was different. Sometimes his hand, offering a kindly pat on the back, landed too low and lingered too long.

Su Li was young, but she wasn't naive. She knew what was going on between some of the clients and the girls from the restaurant downstairs.

There was another room behind the smoking room. Sometimes the girl named Precious, who was fat and had breasts like melons, and other times the mean, scrawny one they called Peony, would disappear into the back room with one of the men, and there'd be a lot of giggling and then a short silence. Eventually the girls would swagger out, and the client would shamble along behind, fall onto a couch, and not even look at Su Li while she prepared his first pipe.

Mostly she ignored it, but tonight Old Wong wasn't there and the other girls, who hated her because she was his special pet and never had to be nice to the men, had been unspeakably rude.

When a new client made a grab for her breast as she handed him the first pipe, Su Li had had enough. She yanked the pipe back and whacked him with it, right across the nose. It was bamboo, and it must have hurt, because he yelped like a kicked dog, and the fat Precious waddled full speed out of the back room and started yelling at her too, and then Peony weighed in. Between the two of them, they shoved Su Li through the door and down the stairs.

Later, she would explain to the amah that if the gweilo soldier hadn't been there for her to land on, she might have broken some bones. As it was, she had lost her dignity.

Freddy got to his feet and looked down into a face that reminded him of a flower.

"Are you okay?"

"Yes. Okay I think."

"You speak English, miss?"

"A little."

"What happened up there? Are you hurt?"

Unaccustomed to sympathy or concern from a man, let alone a gweilo, Freddy caught her off guard. When his next question came out in halting Cantonese, *Sik tzo fan mei?* she was amazed.

Had she had rice? It was the old-fashioned, courteous greeting, born of so many famines, but now only old people used it.

He laughed and switched back to English. "Are you hungry? How about some tea?"

They walked to the Wan Lo Teahouse a few blocks away from the Fortunate, where giant brass urns glinted in the dim light, and the sweet songs of birds could be heard from the dining room upstairs.

He asked her to order for both of them.

"I'm a little hungry," he said. "Maybe some noodles with pork? Or some steamed fish?"

When the bowls and platters arrived, he ate very little, partly because he couldn't take his eyes off her. Not only was she beautiful, but he'd never seen anybody wolf down so much food so fast.

Although they said little during the meal, the silences were comfortable. When Freddy asked for the bill in Cantonese, she was once again caught off guard, so when he asked if he could see her again the next night, what could she say but yes?

FOUR : In the Temple

ON THEIR THIRD EVENING TOGETHER, Su Li takes him to a place where few outsiders had ever been, deep in the labyrinth of Kowloon. Here the streets are reduced to alleys without names, and at the sight of a gweilo in a uniform women hustle their children out of his way. The men stare, defiant and hostile.

Vaguely uncomfortable, he follows her up three flights of rickety stairs and along a passageway too dark to see the eyes he knows are watching them.

When she opens the door, Freddy is reminded of a cave where an animal might hibernate. The windowless room is tiny, yet every inch of space is in use. Cardboard boxes are stacked against the end wall, with baskets and mesh bags hung above them. There seems hardly room for the furnishings: a small cot and a wooden packing box that serves as cupboard and table. On it a small shrine made of red-painted wood. A feeble light from a spirit lamp glows in the little godhouse, illuminating the small statue that occupies it. An orange has been placed in front of the statue, and there's a faint odour of something he has come to recognize as incense.

On the floor, opposite the cot, an old woman huddles on a thin mattress, snoring gently.

"Ah Ming, my amah," Su Li says, putting a finger to her lips. "She only pretends to sleep, until I am home."

They sit close together on the cot, suddenly shy, and Freddy's disappointment hangs over him like a cloud. He'd hoped for a little privacy with this China doll, maybe a little action, and now here's an old granny playing possum. So they sit, whispering together.

"When war ends, you go home?" Su Li asks.

"Yeah, I guess so . . ."

"Where you go, Freddy?"

She likes the sound of his English name when she says it out loud.

"Back home, to Canada."

"Tell me about Ca-na-da."

She says it carefully, mimicking his pronunciation, but slowly, separating the syllables

"Is it cold in Ca-na-da?"

He's been asked the same questions dozens of times by women in the bars of Wanchai. They all seem to know about cold Canadian winters, it's their big talking point. They ask so they can hit him up for a drink, but they're too bored to listen to the answer.

What your name, soldier? Where you from? Ah, Ca-Na-Da! It is cold there, soldier? Buy me a drink?.

But coming from this woman in this place, it's like a different question. She doesn't want a drink or a tip. She really wants to know.

For a minute he considers her question in silence.

"Well, it's winter now, so there'll be a lot of snow. It'll snow every night for a week, and we'll have big drifts, high as you are tall."

He remembers the frozen stillness of a Canadian winter, how everything seemed to be waiting. There was a serenity about winter that he'd always liked, and he wants to share it with her. He tells her about the giant spruce trees in Serena's yard, how their branches grow heavy with overnight snow, droop low under the weight of it, look like the wings of great white birds, like giant crane wings. He tells her about the smell of a winter night, the smell of pine needles when you crush them, the smell of wood smoke. He tells her how snow sounds when it's coming down.

"When the snow falls, if you stand real still, you can hear it hissing past your ears," he says.

He makes a soft hissing sound, a snow-falling sound, and tickles the back of her neck with one finger, so she laughs. Her breath is warm on his cheek.

He nods toward the shrine.

Tell me about that, he says to Su Li as the light of the flickering spirit lamp casts shadows on the small figure within the little red shrine. It's a woman in a white robe, eyes downcast, but there's a suggestion of a smile, as though she has a secret.

Tell me about her, he says.

Voice full of wonder, Su Li tells him a story about a young woman who refused to obey her wicked father and marry somebody she didn't love.

"She starves. She dies! But when she goes to meet ancestors, she becomes Kuan Yin, Goddess of Mercy. Loved by everybody. Especially women."

Su Li smiles, pleased with the happy ending.

"She brings my amah and me here, from old village!"

He likes the sound of her small voice, soft as a child's. He watches her eyes grow wider and darker as she talks. Freddy takes Su Li's hand and strokes her fingers, such long, delicate, fragile fingers on such small hands.

"I hope your goddess sticks around until this is over," he whispers.

Every night for a week, Freddy went to the Fortunate Noodle House to pick up Su Li after her shift. She wasn't sure why she didn't tell him about the smoking room and the men upstairs. Instead, she let him think she was a waitress in the noodle house. By the time he arrived, she was always standing just outside the front door, waiting.

Freddy has no special job in the army. He follows orders, even when they make no sense. The marching, the drilling, yes sir, no sir, all the saluting. It all seems faintly ridiculous, but like Mick says, it's the army, what else do they know?

His knowledge of Cantonese is considered an asset and from time to time he's useful as an interpreter with the coolies who work around the barracks at Sham Shui Po, but the local speech is too fast, the sing-song accent too complicated in its risings and fallings, and he struggles with it. Except when he's with Su Li. With her, he often speaks basic Cantonese, the way he learned it in Yip's kitchen.

As the days passed, Freddy spent less time with Mick and Tony and counted the hours until he could see Su Li again. He had no intention of falling in love with this Chinese girl. He knew the impossibility of

154

such a relationship. Still, beyond his eager physical need for her there grew a tenderness he'd never felt before, not during his brief fling with Zena, certainly not with any of the girls he'd met since.

In the first week of December 1941, Hong Kong was like a party that was winding down, guests lingering too long, food and drink depleted, the band packing up to leave. On those evenings Freddy and Su Li wandered the streets like two happy children, and Su Li became his guide.

"Cloud ears." She held up dry, dusty mushrooms. "Shark's fin," she said of a silvery triangle of delicate-looking cartilage. "Ginseng," she told him, pointing to a pale, weirdly twisted root with two divisions, like two long, dancing legs. It reminded him of the carrot he'd once pulled in Serena's garden, the one that had run into a rock and divided itself into two separate roots, defiantly growing on both sides.

"Make men strong," she said, looking sideways at him now, smiling. "Warm your blood."

He bought her a plum so he could watch her eat it. Watched as her small white teeth pierced taut black skin and plowed a furrow through yellow flesh. Watched juice dribble off her chin, laughed, wiped it off with his handkerchief. Watched as she nibbled the pit, surprisingly small for such a large plum. Saw her turn the pit in her mouth with her small pink tongue, suck on it, cradle it within the warmth and softness he knew was there.

Freddy envied the plum.

That evening she took him to a small temple where Kuan Yin had her own altar. Su Li had made special preparations for this visit, scouring the markets for what she needed, wrapping it all in a cloth: three incense sticks, a small roasted chicken, a packet of sticky rice rolled in a lotus leaf, three oranges she had liberated from Old Wong's place last night.

On the way, blackmarket peddlers grinned from doorways, opened their filthy cloth bundles like magicians, unfurled them at her feet, displaying a few bananas, flashlight batteries, cans of condensed milk, matches, as though they were offering gemstones before royalty. One man with a face like a fox had a suitcase full of jewellery: jade, bracelets, earrings. Su Li's ears were pierced, but her gold earrings had been hidden away for safekeeping. Not good to wear gold now, the amah said, too many crooks.

One pair of earrings caught Freddy's eye. They were shaped like teardrops, and they'd been carved from old jade, polished to a translucent sheen. They reminded Freddy of the milky green colour of moss on a pine tree.

"I want these," he said, holding the earrings.

For whom? she wondered, watching him pay for them.

Outside the temple, a woman sat on a low stool by the door. Her eyes were concealed behind dark glasses with small round lenses, and she was chanting over her stock of amulets and charms.

"Soothsayer," Su Li told him. "She sees your future."

"So ask her this: Am I alone? Or is there somebody in my future with me?"

He was teasing her, and she smiled, touching his sleeve, leading him past the soothsayer and through the door of the little temple in Ning Po Alley.

"First we find Kuan Yin."

In the dark temple, a pearly haze of smoke and ash drifted down from giant coils of incense. Bright objects were captured in pools of light from candles and hanging lanterns that reminded Freddy of the wonderful six-sided lanterns Yip always hung at Christmas. Freddy's eyes wandered over the tarnished brass, the gold leaf on red pillars, the tall red and gold screen, the carved dragons cavorting across the ornate altar. It was gaudy and smoky, nothing like Serena's church back in Edmonton, yet there was something familiar about the incense, something oddly comforting about the sight of human beings lost in prayer.

Su Li sought out her goddess, a smaller effigy on the altar dominated by major deities.

Again Su Li touched Freddy's sleeve—"Here, Kuan Yin is here"— and she opened her bundle and proceeded to lay out her offerings on the cloth square as though laying out a picnic: the chicken, the sticky rice, the oranges.

Freddy stood in the shadows, watching as she knelt and began the ritual prayers. Tucking her feet underneath her small body with toes pointing inward, she put her hands together in supplication, touching her forehead to the floor three times as she performed the kowtows she knew the goddess would expect. He thought again how like a child she was. Her hair was coiled in a heavy bun, but wisps had come loose on the back of her neck. She seemed so innocent, so vulnerable.

Su Li held a cylinder of bamboo sticks in both hands and began shaking them, eyes on the goddess. *Chuka-chuka-chuka.* Eventually one stick worked its way out, and she rose and took it to the only man in the temple, a bored greybeard who had been reading a paper over in a corner, for even now the prolific Chinese press continued churning out newspapers.

"I have asked for your future," she said as the old boy noted the number of the stick and handed her a slip of thin paper. Gathering up her offerings, she led Freddy outside and handed the paper to the soothsayer, who continued to look straight ahead.

"Her eyes are blind, but she sees inside," Su Li explained. "She sees everything."

The woman ran her hands over Freddy's forehead, his ears, his cheekbones. The hands were fluttery, dry as onion skin, her touch as light as moth wings. She muttered rapidly to Su Li in Cantonese, who replied in urgent tones, speaking too fast for him to understand.

Su Li had been squatting in front of the woman, but now she stood up, turned abruptly, and tugged on Freddy's sleeve.

"We go now. Please, Freddy, we go."

He could tell she was upset.

"Well? What did she tell you?"

"Nothing. She is not so good as I thought. She knows nothing. Pah! Stupid old woman. Just takes our money. She knows nothing."

The evening had grown chilly, and Freddy suddenly shivered. Su Li reached up and touched his face.

"You are cold, Freddy?"

He took the hand in both of his, kissed her palm.

"No. Somebody just walked over my grave."

"*Grave?*"

Su Li knew that word. Her eyes went wide with fear, and he laughed at the expression on her face.

"It's just a saying we have in Canada. 'Somebody walked over my grave!' We say it when we shiver for no reason. It's like a joke. It doesn't mean anything."

"Really, Freddy? You promise?"

▲　　▲　　▲

FREDDY BEGAN TO plan a special evening, one that would set a certain mood. For openers, he wanted to take Su Li dancing, and he asked Tony for advice.

"Must be a hot date, Fredo. Maybe tonight's the night, eh?"

"Watch your mouth, Tony, this girl's special. Pick somewhere nice, with a little class, okay?"

When the elegant-looking woman standing outside the Fortunate spoke his name, he hardly recognized her. Instead of coiling her hair neatly and pinning it low on her neck, Su Li had brushed it loose, and it hung straight and smooth, well below her shoulders. She had fastened one side behind her ear with a red flower, and she was wearing the red silk cheongsam that had recently become her uniform in the smoking room.

In the dim recesses of the Golden Bamboo Club, small tables are arranged around a dance floor. Su Li is dazzled, delighted with the rose-tinted shade on their table lamp, the velvet chair Freddy pulls out for her, the waiter in his shiny tuxedo. Freddy orders a beer for himself and a Coke for Su Li, and she's thrilled with the long-stemmed glass, the clinking ice cubes, the crowd of well-dressed men and beautiful women.

"Oh Freddy, so lovely," she breathes.

The band launches into "I'll Be Seeing You."

"Su Li, will you dance with me?"

He takes her in his arms. Something between elation and sadness washes over Freddy, for he is falling in love with this Chinese girl.

FIVE : The Ceremony

IN A WORLD OBSESSED WITH measurement, the speed of light, the distance to a star, an enduring mystery remains: how long does it take to fall in love? Is it a week? A year? Or some bolt-of-lightning nano-second that renders the victim helplessly, hopelessly besotted?

Freddy had known Su Li less than a month. In that time his world had moved to the edge of cataclysm, yet life had never been so sweet. He wanted to know everything about her.

Are you an only child? *Yes.* What are your favourite things to eat? *Rice and small shrimps steamed in lotus leaf. Yellow plums.* Have you ever had a pet? *No, Freddy. What is pet?* What happened to your parents? *They die.* What do you remember of your home? *Swimming in river. Story after supper. Mother's voice.*

At night when you sleep, do you dream about me? *Freddy, why you want to know so much?*

He tried to be happy with this lovely girl, to play silly games and tease her until she laughed, to enjoy making other guys jealous because she was beautiful and she was his, yet something dark hovered in the back of his mind.

In war, young men feel the first breath of their own mortality. Then comes the silent plea to whatever gods might be listening: don't let this be my last love, last dance, last warm body. And they plead with their women. Hold me, make love to me, promise me.

Wait for me.

"Su Li, I love you."

She smiles. This is just talk.

"Thank you, Freddy. I love *you.*" She's returning a courtesy, a polite response to a North American male. This much she has learned, working upstairs in the Fortunate.

"You don't understand. Su Li, I want to marry you."

"Marry? Marry *me*?" He hears her indrawn breath, for this is a preposterous idea. "No, Freddy. Not possible!"

He expects this, and he's ready.

"Yes, Su Li. Possible! Hey, it's 1941! There's nothing for you here, not now. Marry me. Tonight! The war won't last long. Couple of months, maybe three. As soon as it's over, I'll take you home with me. To Canada. Hell, I even have Chinese friends. In Edmonton, Yip and the guys. They'll be crazy about you!"

Ignoring the bewilderment in Su Li's eyes he rattles on.

"You must know a priest, somebody who can perform the ceremony. Maybe that old guy we saw in the temple?"

"No, Freddy! Ah Ming, my amah, would not agree."

And there's another reason, one she keeps to herself. Freddy is a white man. A gweilo. The Chinese have never trusted his race. These people, British, Canadian, they are all alike. Foreign round-eyes. Invaders. Chinese have hated them since the Opium Wars. She, a Chinese woman, marry a gweilo? A natural inferior? Not possible.

There is another matter. How to explain to the amah what she feels for this soldier? She has no Chinese words to describe it. Her vocabulary lacks the term for tenderness, let alone for desire.

No. Not possible.

Pragmatic in all things, the Chinese had always arranged marriage between families for mutual benefit. Parents, with the help of a go-between, made these decisions, for what had love to do with marriage? Later, affection might develop, but the marriage itself was serious business.

Su Li understood, young as she was. She knew the amah would never agree. Although she wasn't family, the old nursemaid had become her surrogate mother, and her word was law. She would shriek and tear her hair, and call on the gods to make this ungrateful, foolish girl see reason.

Even if she could get past the amah's deeply held prejudice against the white race in general and white men in particular, marriage was a long procedure, requiring the services of a go-between and several months of ritual. There were the ceremonies for betrothal, the five rituals on auspicious days only, the exchange of the eight characters. No, she told herself again, it wasn't possible. No more to be said.

Freddy wasn't entirely naive about their situation. He knew the army wouldn't consider his request to marry a Chinese woman. Not now, not in a million years. She wasn't even a citizen of Hong Kong; she was a refugee, a stateless orphan from China.

It was a testament to his golden tongue and his faith in miracles that in spite of all this, Freddy persuaded Su Li that they should broach the subject with the amah.

"Honourable Ah Ming," he babbled, red-faced but determined. "I want to marry Su Li. We would like your blessing."

There. He'd said it.

To their great surprise, the amah didn't rage or wail. Neither did she beat her head against a wall as Su Li had predicted. She sat quietly, puffed on her little pipe, stared impassively at Freddy with gimlet eyes slightly narrowed. She could see the sweat beading on the boy's forehead, see the girl beginning to squirm. Good. She took her time, considering the situation from its many angles.

True, he was gweilo, naturally inferior to Su Li, to all Chinese. Still, the girl's future here was impossibly bleak. Once the Japanese invaded, no woman would be safe, least of all a young and beautiful one like Su Li. Even if she should survive the inevitable horrors, beatings, rape, she would be ruined. No longer a virgin. No Chinese man would marry a non-virgin, especially one who had been used by those pigs in the Japanese army. They were worse than white men.

It was clear to the amah that this barbarian boy, though far from ideal, was the solution to the worries that had haunted her nights for so long now. Once again, Kuan Yin had thrown a rope into their bitter sea, and they must seize it. Su Li would marry the ignorant gweilo boy-soldier. No more to be said.

She spoke to Su Li in the old dialect, the one from their village in China.

"All winds are evil now, and we must survive. This gweilo? Maybe not so bad."

Su Li sat in stunned silence while the amah puffed on her pipe and spoke slowly, still in the old dialect, musing out loud on her plan of action.

"Astrologer must be consulted. Auspicious day must be found. Tomorrow I will speak to Mrs. Wu—only go-between in Kowloon City who won't pick our pockets."

The amah seemed suddenly tired, and she waved them away and curled up on her mat, muttering that she needed to sleep.

Su Li grabbed Freddy's arm and pulled him out of the room before the amah could change her mind, a mind that must surely be slipping.

The amah bounced up as soon as they had gone. There was much to be done. But first she placed a small bowl of cold rice in Kuan Yin's godhouse and lit three sticks of sandalwood incense. As an afterthought, she lit the red candles she had been saving.

Thank you, Kuan Yin. Much gratitude. Once again, you rescue us from a bitter sea.

A   A   A

THE NEXT MORNING the amah set off through the clamorous streets to find the astrologer.

"I will speak plainly," she told him. "My foolish niece wishes to marry a barbarian. A gweilo boy-soldier. Not worthy of Chinese wife, but what choice do we have in this terrible time?"

The astrologer stroked his thin white beard and nodded. There was wisdom in the old woman's words. There was also a fine gold bracelet, discreetly placed on the table between them.

"Like the willow, we must bend in the wind," he concluded brightly. "Otherwise, we break."

So the amah and the astrologer huddled together over the vital statistics: the hour, day, and year of birth for Su Li and Freddy. With her encouragement and a few coins across the small table, events shot forward with lightning speed. An auspicious day, usually not available for months, miraculously appeared only two days away.

Satisfied, Ah Ming now produced her go-between, one Mrs. Wu, an old crony from her repertoire of strange acquaintances. By noon, the two were in conference in Ah Ming's room.

Mrs. Wu was a round, soft dumpling of a woman who'd always been too fond of dim sum. Although widowed herself, she had become an expert at arranging futures between men and women.

But now the marriage business was in a slump. Families that would have demanded two or three applicants before choosing the right one were making unthinkable compromises. Some were actually encouraging their daughters to become singsong girls, selling their bodies to support the family. These days, Mrs. Wu was lucky to have one customer a month, and the stress was beginning to tell on her. She had taken to colouring her sparse grey hair with a coal-black dye and painting a slash of scarlet lipstick on her chalk-powdered face. Above her small black eyes she designed high-arched eyebrows, so she wore an expression of perpetual surprise.

After the usual greetings, Ah Ming asked her to sit down. Mrs. Wu's face lit up when she saw the box of savoury pastries Ah Ming had provided, for although such luxuries were increasingly scarce even for the wealthy, the amah had her sources, and these had fallen off a pastry cart at no less an establishment than the Peninsula Hotel, where one of Old Wong's distant relatives happened to be a cook.

The two women closeted themselves in the amah's room over several cups of weak tea while the details were discussed, and in the end, a sensible path became clear.

This marriage, strange as it was, must go ahead with all possible speed. The barbarian groom must of course supply certain assurances, the most important of which would be an agreement to purchase legal status for Su Li and Ah Ming as Canadian citizens. It was not easy to do these things, yet they were done often enough. Canadian birth certificates must be found and paid for. Mrs. Wu knew a man who dealt in just such matters as these.

"Canada is not so easy for Chinese. They don't want us. We must find other ways. She will be a paper child."

For Su Li, it would be relatively simple to find a Chinese Canadian man who, some thirteen or fourteen years ago, would have visited his wife in China, at which time she might have conceived a child. That child, with its Canadian Chinese father, would now be entitled to a Canadian passport. The small detail, that no such child had been born, or at least had not survived, was of no consequence.

With the Exclusion Act of 1923, Canadians had slammed the door on Chinese immigration. It was only justice that such a government could now be so easily duped.

For the amah, it would be necessary to find a Chinese Canadian woman of her approximate age, who had no further need of such a passport. Possibly she had already gone to her ancestors, but as nobody bothered to inform the government of such details, Ah Ming could simply take over her identity. Tricky but possible.

All of this would cost a lot, but if the barbarian wanted to marry Su Li, it was right that he should pay a bride price. After these negotiations had been completed, the marriage could proceed.

It was left to Su Li to explain the finer points of all this to Freddy.

"You mean she wants me to buy a wife? To buy *you*?"

"No, Freddy. Not buy. Bride price is Chinese dowry."

"And she wants me to buy you a Canadian passport? Her too?"

"Yes, Freddy, she knows how to do this thing."

He looked down at her face, at the beginning of a small frown of apprehension, and he sighed.

"Okay, Su Li. I love you, and I'll do any damn fool thing I have to. Once we're married, everything will be all right. Tell the old girl I'm in."

He agreed to Mrs. Wu's version of an installment plan: down payment now, full payment on day of marriage.

And so Mrs. Wu took Freddy in hand, guiding him through the purchase of ceremonial gifts, and the following morning she personally delivered the first of them on his behalf: a small red laquered box of cakes, courtesy of the Peninsula's back door. On the lid, a broad paper ribbon was inscribed with the characters for double happiness. Excited, she made her way to the room in the alley, huffed and puffed up the stairs, presented her trophy. The amah smiled when she saw the box.

In turn, a second red box made its way past the curious sentry at Sham Shui Po barracks to Freddy, containing one of the cakes he had sent her, and her affirmative reply to his proposal.

Once again, Mrs. Wu huffed her way up the many stairs, this time with a package of tea and the jade earrings Freddy had bought near Kwan Yin's temple. With the last of the ceremonial gifts, the bargain was sealed. Mrs. Wu heaved a great chin-wobbling sigh. What should have taken weeks or months had been accomplished in only one day.

That night Freddy went back to camp and broke the news to Mick and Tony. He decided to say it fast.

"I'm getting married. I'm marrying Su Li. The Chinese girl you met outside the Fortunate. I just wanted you guys to know."

Mick broke the stunned silence.

"The hell you are. You can't marry a Chinese woman. They'll have you up on charges. You'll be court-martialled."

"Fredo, my idiot friend, you can't bring a Chinese woman into Canada!" This from Tony, when he finally found his voice.

Freddy resented the suggestion that Su Li was less than perfect in any way.

"Why the heck not?" he demanded, ready to fight.

"It's illegal. We brought my uncle Sal over from Sicily last year, and the immigration lawyer said he was lucky to get in. Jeez, Fredo, it cost my old man a fortune in bribes! And we're Italian! Lucky he wasn't Chinese."

"What does that have to do with anything?"

"Because we have an Exclusion Law."

"What's that? Never heard of it!"

Tony shrugged. Because of the Sicilian uncle and assorted other relatives that had flocked to the Cecci home in north Winnipeg, and due to his brief flirtation with a law degree, Tony knew something about Canadian immigration procedures. Still, he couldn't explain the finer points of legislation passed by some old geezers in Ottawa during the 1920s, so he kept it brutally short.

"It means if you're Chinese, female, and poor, you can't get into Canada. Not legally anyway."

Freddy felt his face burning. He wanted to punch somebody in the mouth. But Tony wasn't finished.

"Listen, Fredo, you've spent a lot of time in that restaurant back in Edmonton. How many Chinese women did you ever see in Yip's café?"

Freddy thought about those convivial nights in Yip's kitchen, all the old boys gathered around the table, even the younger ones, eight or ten guys most nights. But no women, except for Zena, who was white. Not one Chinese woman. Not in Yip's kitchen, not in the Thousand Year Trading Company where Yip used to send him for vegetables. He could have counted on his ten fingers the number of young Chinese women he'd seen in Edmonton in all of his seventeen years.

He remembered something else too, something Yip had told him that he'd never understood.

"I was a paper son," Yip had said. "One time Chinese baby die in Canada, so I take his place. I come to Canada. I never have my own name. Only his."

Then there was the photograph on Yip's wall, of his family in Hong Kong. No visits to Canada. He hadn't thought anything of it at the time.

"Freddy, use your head. You've only known this girl five minutes." Mick was being his usual reasonable self.

"I know! I know, and I don't care! I love her. Just help me out here! What the hell can I do?"

"Have you talked to anybody else about this?" Tony asked.

"Mrs. Wu. She's sort of a wedding manager." He didn't want to use the word *go-between*. It sounded too foreign.

"She told Su Li I'd need to pay for her passage and documents up front."

Tony nodded sagely. His experience with shepherding his own relatives past government watchdogs had taught him to spot loopholes, and Canadian immigration was a veritable sieve.

"The old girl's right. You'll be buying passports for both of them, and let me remind you again, it's not exactly legal. You'd need to get a passport that was originally issued to a Chinese woman about the same age as Su Li. Which, by the way, would be what?"

"Fifteen," replied Freddy in a low voice, adding a couple of months.

"How old? Did you say *fifteen*?"

Freddy nodded unhappily. Tony's jaw dropped. Mick whistled.

"Fifteen! Sweet Jesus, Fredo. That's not a woman, that's jailbait! Which reminds me. Exactly how old are you, my friend?"

▲   ▲   ▲

ON DECEMBER 5, excitement crackled in the Kowloon alley where Su Li and the amah lived. Nowhere on Earth does rumour travel as fast as it did in those Chinese streets, and everybody knew about the wedding.

The amah had risen earlier than usual and was already dressed in her black pyjama suit, which she had washed and pressed with a heated stone. Yesterday she had scoured the few remaining wet markets for a pummelo with leaves, and bargained hard, for it was only the leaves she wanted. This morning she put them in her tin basin with hot water for Su Li's bath.

"Pummelo purifies," said the amah. "Traditional for bride."

Then she helped Su Li into the red tunic she had managed to scrounge. It was borrowed, and wasn't a proper full-length wedding *kwa*, and instead of the many embroidered golden dragons that should have been cavorting on it, there was one small yellow dragon. It had been hastily embroidered by Mrs. Wu, who had flung herself into the wedding plans with more than usual enthusiasm in anticipation of a generous tip and because she had so little else to occupy her time these days. The tunic had a high mandarin collar, and with it Su Li wore a serviceable pair of black silk trousers.

On her head the amah placed the borrowed bridal headdress, compliments of one of Mrs. Wu's other clients.

"Ward off evil spirits," said the amah, tying a small, mirrored amulet the size of a locket around Su Li's neck.

Finally she draped the red veil over Su Li's headdress, and was relieved when it fell all the way to her shoulders so her face would be decently covered.

Both old ladies stood back and admired their handiwork, and the amah looked a little sad so Mrs. Wu offered a lewd joke to lighten things up a bit, after all, the wedding night was at hand, but the amah shushed her.

Shortly they heard the popping of firecrackers and the tootling of wind instruments, for Mrs. Wu's three musical cousins had been conscripted for the occasion. The band was distinctly out of tune, but nobody expected anything else, its sole purpose being to distract any evil spirits that might be jealously lurking.

Su Li's heart began to race. This was her moment. Her groom was coming.

It was all backwards, of course. As the bride, she should have approached the groom's home.

"His home is far away, in Gold Mountain," the amah explained to those who had gathered in the hall. "Soon enough we go there. For now, groom comes to bride."

She patted Su Li's small hand.

"A fish must sometimes swim upstream. No more to be said."

Mrs. Wu led the parade. Freddy, accompanied by Mick and Tony, carried a bottle of rye. They were followed by the cook from Old Wong's restaurant, carrying a roasted piglet with a red hibiscus blossom tucked behind one crisp brown ear. The amah was pleased. This treasure would distract any lingering demons and would also be placed before the shrine where Kuan Yin lived. Later of course it would be eaten, savoured to the last dribble of grease during a modest wedding feast at the Fortunate Noodle House, where Old Wong would be happy to act as host so long as the barbarian groom footed the bill. Seeing the pig, that most reliable of omens for prosperity, spirits soared.

Now two red candles and three sticks of sandalwood incense were lit in front of Kuan Yin's godhouse. The amah and Mrs. Wu directed Freddy to come in and sit beside Su Li, who was already seated on the narrow cot, hands demurely folded, face concealed beneath the red veil. Although it wasn't customary for the groom's supporters to take part in the ceremony, Mick and Tony followed him into the packed room anyway, crouching to get through the door, joining the crowd that now included the amah and Mrs. Wu, Su Li and Freddy, the man in charge of the roasted pig, two of the three bandsmen, and Old Wong, who had appointed himself Su Li's surrogate father for this day.

If it had been possible to bustle around in such a cramped space, the two old women would have done it. Instead, Mrs. Wu and the amah were forced to move slowly, stepping carefully among the band, the roast pig man, Old Wong, and Freddy's two large friends while offering the couple ceremonial cakes, tea, and wine. Then Su Li's hand reached for Freddy's, and the two of them knelt before the upended packing crate on which rested Kuan Yin's shrine and the ancestor tablet, the one rescued by the amah after the Japanese rabble had killed Su Li's parents.

Su Li made several cramped kowtows before the improvised altar, and Mrs. Wu offered the couple ceremonial wine in two small cups tied together with a red cord. Ah, sighed the amah, as both of them sipped the wine and firecrackers began popping again in the corridor.

Mrs. Wu announced that the ceremony had been concluded to her satisfaction. Freddy, whose Cantonese was sufficiently good for him to add a few words of his own, solemnly thanked the amah and promised to care for Su Li for the rest of his life, causing a ripple of astonishment among the assembled Chinese.

"Wah! The gweilo speaks Chinese! Wah!"

Then he added a western touch by raising Su Li's veil and kissing her gently on the lips.

Tony and Mick, overwhelmed by the unexpected loveliness of Freddy's new bride, slapped his back, shook his hand, and gave Su Li discreet pecks on the cheek, scandalizing both the amah and Mrs. Wu. The band began to tootle again, and firecrackers snapped and popped in the hallways, putting the entire ramshackle neighbourhood at risk of fire. Everyone who had been part of this unusual ceremony felt something they seldom experienced these days: a small ripple of joy.

The amah and Mrs. Wu, led by Old Wong himself, ushered the few invited guests off to the Fortunate, where waiters bowed them through the door and Mick and Tony eventually divided a hefty bill, having already dispensed red envelopes of luck and money for all the staff. The amah beamed, if not in approval, at least in relief. Mrs. Wu smiled broadly beneath her surprised eyebrows and tottered into the night, clutching her fee and a package of sweet bean pastries.

SIX : Honeymoon

AFTER THE WEDDING PARTY LEFT, Freddy and Su Li went back to the amah's room while Su Li carefully folded the borrowed veil and put it on the cot, along with the borrowed headdress. She touched the gold tassels and the strings of fake pearls. For a while she had felt like an empress.

Freddy put his arms around her and nuzzled her neck.

"I have a surprise for my new wife. Pack your clothes."

"Why, Freddy?"

"Can't tell. It's a surprise."

"Please? Tell me surprise?"

"We're going on our honeymoon."

"Freddy, what is honeymoon?"

Laughing, he took the amah's string market bag from its nail on the wall and handed it to her, for he knew she didn't own a suitcase, and in fact she had nothing to pack but one clean tunic, a pair of trousers, and the red cheongsam Old Wong had given her, the one he'd recently required for work in the smoking room above the Fortunate.

In the street Freddy hailed a rickshaw, and they travelled south-west, across Boundary Street to a busy market street with a crush of five-storey buildings, their recessed balconies hung with banners announcing such enterprises as the Excellent Jewellers, the Sincere Teahouse, and the Heavenly Cloud Hotel. From the top floors of almost every building, long bamboo poles extended out and up, sailing the day's laundry high above the busy street to catch whatever breeze it could.

Their progress was slow, as the district was bubbling with the traffic of late afternoon, and the rickshaw driver had to force his way through the crowd of vendors and shoppers and the homeless who simply lived on the pavement. On a side street known for its short-time hotels, Freddy told the driver to stop by a narrow building on a corner, where the Hotel Ozmanthus occupied the third floor. There were other hotels in the building, single-floor love hotels where Chinese girls and their escorts could rent a room for a few hours, no questions asked. Tony had recommended the Ozmanthus for that reason, overcoming Freddy's objections with logic.

"Listen, Fredo, you gotta face facts. You two aren't going to get into the Peninsula together, are you? Even if you had the bucks, eh? Let me fix you up in a place I know. It's not the Ritz, but it's clean and it's in your budget. Hell, Fredo, I'll get you the honeymoon suite!"

Tony had personally visited the Ozmanthus during a couple of memorable nights, and he favoured a certain corner room overlooking a busy market street. It wasn't big, but it was airy, with tall shuttered windows and a small recessed balcony.

During a preliminary tour of inspection Freddy had pronounced it suitable and booked it for an unheard-of length of time: two nights, paid in advance. The unusual booking had been accompanied by a generous tip, which not only pleased the scrawny desk clerk but gave him good face. He quickly offered Freddy tea and sent a runner in search of the owner, Mr. Tang, who scuttled along to meet the crazy gweilo who had done such a thing.

Thus were soap and towels negotiated, and a tea basket, to be delivered each morning to Mrs. McKee, after Freddy had left for the base camp at Sham Shui Po. All would be taken care of, Mr. Tang assured him. His welfare and that of his lucky bride-to-be were in the best of hands.

Despite Mr. Tang's disbelief that any such wedding was about to take place, and notwithstanding his private scorn for any Chinese girl who would marry a gweilo, especially one who brought her to his hotel, he was in all things a pragmatist. Business was business, and who knew how long he would be able to operate? When the Japanese came, as he knew they would, all gweilo would be dead or gone, and paying customers would be scarce. The Ozmanthus would be no more than a smile on the faces of a few former clients, sorting through their memories in old age, should they live so long.

When their rickshaw pulled up outside the hotel, a small boy who had been sent to watch for them skipped up the stairs to say they were coming, and when Mr. and Mrs. McKee arrived at the spartan reception area of the Ozmanthus they were met by the simpering desk clerk and Mr. Tang himself, who first offered tea and then bustled importantly ahead of them down the hall to open the door.

It was the hour of the night market, when the street below their room reinvented itself and the serious haggling of the day gave way to more leisurely pursuits. The voices of women lost their shrill tones and took on a twittering, chirping quality that reminded Freddy of birds. Busy over their charcoal braziers and soup pots, they cooked whatever they'd been able to find, and the good spicy smells floated up from the street, filtering through the shutters.

Su Li took it in all at once: the street sounds, the tall shutters, a slowly circling fan, the gauzy mosquito canopy over the bed. In an alcove, behind a folding screen, stood a greater luxury than she had ever experienced—a huge white porcelain bathtub with the feet of a lion. A magnificent tub, big enough to stretch out in, head to toe with room to spare. Big enough for a whole family to bathe in. Two threadbare towels hung over the side, and a small bar of soap had been placed on one of them. Soap! How long since she had even seen soap, let alone had a bar of her own?

Mr. Tang was proud of this particular amenity. Some hotels might have offered a drippy shower pipe, draining into a sloping corner of the tiled floor, or a communal hose in a mildewed lavatory somewhere down the hallway. But this! The biggest bathtub in the world, with burnished brass taps and a long brass faucet. This was beyond dreams.

Su Li squealed with pleasure. She bounced up and down. She laughed. She flung both arms around Freddy and chattered at him in rapid Cantonese. She skipped over to the tub and ran a hand along its smooth edge. Mr. Tang bustled over and bent to turn on the taps.

172

They watched as a feeble dribble of rusty water trickled out, then stopped. There was a breathless moment of disappointment, but Tang raised a reassuring hand, soon followed by terrific clanks and groans from deep within the Ozymanthus's plumbing as the hot water made its slow, deliberate way to their room and at last gushed out in a cloud of steam.

Freddy paid off the hovering Tang and closed the door. His bride had flung open the balcony shutters, delighted with the street life three floors below.

"Su Li, are you hungry?"

She was not. She was too excited to eat.

"Why don't you try out the tub?"

He turned the taps on full blast and waited for a show of reluctance from his new bride, possibly some initial protest, for he had no idea how a Chinese wife was expected to act on her wedding night. He was a little surprised when she immediately began to take off her clothes.

There was nothing coquettish about Su Li. Peony and Precious had filled her in on what happened in the back room with special clients, so she wasn't completely ignorant of matters between men and women. Now she simply undid her tunic and let it slide off her shoulders. She stepped out of her trousers, raised her arms, pulled the combs out of her hair and let it cascade down her back. Naked, she climbed into the tub like a happy child who had been given permission to strip and hop into a paddling pool.

Freddy was shocked to see how thin she was, how fragile; her hips so narrow, her backbone clearly visible. When she turned toward him, he saw that her breasts were barely formed above her ribcage, and her pelvic bones were prominent above the small triangle of pubic hair.

She watched him loosen his tie, take off his shirt and pants and hang them neatly over the bamboo screen. Suddenly conscious of his own nakedness, he turned off the light over the bed and lit one of two red candles Tang had left them. Su Li slid under the water, fully immersed except for her nose. Her hair fanned out behind her like black silk, and for a long moment he simply watched her before he climbed into the tub behind her.

They laughed as water sloshed over the edge of the tub. He began soaping her back and shoulders and she made small, appreciative noises that reminded him of a contented kitten being stroked. His hands moved over her shoulders to her breasts, and he felt her nipples harden under his touch.

Like a small, slippery fish she wriggled around to face him, solemnly returning his gaze. Wondering, he took one of her nipples into his mouth.

Hearing her indrawn breath, he lifted Su Li to her feet and pressed his lips against the velvet softness of her stomach. He pulled her down again and she wrapped her legs around him.

Time stopped for Su Li and Freddy, in the way that it does for new lovers. They had all night, an infinity, all the way to morning.

The first candle burned itself out.

▲　　▲　　▲

ON THE MORNING of December 6, 1941, headlines in newspapers around the world ran more or less like this:

Japanese Bomb Pearl Harbor.

The bombing of Singapore and Manila followed within hours. Then it was Hong Kong's turn.

Early that first morning, when Freddy kissed his new wife goodbye, he assured her he'd be back around four o'clock. They'd go to the Fortunate Noodle House for a celebration and take the amah with them.

But when he got back to Sham Shui Po, the camp was in an uproar.

"We've been ordered out," Mick told him, stuffing essentials into a duffle bag.

"Ordered out where?"

"Evacuation! The Japs bombed Honolulu and Manila. We'll be next. We're headed over to the island. Tony's out with a patrol, blowing up anything the Japs could use. They're starting with the cement plant and the power station."

At that moment the CO appeared, bawling at the men to move faster. He needed work parties to set explosives and destroy the railway tracks, a fuel dump, and what was left of the airport at Kai Tak.

"I don't have experience with explosives, sir," Freddy protested, but the CO, a red-faced man that Freddy rather liked, slapped him on the back.

"Don't worry about it, son. Figure out which end to light, then run like hell and get your head down till it blows."

Just then two loud explosions shook the building. They were followed by a third, from the direction of the water.

Boom! Again the building shook, and they all ducked, expecting the roof to fall in.

"What the hell was *that*?" Freddy yelled, and the CO grinned at him.

"We're blowing up the freighters in the harbour so the Japs can't get 'em."

In the early afternoon, Freddy left for Kai Tak with his platoon. The airport was right beside Kowloon City, not far from the Ozmanthus, maybe he could slip away and find Su Li and the old girl. He had to get them on a ferry and across to the island before the Japs arrived, and he knew that wouldn't be long.

SEVEN: Searching

THEY WASTED HOURS AT KAI TAK, and nothing went well. The CO gave new orders. They were not to go back to their barracks but to head straight for the pier.

"The ferries are still running, but nobody knows for how long. Some of our men are already there. Leave now," barked the CO. "Get on anything that floats. We'll reassemble on the Hong Kong side."

Freddy felt his stomach fall through his shoes.

"I can't leave," he told Mick and Tony. Desperation made his voice crack. "I'm going back for Su Li. I have to get her on a boat."

"You'll never find her now," Tony argued. "She's likely already left. She and the old granny."

"They're no fools, Freddy," Mick said. "Those two can look after themselves in this crowd better than we can."

But Freddy wasn't convinced.

"I'll meet you over there," he yelled. "I'll be back. I have to find her!"

He took off at a run, managed to commandeer a rickshaw, and sent the young driver pelting through the streets to the Ozmanthus Hotel. The trip should have taken a few minutes, but now, fighting the crowd, it took nearly an hour.

"Wait for me," he told the driver. Freddy flew through the door and took the stairs two at a time, but to his dismay the building was in chaos. Narrow hallways were clogged with people attempting to leave. Men in business suits, girls in evening dress. Women with huge bundles. Some carried or dragged small children. Where had they all come from?

At the reception area of the Ozmanthus, Mr. Tang busily cleaned out a safe and stuffed money into two cloth bags. He was no help. He only knew that Su Li had left with an old woman.

Freddy raced downstairs, but his rickshaw was nowhere to be seen. Spooked by the growing chaos in the street, the boy had run away. Bloody little coward, Freddy swore, and shoved his way through the crowd, heading for one of the only two places she might have gone: the Fortunate Noodle House.

Precious met him at the door with a simper on her chubby face.

"Is Su Li here? Have you seen her?"

"Your girl gone. Not come back," Precious announced, pouting. The simper returned and she stroked his arm. "You like Chinese girl? We have pah-tee?"

Unbelievable, thought Freddy. She doesn't give a damn about Su Li.

"Where's Old Wong?" he demanded.

"Gone. Collect money. Maybe come back. Maybe not."

Shoving Precious aside, Freddy ran back into the street. He didn't think it was far to the Kowloon tenement, and he headed southeast, toward the tumbledown building where she and the amah lived.

Freddy had never known a crowd like this. There had been no announcement, no general alarm, yet somehow these people sensed impending disaster. They knew the army was abandoning Kowloon like rats jumping ship, and the entire population seemed to be on the move, swarming toward the harbour.

They were converging in Chatham Road, so he knew the mob would spill eventually into Tsim Sha Tsui, ending up at the water-front, joining hundreds, maybe thousands of others from Mong Kok and Yau Ma Tei, and all of them would eventually funnel onto the same narrow docks in Victoria Harbour.

The luckiest among them would board Star Ferries, as long as they continued to run; or they'd scramble onto one of the kaidos, the water taxis that still buzzed around the harbour. They'd find something that floated, board it, commandeer it if necessary, for the Chinese had no illusions about what would happen to them once the Japanese arrived.

Fighting through the mob, he felt like a fish battling upstream, so he struggled toward the outer edge. In a quieter side street he heard the crystal sound of shattering glass, and he knew that the true entre-preneurs were at work. The looting had begun. Windows smashed, shops stripped, anything that could be moved was fair game. Sacks of rice, liquor, electric lamps. Upholstered chairs. Rugs. Doors were being lifted off their hinges.

In front of him, a ragged coolie darted into the street. On his head he wore a stack of women's fancy hats, their broad brims wobbly with feathers, ribbons, silk flowers. Over his shoulders he'd flung several men's suits and a fur stole, and he'd looped one car tire over each arm, as though they were bracelets. His bare feet slip-slapped along the street in an odd, penguinlike shuffle.

When he saw Freddy he hesitated for a fraction of a second. Men in uniform had already shot looters, but he gambled on Freddy, flashed a toothless grin, and slip-slapped away, as fast as his burdens would allow.

The perimeter street of Su Li's neighbourhood was oddly deserted, but he found the opening in the wall where she had taken him that first night. Even this pitiful sanctuary seemed abandoned, and he stopped to catch his breath, listened, heard nothing louder than the thumping of his own heart. Something moved behind him, and he whirled as a rat skittered across the alley.

"Su Li!"

He yelled her name. Darted this way and that in the maze of pas-sages. Got lost twice before he found the entrance to the rickety stairs and the door that still bore the double happiness paper the amah had pasted there to celebrate his wedding. It seemed so long ago, yet there were the remains of spent firecrackers, red papers bright in the gloomy passage. Maybe the two women were huddled inside, waiting for him. He wasn't much good at prayers, but now he heard his own voice, *Please, God, please let her be here.*

"Su Li!"

He threw his weight against the door, hoping it would be barri-caded in some ingenious way and he'd find them there, terrified but trusting, waiting for him.

It flew open so fast that he fell into the room, where the lingering smell of incense and the amah's clove-scented tobacco washed over him.

"Su Li!"

He howled her name into the empty little room, his voice cracking as he swept his flashlight all around, but there was no place to hide here, no possible concealment for an old woman and a small, frightened girl. There was only the careless debris left behind when people suddenly leave a place with no intention of coming back.

Somewhere a door slammed, and Freddy knew he wasn't alone, that there were watchers and listeners all around him. Behind secret panels, beneath trapdoors, the Chinese were battening the hatches. They would stay hidden in their cellars and burrows and cupboards, and behind their false walls, until the Japanese broke the doors down or burned the place to the ground.

He fought his way toward the pier, pushed through the mob, moved faster now that he travelled with the flow of pedestrian traffic. The loud *thrummm* of an aircraft engine made him look up, just as the lone Japanese Zero swooped over the street, so low he could see the pilot grin when the guns began to spit. Bullets tore into the crowd. A section went down, and their collapse had a strange order to it as one body fell upon another, then another, and so on, like dominoes. In seconds, the roar of the departing Zero was replaced by the screams of the wounded. Ignoring their frantic wails, Freddy kept moving.

Ferries had been running all night, carrying more civilians and army stragglers over to the island. Freddy's outfit had boarded the last ferry, the *Morning Star*, with Mick and Tony being the dog's tail, hoping he'd show up. Freddy was the last man in uniform on the pier, and he fought off terrified Chinese who pulled at his clothes and yanked on his arms, for if he could be held back, surely one of them could take his place. The ferry was overloaded with men in khaki, but on the starboard side, leaning precariously over the rail, he saw Mick and Tony scanning the crowd. He yelled, and they spotted him just as a Chinese deckhand began to haul up the gangplank.

"Jump, Fredo," Tony yelled and shoved the deckhand out of the way. Mick reached for him, hands outstretched.

"Jump, you crazy bugger! Jump!"

Freddy jumped and felt his right foot slip on the wet metal as he lost his balance, but then Mick's hand fastened around his wrist, pulled hard, and he was on the deck. Company D cheered wildly. Freddy kept his eyes on the Kowloon dock until it was no longer possible to recognize faces in the howling mob.

EIGHT : Waiting for Freddy

ON HIS FIRST MORNING AS a married man, Freddy had kissed his sleepy wife goodbye and left her in the room at the Ozmanthus.

"I have to go, Su Li. No choice."

At first she slept, revelling in the unaccustomed luxuries this new husband had already showered upon her: big bed, clean sheets, wonderful, marvellous, thrilling bathtub. Hers, all hers, for the rest of the day, until he came back to claim her. The hours stretched sweetly ahead, all the time in the world.

She filled the tub and took another bath, with water right up to her neck, smiling because some parts of her body felt sore and a little bruised. She thought of going downstairs, into the streets, maybe dropping in on Old Wong and the girls at the Fortunate for tea. She was, after all, a newly married lady, no longer expected to do her shift in the smoking rooms. That dirty business would now be left in the hands of Peony and Precious.

But what if Freddy came home early and she missed him? Su Li picked up his mandolin and plinked tunelessly at the strings. Bored, she curled up in the middle of the bed and fell asleep, so soundly that she didn't hear the distant thrum of the first Zero, nor did she recognize the muffled boom of the explosions. When footsteps approached in the hall, she bounced off the bed and stood by the door, ready to fall into the arms of her new husband, but the footsteps hurried past. The bars of light coming through the shutters had changed, and she knew the afternoon was waning.

As evening descended she lit the second red candle, opened the shutters, stepped out on the small balcony, and looked down upon the street. Something wasn't right. It was still crowded but somehow different. Now and then she heard thunder, or so it seemed, and there were strange flashes of lightning in the sky. Increasingly uneasy, Su Li went back to the bed to sit cross-legged and watch the candle. He'll come when it burns halfway, she told herself, but when it had burned halfway and a little more, she felt fear rising around her like cold water.

There's still some candle left, she told herself. When it's burned halfway again, he'll come. And she listened carefully to the street, not daring to watch the candle too closely, hoping the night cooks would return, for it was the hour when the food vendors had been busiest and loudest. But nobody called out their specialties under her balcony.

Su Li's heart beat hard at every footstep, every rustle outside her door.

Why hadn't he come back? Had he lied to her? Had she been a silly girl, abandoned by a white soldier, a phony gweilo who only wanted to play for a few days with a Chinese woman?

No. He wouldn't have gone to such trouble with the wedding. He wouldn't have whispered such sweet words all night long.

Then a new worry. Maybe he'd been attacked in the street, killed by thugs who roamed the alleys and preyed on anyone who walked alone. By now his body could be cut in little pieces, for the razor-sharp chop was the number-one favourite way to dispose of unwanted corpses. At the thought of Freddy's lifeless body being tossed over a cliff into the South China Sea, she whimpered out loud.

When the candle had burned to the size of her little finger, she again heard footsteps approaching, and this time they stopped at her door. She held her breath, for by now some sixth sense had kicked in.

This was not Freddy.

She heard the amah's voice.

"Su Li, unlock door!"

She flung the door open and threw herself upon the old woman.

Ah Ming sighed heavily, for she, too, had been waiting, hoping, but word had spread through the neighbourhood like a black wind. They had to leave, escape from Kowloon while they still could. There was not much time left. Even now, they could be too late. She cajoled Su Li into packing her small bundle.

"What if he looks for me in the old place? He could be there, waiting!" Neither woman believed this to be true, but what else could they do? At the very least, they could pretend to hope. Su Li refused to believe she had been abandoned.

"He will come back. Not here, maybe. But he will find me," she told the amah. "He will find me."

The amah hustled the reluctant girl into the hallway.

"Wait," Su Li cried and ran back to the room to collect his mandolin.

▲ ▲ ▲

WHISPERING IN THE dialect of their old village, the two women hatched a plan. For the second time in their lives together, the amah tied necessities into two bundles. They would look for Freddy, the amah would help Su Li search, but they must be prepared to move. The room in Kowloon, their home for the past four years, is no longer a refuge.

In the darkness, the women hurried through side streets to Sham Shui Po Barracks. Maybe she could talk to the sentry, leave a message, but when they arrived the gate was open and the camp was in darkness. Even the little guardhouse at the gate was empty. It was eerily quiet.

"Nobody here," said the amah. "No more to be said."

They turned back, moving warily, for the bombing was terrifying, earth-shaking. It was approaching three o'clock in the morning, an hour when there was usually a lull in the frenetic activity of Kowloon, the last of the night people having gone to roost. Yet on this night the streets were as busy as high noon, and ragged people scurried here and there, gathering in knots, dispersing, gathering again.

The amah approached a woman about her own age, carrying a baby on her back and leading a small child by the hand. A bundle was slung over her opposite shoulder. She spoke to the woman in the old language.

"Where have you come from?"

"From China. Beyond the New Territories."

"Where are these people going?"

"They run from the Japanese. No time to waste, Japs come soon!"

"What about the Canadians? The ones at Sham Shui Po?"

"Gone. To Hong Kong Island. They run away. Leave us for the Japs. Pahh!"

The woman spat in the street and turned her back, hurrying toward Chatham Road. Su Li ran after her.

"Wait, Mother! Where are you going?"

"To the ferry. To Hong Kong Island. Where else to go?"

It took the two women more than an hour of pushing and shoving through the crowds to find the ferry dock. Just as they reached it, a group of Punjabi soldiers clattered along at a dead run and forced a space in the protesting mob. They set up a machine gun and faced it up the road, and another sort of desperation took over. Frantic people leapt onto anything that floated, small sampans or kaidos, because the Star Ferries had all docked on the Hong Kong side. Su Li and the amah clung desperately to each other's hands, but they were being pushed back by bigger, stronger people.

The word passed through the crowd. Japanese coming! Coming now!

Then, in the first light of dawn, little men in rubber-soled shoes marched toward the pier with their rifles pointed, waist high, bayonets fixed. The pier erupted in total chaos. Women with children fought their way to the edge, hoping to jump onto a boat, only to be trampled underfoot or shoved off into deep water. Those who couldn't swim soon drowned.

The Japanese advanced, raised their rifles to their shoulders, and opened fire. The terrified Chinese screamed, pushed frantically, fell quickly as the bullets ripped into them.

At the edge of the pier, Su Li took a firm grip on the amah's free hand and pulled hard. When Su Li jumped, Ah Ming jumped too, but it was a good six feet down to the water and then Su Li had to swim an awkward sidestroke, hauling the terrified old woman with her.

Su Li had spotted the man at the tiller of the overloaded sampan, and it seemed that he slowed down, just until she reached the boat and grabbed the rope hanging over the side. Then the motor roared and she hung on hard, clinging to the amah with her other hand. They might have been in the water fifteen minutes, no more than that, because the sampan owner made all the speed his small motor could muster, headed for North Point.

If he noticed the two women he was towing, he gave no indication of it, even when he cut the motor. Su Li managed to swim the last few yards, and as she hauled the old woman ashore, Ah Ming still clung to her sodden bundles. Together they stumbled onto Hong Kong Island and collapsed on the stones, fighting for breath.

From across the water of The Fragrant Harbour, they heard the screams. The noise of the killing went on and on.

The amah recovered her wits first. Ever-resourceful, she had an address from Old Wong, some hole-in-the-wall on Fenwick Road. It was all they needed, while waiting delivery of the merchandise the amah had ordered.

During the first days of the Japanese invasion of Kowloon, Freddy and Su Li kept a strange vigil, each watching, hoping. If they gradually gave up hope, it was because they had more pressing concerns, for the Japanese were about to invade the only remaining refuge, Hong Kong Island.

General Sakai had sent a delegation to the island to accept the inevitable surrender. Governor Young's one word reply, "No," puzzled and infuriated the Japanese officer, who had expected a quick rout, given the well-known Caucasian reluctance to die in battle.

The Japanese were well equipped, and after five years of fighting their way through China, they were used to war. Now the bigger guns were turned on the island.

The Japanese artillery was deadly accurate, and they made mincemeat of the anti-aircraft and machine gun placements along the north shore. The city was soon in flames, and soldiers became firefighters.

Garbage piled up and bodies, both animal and human, were left to rot. Only the rats, who didn't seem to mind the maggots, fattened and thrived. Bit by bit, the remaining shreds of civilization began to unravel.

Every morning, a truck with loudspeakers drove through the city, blaring at the Chinese to burn or bury their dead. Human waste became a serious problem, and an appalling stench hung in the alleys, but the amah understood. Why would a coolie who had barely escaped with his life worry about where he emptied his bowels?

The dive bombing started, and Japanese Zeroes flew over the harmless defence line on the north shore, into the heart of the small island.

Yet among the Chinese, the much-depleted wet markets still offered cabbages, garlic, a handful of scallions. A few live fish flopped in their baskets, caught by some intrepid fisherman who had escaped the bombs. Meanwhile, Su Li and the amah waited patiently for delivery of the package Old Wong had promised.

Every morning, the two women ventured into Fenwick Street for supplies. They haggled for rice, waited in soup lines, scrounged just enough food to get them through that day. Every evening, they returned to the tiny room where the amah had once again set up a little shrine for Kuan Yin, and she thanked the goddess for her mercy.

Su Li also said prayers.

Please, Kuan Yin, merciful goddess, protect my husband, protect Freddy McKee, wherever he is.

NINE : Su Li's Christmas

NOW THE PLANES CAME EVERY night, their engines vibrating with a pulsing rhythm like the muted beating of a human heart.

Thurumm, thurumm, thurumm . . .

Then the bombs fell, solemn and silent on the way down, a pompous descent earthward to explode with terrifying might.

Su Li's heart beat wildly, and the two women huddled together in a corner of their small room, the amah sheltering the girl's body with frail old arms, as though she could beat off the bombs with her two hands.

On the morning the gweilos called Christmas, Ah Ming knew it was once again a day of decision. Time was running out.

The tea leaves in the pot had been used so many times, there was no flavour left, but the old woman didn't throw them away. She let them dry and spilled them into a small pouch. Tea leaves could be chewed, if there was nothing else.

Water was a problem. Who knew how much longer the communal tap would run at the end of their street? It had been reduced to an hour yesterday and the lines were so long that many people didn't get any. There was nobody to keep order, and fights broke out.

"Look, they fight over the water while it spills," the amah grumbled to Su Li.

"They're thirsty, Amah."

"Thirsty fools, to waste precious water."

Now they ate the last of their rice. The amah made congee and they slurped it hungrily, without anything else, no peanuts, none of the bitter green herbs Su Li liked to stir in for health and flavour. Just a scant handful of rice boiled into a thin porridge.

"The governor has set up a new food line near the docks," Su Li said. "We must go early, the line will be long."

The amah made a derisive noise, pursing her lips and blowing.

"Useless man, this governor. Does he wait for water at a communal tap? Does he stand in line for rice? Pah! We have no time to stand in line for his soup!"

"But, Amah, we're hungry," Su Li pleaded. "We have no food. And I must look for my husband!"

Su Li's voice had developed a whining tone, and the amah scowled. Foolish child, to worry over the gweilo soldier. Probably dead. His money they would use, but he was gone. No more to be said.

The lack of food was a different matter. The amah turned her attention to the bag of much-used tea leaves, tying the top with a bit of thread she'd saved, hefting it thoughtfully in her palm.

Ah Ming has survived famine before, and even in the good times, she hoards. The last grain of rice, the final pinch of tea. Anything and everything has been kept and cared for, against just such a time as this.

For today, what was a little hunger? The empty feeling in their stomachs didn't matter and the weakness of the body could be staved off a little longer. But she knows the hiding is about to begin, and for that, they need food.

"Last night I dream," she tells Su Li. "Fox at door. Shows sharp teeth, then runs away."

"What does it mean?" Su Li asked the amah, hoping for news of Freddy, for the amah's dreams were usually accurate. "When will my husband come back?"

"Fox is sly demon," said the amah. "Brings evil news. Gweilo soldiers will run away from this island, as they ran from Kowloon."

Su Li began to cry.

"But what can we do? Where can we go?"

Not far away lay another island. Some called it Broken Head, others called it Lantau, but it was known among Hong Kong Chinese as Tai Yue Shan, Island of the Big Mountain. It was twice the size of Hong Kong Island, with a range of low green mountains running down its spine, and hills and valleys enough to hide two women for a long time. Years, if need be.

"Some distant kinsmen live on an island. There is a village."

If they could reach Broken Head, she felt certain they could survive. They could live on small wild animals, snare the ever-present rats, net a fish. They could eat roots. If necessary, they could eat grass. She had done it before.

As the youngest daughter of a farmer who had moved his wife and nine children to southern China in the wake of one famine after another, she could make soup out of a stone. They would find the village of her ancestors. They would survive.

But how to get to Broken Head? Late that night Ah Ming knelt in front of the little red godhouse. She had nothing better for the goddess, so she laid the precious bag of tea leaves at the foot of the statue and kowtowed three times.

Help us, merciful mother. Canadian husband you sent Su Li is gone. Maybe dead. Merciful Kuan Yin, rescue us once more from the bitter sea. Help me find a boat.

The amah's nose twitched as the smell of frying fish crept into the room. Her empty stomach growled. Cooking? At this hour? Somebody with the luck to catch a fish or steal one?

The amah laughed out loud. A miracle! A fish being fried in the middle of the night reminded her of Old Wong's brother-in-law, the fisherman! Old Wong had once sent her a gift of a fresh garoupa, straight from his brother's boat. She cooked it with spring onions and ginger, and as a courtesy she had sent back a box of small cakes.

The brother-in-law had a boat somewhere near Aberdeen, in the typhoon shelter. She would find him. A bargain could be struck.

Thank you, Kuan Yin, the amah breathed. *Thank you for mercy.*

TEN : Boxing Day

ON THE MORNING THE GWEILO called Boxing Day, the amah made her move.

As the two women stepped into Fenwick Street, acrid smoke billowed in great black clouds from another fire near the docks. Though it covered the sun and fouled the air, it couldn't disguise the smell of putrifying flesh. Hong Kong's heat and penetrating dampness wasn't kind to the dying or the dead, and the unseasonably warm weather that had marked Su Li's wedding day was followed by days of rain and low cloud.

The street was deserted, but at the shop where they had bought their last rice only two days ago, a small body sprawled halfway through the open door. The amah nudged it with her foot to see if the unlucky person might still be alive.

"A woman, not long dead," she muttered, talking to herself. "Limbs not stiff."

Grasping the body by one arm, she dragged it into the shop. The small space had been looted, every shelf smashed. Empty sacks littered the floor. Halfway up the doorframe a bloody handprint told what must have happened here, how this woman tried to escape. The looters had planned to burn the shop; there were charred patches on the floor and the place reeked of smoke.

"Unlucky for her, lucky for us," said the amah. "Quick, help me. Take her clothes!"

Su Li couldn't believe what she was hearing.

"But why? They're dirty! They have holes! Her tunic is ragged. Why do you want them?"

"So many questions," barked the old woman, dragging the soiled trousers off the corpse as though she robbed dead bodies every day. "Take off your tunic."

"What? You've lost your mind, you crazy old woman," the girl cried, but the amah yanked Su Li's tunic over her head and began wrapping the dead woman's thin trousers around her chest like a scarf, spinning her around, once, twice, pulling the material so tight that the girl's small breasts were completely flattened and she could hardly breathe. The amah knotted the binding.

"You hurt me," Su Li whimpered. Paying no attention to her protests, the amah tugged off the dead woman's tunic and held it out to Su Li.

"Now this."

"No! She's dead!"

"Thank the gods for that," replied the amah as she wrestled Su Li's arms into the ragged garment.

"She might have lice!" protested Su Li.

"Lice? You worry about lice? Stupid girl, be glad this poor woman died so you could wear her ragged coat. Be glad you are still alive to carry her lice for her!"

In the back corner of the shop, the rice merchant had a simple kitchen. A wok, a charcoal burner. A cleaver hanging on a nail. The amah tested it with her finger, found it sharp, nodded approvingly. Doubtless the woman had been a good cook. With the chopper in one hand, she grabbed Su Li's long silky hair in the other; held it near the top of her head, as though she was going to pick the girl up and dangle her off the ground.

"Amah, no!" Su Li screamed and twisted her head in the old woman's grip, but it only put tension on the length of hair the amah was sawing, and it came off quickly.

Su Li began to sob.

"Amah, my beautiful hair! Why?"

"More questions! What good is beautiful hair when the Japanese catch you? Better you be ugly."

She continued hacking at Su Li's hair until only a few short, unruly tufts remained. Then she turned her attention to the wok, which was filthy with soot. Su Li had given up protesting, and after the amah smeared dirty streaks across her face, not even Freddy would have recognized his wife.

She had been replaced by a grubby little street urchin.

The amah rolled the dead woman over on her stomach and draped an empty rice sack across her naked buttocks to preserve such modesty as she could on behalf of the departed spirit who might still be hovering. Then they left the shop.

The rest of the day supported the amah's dream. There were omens everywhere. When they turned the corner from Fenwick Street into Jaffe Road, two more bodies lay across their path. Two men. One was skinny, with sharp, cadaverous features, and it crossed the amah's mind that he might have starved to death except for his fancy clothes. The other was shorter and decidedly fatter. This one hadn't missed many meals. Both were dressed western-style, in suits. The fat one lay on his back, arms and legs splayed out, eyes staring, and his coat had fallen open to reveal an entire row of inside pockets, cleverly designed to conceal a host of things. Su Li pointed to a hole in his forehead, small, neat, very little blood.

"Police shoot looters," said the amah. "Good thing."

Bending over the bodies, she patted down their pockets. From the top pocket of the fat man she extracted a woman's gold bracelet, a man's watch, and several gold rings tied together with silk thread. With a grunt of satisfaction, she pocketed the jewellery, then steered Su Li around the corpses and along Jaffe Road.

As they continued toward the amah's destination on Cat Street, where Old Wong had taken up residence, they suddenly heard the excited babble of voices coming closer. People poured into Jaffe Road from other streets, hundreds of people. Refugees and paupers mingled with the wealthy and their servants, and everybody rushed aimlessly in all directions, like ants whose protective log has been kicked and broken open. The old and the feeble hobbled on canes, and women, bent nearly double under huge bundles, dragged whimpering children. Rickshaws, carts, bicycles, and an assortment of other vehicles clogged the street. Two ancient trucks and a luxury car were in a standoff at a main intersection, all three drivers honking and yelling. The farther they went along Jaffe Road, the worse it got.

On a side street with many nightclubs, soldiers were smashing liquor bottles. So many bottles, so much red wine sloshing out the door, pouring over the paving stones like a river of blood.

"So the Jap soldiers cannot get liquor," confided the amah. "Japs drink, they go crazy. Kill everybody."

The amah had made a mental list of necessities and divided it because each list required the special services of a different black-market bandit. Such men were controlled by the triads, so these negotiations were delicate matters, requiring patience and skill. One wrong word could cost your life. But as much as she hated and feared these men, in some matters they could be useful, for who else would have access to the supplies two women would require for their coming journey?

"Be careful," said the amah when Su Li headed out. "Trust nobody."

Su Li was to find a flashlight with batteries if she could, candles if she couldn't. Matches they must find in any case. The amah would ferret out rice and tea, and if she was lucky, a little dried fish. She let it be known that she was in the market for a small Japanese flag. If they were captured and it became necessary to improvise instant loyalty to the Japs, the flag would be useful.

Most important of all, the amah would assure the delivery of a handgun, previously arranged at great expense with Old Wong. Neither woman had any idea how to use either a pistol or a revolver, but for now the security of owning the weapon was essential. When the time came, they would learn to fire it.

ELEVEN: Escape to Broken Head

ON DECEMBER 27, 1941, General Sakai rode his white stallion in a victory parade through the main streets of Hong Kong Island, with thousands of Japanese soldiers marching behind. Sixty-two planes from the Japanese air force flew low over the parade route, dropping leaflets that declared their victory and exhorted the Chinese to welcome their new masters.

Trust in the Kindness of the Japanese Army, the pamphlets declared in English and Chinese. For his part, Sakai found the surrender puzzling. Certainly their British enemy had little choice, but why the disgrace of giving up when they could have had a glorious death?

"What cowards they must be, to have surrendered so easily," Sakai mused to his aides. "War has a glorious order: a man fights, he is victorious or he dies in battle. Or he chooses an honourable death. *Sepuku!*"

This morning's parade route was lined with thousands of Chinese, most of them cheering wildly, many of them waving hastily acquired Japanese flags as their new landlords rode past.

Sakai saw the flags, but he wasn't fooled. Not for a minute. Stupid Chinese. He had plans for them. Slaves were always useful. Some of the women were quite attractive, especially the young ones. As soon as this parade was over, he would declare all Chinese women prostitutes.

At the back of the crowd, two Chinese stood in watchful silence. One was an old woman with wispy, dishevelled hair. She wore no jewellery, and her ragged coat over a dusty samfoo wasn't worth stealing.

Standing beside her was a miserable brat of a boy, scrawny and dirty-faced, teeth black as though badly decayed, scalp caked with mud and soot. This urchin wore the ragged clothes of a coolie's son, and was probably not too bright. It would have been clear to anyone watching this pair that they'd be useless to the Japanese.

The tattered old woman and her companion wasted no time gawking and cheering with the rest of the crowd. Temporarily occupied with the obsequious fawning of their new subjects, the Japanese would be distracted, if only briefly. It bought a little time for those who knew what to do with it.

The amah knew this reprieve would last a few hours, until the victory parade was over and the rabble of peasant soldiers were turned loose on the population. What would happen after that was too terrible even to think about.

Ah Ming patted a bulky object concealed under her samfoo. The handgun was a Radom, a pistol the Polish army had adopted in some earlier battle. According to the skinny twelve-year-old gunrunner who delivered it to her, it spit bullets like a dragon.

Wong's agent was wise beyond his dozen years. Darting in and out of various hidey-holes in Hong Kong since he was old enough to walk, he had become a street-smart kid with a glib tongue. One look at the ragged old woman and he decided he had the wrong customer, more likely in need of a crutch than a pistol, but he changed his mind when she snarled at him and waved a gold bracelet under his nose. He was a businessman, and a greedy one at that. Out of respect for her age, he took the time to instruct the amah on the weapon's provenance and use.

"See, Mother! It has a catch here, on the side. Keep it loaded. Hold it with your thumb, like this, to block the firing pin while it lowers the hammer. It will always be ready to fire," he told her. And then, with a swagger, "Trouble comes, who has time to load a pistol?"

The Radom weighed about two pounds, and he pointed out that it would be relatively heavy for a woman to carry around, rather like having a small melon weighing down her pocket, but he assured her he had personally shot a man with this very gun and could guarantee its accuracy.

"Now hold it in both hands. Move the hammer back and squeeze the trigger."

Satisfied, he snapped a clip of 9mm cartridges into the handle, put the pistol in the amah's hand, and walked away, shaking his head. What was the world coming to when old women ran around with loaded guns concealed in their tunics?

Through deserted side streets they stole away. Pausing only to pick up their few small bundles, they walked steadily south, over hills and through a valley by a route only the Chinese would know, until Su Li could smell the ocean. The amah had reached her goal: the typhoon shelter in Aberdeen.

The harbour was crammed with sampans and small junks, for few of these people dared venture far to sea with the Japanese everywhere. Some invisible signal passed between the amah and one of the men on the water, and the two women boarded a certain sampan, squatting under the flimsy shelter while the amah bargained with the owner. Finally she agreed to an exorbitant price, which had to be paid into his filthy palm in gold, and even then she had to wait, fuming, while he consulted with his scrawny crow of a wife. Only then did he rev the small motor and nose through the crowd of boats in the typhoon shelter, into the channel, and across a narrow arm of water to Lamma Island, where another boat waited, a nondescript fishing junk.

The junk belonged to Old Wong's brother-in-law, and more gold changed hands as the two women scrambled aboard, crouched low in the prow, clutched their bundles, and took note of everything around them, for now their lives depended on spotting trouble before it spotted them. As the motor sputtered and they moved ponderously around the point and across the West Lamma Channel, Su Li watched the handful of other deepwater junks owned by the bolder fishermen, the ones who fished far into the South China Sea. Lights of scattered villages winked from islands they didn't recognize, and she thought how welcoming they looked. She devised a fantasy in which Freddy waited for her in one of those villages, in a safe house, a small, warm hut where nobody, not even the Japanese, could find them.

The amah knew better. Lights could mean danger. It was rumoured that a band of Chinese guerillas were holed up on one of the islands.

Eventually the Japanese were certain to figure out where they were hiding, and the reprisals would start.

In the darkness, with no running lights, the fishing boat skirted the south end of Peng Chau. Around midnight they put in at Silvermine Bay, on the east side of Broken Head.

No words passed between the fisherman and Ah Ming, and while he studied the shoreline she and her small, ragged companion clambered over the side. The strange-looking pair slipped away into the night, avoiding the handful of lights still burning in the village. Too tired to worry about the possibility of poisonous snakes or roving bandits, they fell asleep in a field, and before sun-up they were walking again, heading up a valley in the direction of the low green mountains that formed the spine of the island.

The final provisioning had not gone well in Hong Kong, and they hadn't eaten for two days. They had a small pouch of rice, but no way to cook it, and Su Li grew so hungry she felt faint, so they divided the last small piece of dried fish. It wasn't even a mouthful each, but they savoured the final salty flakes and licked their fingers.

Trusting nobody, the amah avoided the few isolated buildings, but late in the day they came upon a small farm with a swept courtyard where a single yellow pumello hung on a tree. The only sound was the faraway barking of a dog, and there was no human being in sight, so Su Li went boldly in and picked it.

They hurried away from the garden and hid in some brush beyond the path. Careful to waste nothing, they stripped the membrane off each section with their teeth and chewed it first, cherishing the slightly acidic taste. Wonderful was the aroma of the fruit, the sweetness of its red flesh, and the juice, for the salted fish and the walking had made them as thirsty as they were hungry. The pumello was full of bitter seeds, and these too they ate, nibbling them like peanuts. After the fruit was gone they ate the peel, chewing the thick, knobbly rind as long as they could.

By evening they had crested the mountain and were travelling down the other side, through a valley. As they sat down for a few minutes' rest, the taste of the stolen fruit was still in Su Li's mouth, and its perfume lingered on her fingers. She knew that the amah had wanted to keep the peel, to horde it until it dried so they could eat it another day, but Su Li was past such saving ways. She knew now why people ate their own dogs. Her hunger was deep, and it made her angry.

Daylight faded, but they kept walking. When they crested one final hill and saw below them the few lights of a walled compound, the amah recognized certain marks on the double wooden gate and the flat stone that formed its base. This was the village of her kinsmen.

These three items, two massive wooden doors and the broad, flat stone, had been carried here on the backs of her Punti ancestors, all the way from their home village in South China. The objects were well known in the stories that had been passed down and down, through generations of her family, until they no longer knew what was fact and what was story, and the amah was grateful that these three things at least had been the truth.

The village consisted of a few small mud-brick houses connected one to the other to form part of a wall around a central U-shaped courtyard. The roofs were of terra cotta tiles with upturned corners, and a higher wall extended across the front, with the sturdy double doors of the gate opening inward to the enclosed courtyard, so the little village could become a fortress if need be.

"We have found it," the amah said, for she knew the mark of the Punti, those good farmers who had travelled so far to escape some other army, now long past and forgotten, except in the stories.

If two more mouths to feed were not exactly welcomed by the surprised members of the amah's clan, they were at least tolerated on the basis of distant kinship. The headman assigned their quarters: a small shack formerly occupied by three sheep, all eaten in a period of hunger, for these people were farmers, not fishermen. The sheep had been replaced by a single pig, amazingly fat considering its Spartan diet. A flock of brown ducks were being raised on a pond outside the wall. The ducks supplied meat more successfully than the sheep had ever done, with the luxurious bonus of eggs.

Their new home had one high barred window, and a dirt floor, easily swept with a twig broom. The two women would pass the next four years living in this simple room, working from sun-up to sundown as farmers, growing vegetables and caring for the ducks and one well-upholstered pig, a different pig each year as the mature one was slaughtered and replaced.

Su Li and the amah worked side by side in the gardens, and there among the cabbages and corn plants the older woman took pride in keeping up with the younger one.

Su Li kept to herself. She made no friends among the women, rejected the sly advances of the men, and ignored the slights and insults of those who openly resented her presence in the village.

One night as they slept, a drunken village man kicked in their door, determined to rape Su Li, but Ah Ming quickly removed the loose brick where she'd hidden the pistol and remembered everything the gunrunner had taught her.

Holding it firmly in both hands, she squeezed off a single shot, which landed harmlessly in the mud wall, for the amah's aim was not as good as her memory. Terrified, the man tried to escape the wrath of Ah Ming. With his pants around his ankles he went stumbling and yelping into the courtyard while the entire village laughed behind closed doors, and his wife came out and beat him with her broom until he begged for mercy.

After that the villagers ignored both of them, which was all they asked.

Sometimes in a rare moment of leisure before sleep, Su Li would unwrap the small bundle she had brought with her. The mandolin looked not unlike one of the traditional Chinese stringed instruments, and she would pluck tunelessly on its strings, caressing its smooth, rounded contours, tracing the mother-of-pearl butterfly with her fingers, letting her mind float backwards. Then, with great care, she would wrap it up again.

Once in awhile the amah would pull out the loosened brick and take the pistol out of its oilskin wrapping, checking to see that all was well with it. Good that she'd had it, she told Su Li. Good that she still kept it, for who knew what the future would bring? Su Li wasn't fond of the gun, but Ah Ming had used it, and Su Li knew that she, too, could fire it if that moment ever came.

A few weeks after the British surrender, a sad parade marched from a temporary prison on Hong Kong Island to the docks. Canadians were to be held either at North Point or at Sham Shui Po. Crowds of Chinese lined their route, spitting, throwing rocks, and yelling obscenities at the foreign devils.

"Look at them! We risked our bloody lives for them, and this is the thanks we get," growled the man who limped along beside Freddy. "I took a bullet for these yellow bastards! Can you believe this?"

Private Freddy McKee, ignoring the pain in his shoulder and ribs when he turned his head, scanned the faces along the route. Was she still alive? Could Su Li have survived the chaos of the past weeks? With the old woman looking after her, it just might have been possible.

At that moment a Chinese woman darted out of the crowd, screeching at the Canadians. She spat at Freddy, and a blob of saliva landed on his chest.

"Bitch," the soldier beside him yelled. "Didn't you see that?" he demanded of Freddy. "See what she did to you?" And he yelled again, "Slant-eyed bitch!"

Freddy would spend his next four birthdays in prison camps.

He would turn nineteen in the camp in Hong Kong. Three more birthdays would pass in a Japanese coal mine.

He would lose so much weight that his flesh would shrink against his bones. His ribcage would become so prominent you could count the ribs by looking at him, and his shoulder and knee joints would look like baseballs with sticks attached. He would see things that became part of a living nightmare, things he could never shut out, even when he slept.

But on that January day in 1942, he could find no anger for the Chinese woman who spat on him.

"Ah, forget it," Freddy said in a voice so tired it was barely audible. "They're just hedging their bets."

TWELVE : In Gold Mountain

Lantau Island, 1945

A DAY CAME WHEN THE village headman approached the amah with news.

"Foreign war is over," he said. "Turnip-heads gone. Time you go too." Then, for emphasis: "You go now."

Ah Ming and Su Li tied their few belongings into the same two bundles they had travelled with four years ago. Without saying goodbye, they headed over the ridge of Broken Head. In Silvermine Bay the amah made discreet inquiries, and soon they were on a junk, puttering through the crowded typhoon shelter.

In Hong Kong they took refuge with Old Wong, who had reopened his noodle house, and Su Li waited tables while the amah busied herself making certain arrangements.

In the two days after Freddy paid his bride price, Ah Ming had wasted no time. Within hours, she had traded his paper money for the only currency she trusted: gold. Almost five years later, with the help of Old Wong, she used it to wangle two third-class passages on the *Empress of Russia*. Destination: Vancouver, Canada, the place the Chinese called Gold Mountain.

Using their forged passports, Ah Ming and Su Li arrived in Canada as paper people. This way and that, the women found a route into the heart of Vancouver's sprawling Chinatown, where, from his lair in distant Hong Kong, Old Wong had already made certain arrangements. It was their good luck that he had such strings to pull.

The women settled into a small, bare room behind the Silver Dragon, a dim sum restaurant owned by one of Old Wong's amazing collection of kinsmen living in Gold Mountain. But as frugal as they were, they needed money to live, for Vancouver was not Hong Kong.

They had no resources beyond the amah's dwindling stock of gold jewellery, and she wasn't about to part with that. The day came when Su Li and the amah were finally forced to do some business in the Fair Exchange, a pawn shop four doors down the block. They had only three items of value: the pistol, which Ah Ming felt had outlived its usefulness, now that they were safe in Gold Mountain, the jade earrings Freddy had given Su Li, and his mandolin, which the girl was reluctant to pawn. The owner of the shop picked up the pistol, turned it over in his hand, and laughed. He swept back a dingy curtain behind the counter where a shelf held at least two dozen handguns, maybe more.

"Soldier come, need money. Pawn gun," he said, adopting the pidgin speech he used with most of his Chinese customers. "Pistols. Revolvers." He shrugged both shoulders, extended his hands, palms upward. "Too many!"

The jade earrings he declared worthless, which enraged the amah but left Su Li relieved because they'd been Freddy's wedding gift. She clung to the earrings as she clung to her memories of her Canadian husband.

There remained only Freddy's mandolin, and to her horror, the broker offered the amah a modest amount for it.

"Must have money," the amah declared, snatching it from Su Li and handing it over. "No more to be said."

Once again, Su Li went to work as a waitress. Lee Wong, whom Su Li called Third Uncle, owned the Silver Dragon. Both Chinese and gweilo congregated here on Sunday mornings for dim sum, the meal of tea and small delicacies that were Lee's specialties.

The amah installed herself at the back table, the one nearest the kitchen door, where she had an unobstructed view of Su Li's customers and their behaviour.

It was Lee who suggested a job for the amah. She seemed determined to spend all her time glowering from the back table, so why not do something useful, like tell fortunes? A little palmistry, a bit of face reading? Lee even located a trained bird that could pick up a fortune card in its beak so Ah Ming could translate its meaning for the delighted customer. The amah was nothing if not creative, and before long, she had a regular clientele.

Now and then Su Li would walk down the block and peer in the pawn shop window, checking to see that Freddy's mandolin was still there, for she intended to buy it back the minute she had saved enough. Sometimes, if the pawn broker wasn't busy, he'd bring it out so she could run her hands over it, stroking the smooth curve of the back, gently touching the faded butterfly beneath the strings and the shell-shaped metal button where they were attached.

One day when she looked in the window, her heart lurched. Su Li felt tears running down her face. She couldn't help crying, for Freddy's mandolin, with all her happy memories, was gone.

Like most of the Chinese men in western Canada's scattered restaurant population, Yip Lee found reasons to travel to Vancouver. He was doing well in the café, and a yearly holiday among friends and extended family was a good thing.

His cousin owned a laundry not far from the Silver Dragon, and when Yip arrived on a visit in September 1947, he and his cousin gathered the family together for Lee Wong's dim sum.

The party was loud, the food plentiful, and Yip took little notice of their pretty young waitress. The vile Exclusion Act had been repealed, so Chinese women had been filtering into Canada for the past two years and were no longer a rarity. The meal took three hours, and when it was over and his guests had left, Yip tipped the girl generously. Then the cousins took a stroll.

Instead of turning east, past the laundry, they turned west, past the Fair Trade Pawnshop. Glancing idly in the window, Yip came to an abrupt halt. There, reposing on a bit of rumpled velvet, was an old beetle-back mandolin, with a mother-of-pearl butterfly under the strings.

When Yip bought the mandolin, he fully intended to take it back to Edmonton to surprise Freddy the next time he was in town, for there was no doubt in his mind that it was the same instrument. He recognized the worn spot on the butterfly.

Freddy was working in a place called Trout Creek, somewhere north of Winnipeg, so it was a mystery that his mandolin had ended up in a pawnshop in Vancouver.

"Where you get this?" he asked, and the pawnbroker told him about the young Chinese woman who brought it in. Although she still came in to look at it, she'd never been able to afford to claim it back.

The pawnbroker was Caucasian, but he had a passion for dim sum and was a regular at the Silver Dragon. He'd often seen Su Li in the restaurant.

"Maybe you know her," he told Yip. "She's Lee's best waitress."

He began wrapping the mandolin, first in the rumpled velvet, then in brown paper. It was a fine instrument, after all.

"It's quite a story, according to Lee. Seems she was actually married to some white guy back in Hong Kong. A soldier. Canadian, too, one of our guys who got stuck there just before the Japs invaded."

Now he had Yip's complete attention.

"Oh yeah? This Canadian guy. What happen to him?"

The pawnbroker shrugged.

"Nobody knows. Her old nanny told Lee he disappeared right after the wedding. Likely captured."

"So this husband, he die in Japan?"

"Like I said, nobody knows. The girl and the old lady spent the whole war holed up on some island near Hong Kong, and they came over right after it ended."

"Refugee?"

"Nope. The usual way. Seems the old girl arranged it all as part of the dowry. Fake passports, the whole nine yards."

"Very strange story," Yip mused.

"Yeah. Kinda sad, too, a young girl like that, widowed. She won't give any of Lee's waiters the time of day. Still hoping this guy'll turn up sometime. You could ask her about how she got the mandolin. She speaks pretty good English, for a China girl. She's been in at least a dozen times to check on it," he said.

"This guy. Dead husband. You know his name?"

"Nope. Can't say I do. Except, she always calls it 'Freddy's mandolin.'"

BOOK FOUR

Collateral Damage

ONE : The Newlyweds
September 1947

THE MORNING AFTER FREDDY'S CHINESE wife came to Trout Creek, Tom Cat and I went to the cookshack to visit. She was unpacking, and I sat on Freddy's bed to watch. The bed was pretty narrow, and I wondered where Su Li slept.

Mary Leski came in to see if she could help, so I ran home to get my mom, but she was too busy.

By the time I got back, the unpacking was pretty well finished. Freddy's wife didn't seem to have much, and none of it was exciting except for one long red silk dress with a stand-up collar. I noticed a long slit on one side from the hem partway up the skirt, and I figured a seam had come undone so I asked if I should get my mom to fix it. Mom was always sewing.

She said no, and I must have looked funny or something because she laughed. Not like Trout Creek women—when something struck them funny, they threw their heads back and roared. Su Li's laugh was soft and musical, like the top notes on Mom's piano.

"This is cheongsam," she told me. "Dress is for parties." She pronounced it *pah-tees*.

"Oh yeah?" said Mary in an interested voice. "That's some dress! We'll have to have a *pah-tee* so you can wear it."

It was the rest of the suitcase that told us how different this woman was from anybody we knew, or had ever known.

She pulled out a paper-wrapped package, handling it carefully, like it might break, but it turned out to be a bundle of red-painted sticks, or at least that's what we thought. Like parts of a puzzle. When she put the pieces together, it made a little box with one side open, like a puppet stage. Then she unwrapped a white china ornament, a woman holding a vase in one hand. She put the figure in the little house, looking out over the balcony.

Freddy stood in the doorway, watching her work and grinning like he'd found the prize in the Cracker Jack.

"Remember, Freddy? Kuan Yin," said Su Li, bringing the statue out so he could take a closer look.

"But that's amazing! How did you manage to hang on to her?"

Mary asked what the heck this Kuan Yin was, and Freddy said she was the Goddess of Mercy, just like one of your Catholic saints, and Mary crossed herself and said, Holy Moses, what next? And Freddy said, Yup, just like Moses, Kuan Yin showed people how to get out of tight spots when they couldn't figure it out for themselves.

Freddy knelt beside the Chinese woman and ran one hand over the little china figure. "What else did you save?"

"Only this," she said and took a second bundle out of the suitcase. "For you, Freddy."

It was bulky looking on one end, and she used both hands to hand it to him and made a little bow with her head. He unwrapped a funny-looking guitar.

"*Serena's mandolin?*"

"I know you love it very much, Freddy. Mr. Yip buy it back for me."

Freddy put his arms around her and rocked her back and forth. His eyes were closed, and he was whispering words we couldn't understand.

"Ah, jeez," said Mary. "Enough with the mushy stuff! Is it too early for a beer?"

Su Li said no beer, thank you. She explained that this goddess of hers needed to be facing the door, to ward off any bad spirits who might try to come in.

"Oh jeez," Mary said again. "Now it starts."

"What starts?" I asked because I needed more information.

"All the foreign hocus-pocus!"

The next day I was late getting there because my mother had found a thousand things for me to do. Make your bed, Hope. Change Tom's litter box, Hope. Dry the dishes, Hope! When she finally ran out of chores I asked if she was coming to Freddy's to help Su Li get settled because everybody else would be there, but she was still too busy.

Tom Cat and I went anyway.

George Leski was already there, making a couple of nail keg chairs for a table, and Chris Stinson came in with the frame of a double bed.

"Kay will haul the mattress over as soon as we set up the frame. Can't have you two sleeping in that little cot. Freddy could roll on you. Little thing like you, there'd be nothin' left but a grease spot!"

Su Li smiled at him like she didn't understand but it must be wonderful just because he said it.

Steve Popovich came in and started building a shelf to hang on the wall, and Dahlia Rempel arrived from the post office with a stack of old *Ladies' Home Journals*, so Freddy's Chinese wife could practise reading English. As if the room wasn't full enough already, Mary came bustling in with something wrapped in a quilt. It turned out to be a spindly looking geranium in a tin can. She started measuring the window for curtains.

Freddy looked happy. He asked if anybody needed coffee or would they rather have tea? It was like a party. Su Li and Freddy were all smiles. When he had coffee for everybody and a Coke for me, George Leski stood up and offered a toast to the newlyweds, like they'd just been married yesterday or something. Su Li kept on smiling, but Freddy all of a sudden got a funny look on his face.

"Where's Joanna?"

He wasn't asking anybody in particular, but nobody seemed to want to give him an answer so he zeroed in on me with those black eyes of his.

"Hope, where's your mom?"

The room went quiet, and everybody was looking at me. It made me mad. It was like my mom had been left out on purpose, and everybody knew but stupid Freddy.

"She's busy," I told him. "She has a lot of work to do."

Then I gave the rest of them my dirtiest look.

"She doesn't have time to waste, fooling around in other people's business!"

I knew I was going to start blubbering so I got out of there as fast as I could and headed home with Tom.

Freddy loved me. He loved my mom, too, and that was okay because it was different. But now he had this Chinese wife, and it felt like some part of him that had been ours was gone and we could never get it back.

I was barely through the kitchen door when Freddy came in behind me. He didn't even knock.

"Joanna, we need to talk." Then he said, "Hope, you scoot. Please. I need to talk to your mom."

And I got sent to my room again.

TWO : Conversations

JOANNA STANDS WITH HER BACK to the cupboards, facing him.

"Just tell me one thing. Is she really your wife?"

"We were married in Hong Kong by a woman who performs weddings."

"Is it legal?"

"In Hong Kong. Maybe not here. But that doesn't matter anymore. Mick and Tony were at our wedding. Joanna, Mick was my best man."

She turns away, looks out the window, watches a sparrow fluffing its feathers against the cold.

This hurts too much. I thought nothing would ever hurt this much again, but it does.

"I knew her for a few weeks," he said. "Then we got married. Hell, Jo, we were just kids. We had a one-day honeymoon. Then the Japs came, and I never saw her again. Not until she walked off that train two nights ago."

"You never heard from her?"

"How? They rounded us up. Put us in cages. I watched the fence line every day. I thought she might show up at the wire. Women did, the ones with men in the camp. Eventually I gave up hope."

Why don't you just shut up, Freddy? Can't you see what you're doing to me?

Joanna didn't want to look at him, kept her face toward the window, watched the sparrow, prayed she'd wake up and this would all have been a bad dream.

Don't make me listen to this. Please, God, can't we stop now? I've had enough.

But he went on.

"When they sent me to Japan, Joanna, I swear to you, I never expected to see her again."

So that made it all right to go to bed with your best friend's wife?

"You never tried to find her? Afterwards, I mean?"

Freddy's voice rises now. Like this is *her* fault.

"For Christ's sake, Joanna! Three thousand Chinese refugees everyday, like a goddamn river, pouring into Hong Kong. How was I supposed to find her in that mess? What was I supposed to do, look her up in some magic filing cabinet somewhere? Filed under Private Freddy McKee's illegal Chinese wife?

"Jo, the world isn't neat and orderly like you think. Not like it is here. In a war, people just disappear!"

"How dare you talk to me about people who disappear? I had a husband once, a man I loved, the father of my child, and he 'just disappeared.' Do not lecture me about people who disappear!"

"She was a refugee, Jo. A stateless person. Nobody kept records for those people. I figured she'd been caught in the invasion. The Japs were brutal to women. I couldn't even let myself think about what might have happened, what they'd have done to her. It made me crazy. Joanna, she was my wife!"

Stop this. Please, make him stop . . .

Joanna feels sick to her stomach. She feels light-headed, hears her own voice, speaking from a great distance.

"But she's a . . ."

It's as though little flames are flickering behind his eyes.

"She's a *what*? She's Chinese? Say it, Jo. Chinese! It's not a dirty word."

"All right! She's Chinese! How could you marry that Chinese woman?"

The minute she said it, the very second it was out, she'd have taken it back. But his eyes burn, and she sees his jaw clench. When he speaks again, his voice is cold.

"Why *wouldn't* I marry her? Because you don't like *chinks*, Joanna? Isn't that what you good white people call her? A dirty little *chink*?"

She had never seen Freddy like this. So angry. Bewildered by the change, she fumbled for words.

"No! I'd never call her that! I wouldn't! It's just that she's different. She's foreign."

Freddy shook his head and laughed bitterly.

"Yes, she is. And in her country, I was foreign. I wasn't like Mick, with you and Hope waiting for me at home. I didn't have anybody. I didn't know how much time we had left.

"You people here, you safe people with your war bonds and your little ration books for sugar and butter!" He sounded as though his teeth were clenched. "You don't know what it was like. I can't explain. Why should I? You couldn't possibly know what she went through, just to survive. You don't have a bloody clue! None of you do!"

He turned toward the door, finished with this, with her, but she stopped him with a barely audible question.

"So where does this leave us?"

He winced as though she'd hit him, and turned back to face her. She watched a nerve jump under his left eye.

"Jo, please. Please try to understand. She's my wife. Su Li is my wife." The coldness had gone out of his voice. He was pleading again, repeating the words that hurt so much.

"She's my wife."

He stood up to leave. To walk away from her.

"And you, Jo, well, you're Mick's wife. You'll always be Mick's wife."

Joanna's right hand goes to her mouth. She feels her face flushing, as though she's been slapped. She almost expects to feel a welt rising across her cheek. She opens her mouth to speak, but no words come out.

He takes a step toward her, but she shoves at his chest with both hands. Now she finds her voice, and she yells at him.

"You selfish bastard! You've been sleeping with me all summer! Now this woman shows up, this little Chinese dolly, this *wife* you somehow forgot to mention! Suddenly, you develop a conscience? Suddenly, I'm *Mick's* wife? How stupid do you think I am? You didn't care about me, Freddy. I was just a convenient lay!"

"Joanna! Stop this!"

Shocked, he reaches for her, only to comfort her, but the look on her face stops him.

"Don't! Don't you touch me! Just go. Get the hell out of here and leave us alone!"

He leaves, closing the door softly behind him. She holds her breath, hears the latch click, watches his profile pass the window.

She lets the pain take her. Reaches blindly for the table's edge. Misses. Her body slumps to the floor. Joanna cries now, as she has not cried since she lost Mick.

This isn't fair! Mick was my sacrifice!

▲　　▲　　▲

FOR THE FIRST time in her life, Joanna understood jealousy. Night after night, she would stand in the darkened living room, watching the light in Freddy's window. Aching when she saw it go out. It was a physical pain. One she'd never felt before.

Joanna didn't know quite when her feelings began to change. She couldn't hate Freddy's tiny, childlike wife, and the thought of trying to win him back to her own bed never entered her mind. Rather, she began to develop a strange fondness for the Chinese woman, and she realized that in some perverse way it was based on their mutual love for the same man.

This is so Chinese of us, isn't it? A plural marriage. I've read about those. About concubines. I'm like the old wife being pushed aside by the younger woman. Except that I never was your wife, Freddy. So maybe we should just do it that way anyway. You could sleep with me one night, Su Li the next. She'd call me elder sister. Isn't that how they do it in China? Am I losing my mind? Oh God, Mick, why did you have to leave us?

THREE: Socializing in Trout Creek

FOR A FEW WEEKS WE didn't see much of Freddy and his Chinese wife. Mom was too busy, and she kept on finding things for me to do too. Do your spelling charts, Hope. Make your bed, Hope. Set the table, Hope. Jeez! She was driving me crazy.

Then one Sunday she told me Freddy and Su Li were coming to supper, along with Stan, and Mary and George. Stupid Georgie too. I set the table for Mom, and we used the good glasses so I knew it was some kind of special occasion, though she didn't say what.

I watched Freddy coming along the path, holding Su Li's arm with one hand like he thought she might break if he let go, while with his other hand he balanced a lemon meringue pie, my well-known weakness.

"I made this especially for you, Hope," he told me, handing me the lemon meringue. I put it on the cupboard, but I didn't say thanks. I knew it wasn't really for me. I didn't matter to him anymore, now that he had his Chinese wife. Besides, he was busy trying to worm his way back into my mother's good books.

"We'll sit boy and girl, boy and girl," said my mom. "Stan, you're beside me."

Which meant I got stuck beside stupid Georgie. After supper Freddy played his mandolin for a while, but I didn't feel like singing. I was glad everybody went home early.

▲ ▲ ▲

SOON ENOUGH, EVERYBODY in Trout Creek developed a theory about Freddy's Chinese wife.

Chris Stinson, who'd been in France in the First World War and knew about these things, said she was the spoils of war.

Chris's wife, Kay, said she didn't believe they were ever married, that no Canadian Army chaplain would marry a Roman Catholic boy to a heathen Chinese.

Stan had heard from one of the guys at the airbase that Freddy had outsmarted both the army and the immigration people and smuggled her into Canada.

Dumas the Trapper said Freddy won her in a poker game because everybody knew what gamblers those chinks were.

Bertha Yellowquill figured she'd been a holy sister in a foreign nunnery and pointed out that she kept a statue of the virgin in a little shrine, except the virgin looked Chinese.

George was certain that she'd been sold by her starving refugee family, and Freddy bought her as a slave. He'd read about such things in *Life* magazine.

Mary, who had her own sources, said Su Li had been a bar girl, a hooker, and Freddy rescued her from the streets.

It seemed that Joanna was the only person in Trout Creek who didn't have a theory about Freddy's wife.

THE SECOND WEEK IN DECEMBER, Joanna decided to reinstate the Christmas party.

Every year since their marriage, she and Mick had held a big Christmas dinner. For Trout Creek, it was as important a date on the calendar as Mary's annual Summer Solstice Supper.

No formal invitations were ever issued, but the word was passed and the welcome was certain. Men who lived as contented hermits the whole year long would suddenly appear out of the bush on Christmas morning, as though some primeval need drew them together in this darkest, coldest season.

Always, they came bearing gifts. Over the years, there'd been two silver fox pelts for Joanna, a pair of fawn-coloured mukluks for Hope, and homemade toys: a wooden jumping jack with arms and legs that flailed and danced when she pulled a string and a wonderful egg-shaped toy carved from poplar. It came apart in two halves, to reveal a second egg, and a third inside that. The largest egg was stained pink with the juice of wild strawberries; the second was dyed green with a tea of moss and lichen; the third, lemon yellow, coloured with hard-to-get Winnipeg onions, their papery skins hoarded until there were enough to boil up and give the smallest egg its soft yellow colour.

Joanna and Mick had known the skill, effort, and sometimes danger, that lay behind such gifts. How many days did it take to track a bear, tan a hide; how many nights by an oil lamp to lace together a small moccasin or carve a jumping jack?

Guests brought food. Fish caught through the ice, or geese, or roasts of game. Sometimes a jar of summer berries preserved in wild honey or mushrooms pickled with herbs. Always, Baba's famous jellied rooster and Bertha's bannock.

The guests came from as far up the rail line as Churchill and as far south as Le Pas and Winnipeg. They came from Steeprock Mine and Snow Lake and the phantom airbase at Dogrib. A seven-man construction crew crossed the ice on McLaughlin's caterpillar with a skid pulled behind it, a shorter version of the cat trains that hauled logs all winter long. A few of them, like Dumas the Trapper, just walked out of the woods on snowshoes, having come from some obscure cabin miles away on the far shore of a nameless lake.

Before the men showed their faces at the Keegans' door on Christmas, there'd be a stop at McLaughlin's camp for grooming. The Swedes and the French, the Poles and the Ukrainians, all of them puffing and blowing and stomping into the cookshack, eyebrows and moustaches rimed with frost like strays from some long-lost Slavic army. Trimming hair, taming beards, putting on their cleanest clothes, they turned into a pack of schoolboys on their way to a Christmas party, with Stinson's hot spiced punch, the mammoth feast, and carols.

There were always carols. Joanna at the piano, Mick leading the singing. "God Rest You Merry Gentlemen," they sang, and "Deck the Halls," and eventually "Silent Night."

Some of the men had fine voices, and although they'd have taken a beating rather than admit it, they practised the carols ahead of time, singing their hearts out on lonely trap lines under the northern stars.

So on the night of the party, because they were shy men and inherently polite, they'd wait patiently for somebody else to start "Silent Night," and then they'd slip in with their perfectly pitched harmonies, and for whatever time it took to sing that one old carol the little house would ring with music that was beautiful beyond any great choir, anywhere.

After such a sweet song a man is apt to grow too sentimental for his own good name, so Dumas the Trapper would launch into his favourite poem.

"*De Stove Pipe Hole*, "he would announce. "By William Henry Drummond."

And as his accent grew thicker and his gestures more hilarious with each verse, the guests would clap until their hands hurt and laugh until tears rolled down their faces.

Dumas always brought down the house.

Because the time for serious drinking had arrived, Mick would scoop Hope into his arms and cart her off to her bed.

After the telegram, Joanna hadn't the heart to celebrate. Since then, there was never any mention of Mick during Christmas, and no more of the beautiful music they had all loved.

Marg always went back to Winnipeg on the next southbound train after Boxing Day, and in each of those years Joanna had been secretly relieved when she waved goodbye to her sister. It was Mick she had missed, Mick she needed, and at Christmas it was worse.

So when she announced that she was reinstating the big Christmas dinner, Mary was dubious.

"Are you sure? Why now?" she demanded. "You've hardly socialized at all, except for that night at my party."

The thing between Freddy and Joanna had fizzled, as far as she could tell. Joanna refused to talk about it and she could hardly ask Freddy, especially now.

"Mary, Mick would have wanted us to celebrate Christmas," Joanna said. "Remember how he loved our big Christmas parties?"

Mary shook her head, incredulous.

"I don't believe you. You've just spent six years mourning, acting like a goddamn saint, pushing poor Stan away like he had the plague or something, refusing to talk about Mick, making the rest of us tiptoe around his memory like he never existed."

"I did not! Mary, I didn't!"

"Yes, Jo, you did. So are you doing this to prove something to Freddy? What happened between you two anyway? You won't solve anything by putting yourself through this, Jo. Christmas is brutal for sad people."

Joanna made an effort to sound confident.

"I can handle it. Anyway, you're the one who's always telling me to get on with my life. So that's what I'm doing."

For two weeks before the big night, Joanna had her sister, Marg, running all over Winnipeg with shopping lists. She ordered stuffed olives, Christmas crackers, candles, all the frills and ruffles of the parties she and Mick had given. Marg was surprised, but unlike Mary, she saw the sudden party plans as a healthy sign.

Hope was ecstatic. There were so many things to be done, and she loved sitting at the kitchen table making pompoms out of red and green tissue paper.

"I want it to be the best party we've ever had," said Joanna.

"You seriously expect that to happen?"

"Mary, stop fussing. Hope needs to have a proper Christmas again. So do I."

Mary just shook her head.

The morning of Christmas Eve, Stan took Hope and Georgie into the woods to cut a couple of trees, and he set Joanna's up beside the piano, where it stood every year. He anchored it in a pail of coal and put the lights on, checking to see that they all worked.

Joanna cast her eyes over the lighted tree.

"Thank you, Stan. I don't know what we'd do without you."

"Don't you?"

Hope saw him move close to her mother and put his hands on her shoulders.

"Then why don't we do something about it, Joey? You know how I feel."

Joanna turned away and started opening cupboard doors as though she was looking for something.

"Coffee?" Her voice sounded funny, Hope thought. High and kind of squeaky. "I'll make a fresh pot."

Stan just kept looking at her.

"No, thanks," he said finally. "I don't want coffee, Joanna."

He put on the big buffalo coat and walked into the early twilight of the December afternoon.

At six o'clock Hope and Joanna went to meet the train, and Marg was on it. Al the brakeman struggled with a huge box of groceries and armloads of Marg's parcels while she issued instructions.

"Be careful, don't drop it, the red one's fragile. Don't turn the blue one upside down!"

Then she saw Hope and folded the little girl into a hug, enveloping her in a cloud of Evening in Paris. It was Aunt Marg's favourite perfume, and her mom's. Hope thought it was an elegant scent.

"Hope, my angel, you're growing like a weed! And look at you! You're gorgeous!"

In their living room, the tree breathed little gusts of fresh evergreen. They ate toast and omelettes for supper, and Hope started decorating the tree, draping it with paper chains and cut-out snowflakes.

"Where's Stan?" Marg asked. "I thought he'd be here to help decorate."

"No. He had something else to do," Joanna replied.

"That's funny," Marg replied. "He's always here on Christmas Eve. Did you two have a scrap?"

"Marg, leave it alone." Joanna turned to face her sister. "Please, no lectures about Stan. Not tonight."

▲　　▲　　▲

JOANNA'S COLLECTION OF tree ornaments had always been a source of wonder to Hope, who was finally allowed to clip on the beautiful glass birds with the shiny tails.

She watched her mother open the box of special ornaments: a Santa, a bear, a clown, a dog, an angel, an elf. Each one was wrapped in white tissue paper and nestled in its own section of the divided cardboard box.

"Your father bought these for me, Hope, before he went away. Aren't they beautiful?"

A second box held the most wonderful glass fruit. The paint had been applied inside the glass, and the outside had been dipped in crystal beads as fine as sugar, so they looked like frost had settled on them overnight.

"These were made in Germany, Hope. Before the war."

"Mom, isn't it the prettiest tree ever?"

"I think you're right, Hope." Joanna hugged her daughter. "Your dad would have thought so too."

FIVE: Joanna's Party

THAT CHRISTMAS MORNING WAS THE most exciting day Hope could remember in all of her nine years.

She unwrapped a stack of presents, including a beautiful wool coat, deep rose pink with white fur trim. The coat was from Stan.

"That set him back a bit," Marg remarked while Hope modelled it. "I wonder who he's trying to impress?"

"Nobody," Joanna snapped. "He's just a good man."

"Yeah. And the good ones are darned hard to find," Marg replied, but Joanna ignored her.

"I think we'd better get dressed or the boys will catch us in our jammies," said Joanna.

"Well, that would be a start," Marg said, winking at Hope.

Half an hour later Stan and George came stomping in the back door, carrying a stack of long planks. George lugged in a couple of wooden sawhorses, they pushed the kitchen table under the window so it would be out of the way, and set up the plank table for the buffet. It divided the working kitchen from the party space at the other end. Joanna draped it with white sheets and ironed the fold marks out so it looked like a big white tablecloth.

"Marg, if anybody notices these are bedsheets I'll die of embarrassment."

Marg grinned at Hope. Things that would make Joanna die of embarrassment were a family joke, and the list was already so long that no social occasion passed in their home without at least two or three near misses.

By four o'clock the sun had disappeared. By five, the table was ready, candles tucked among the greens, silver gleaming. The tree lights twinkled. Joanna felt almost happy. It was the moment when Mick would have put his arms around her, nuzzled her neck, and said, "Merry Christmas, beautiful."

Mick, we were so good together. Why did you have to leave me?

Around six o'clock the crowd began to gather, and those who'd been at the Keegans' Christmas parties before said right away that it was almost like old times, and to each other, out of Joanna's hearing, they said what a damned shame it was that Mick was gone. He'd been a prince of a fellow.

Nobody said out loud what every man at the party was thinking: that they couldn't wait to get a look at the Chinese woman, the one Freddy McKee called his wife.

▲   ▲   ▲

MOM PUT ME in charge of coats, and I stayed by the front door so I wouldn't miss anybody. When Al the brakeman came in, he had a friend with him, a thin man in a uniform with three rows of coloured ribbons on the front of his jacket. The man talked funny, like he had marbles in his mouth. Mary said it was because he was a Limey.

Mom was wearing her new black Eaton's catalogue dress with white coin dots, and her red party shoes with the toes out, even though it was winter. She'd painted her toenails bright red, like her shoes. Aunt Marg told her she'd stop traffic if she was in Winnipeg.

Baba Popovich sailed in wearing a new green babushka with red roses, carrying jars of her secret-recipe jellied rooster. Steve was right behind, with a roaster full of cabbage rolls. Dahlia and Deaf Gilbert were next (mince tarts and pickled jackfish), then Bertha Yellowquill with her special raisin bannock the size of a frying pan.

When Uncle Stan came in, he said a lot of nice things. "Smells terrific in here! Joanna, love the shoes. Hope, pretty as a picture. Marg! You're ravishing! Marry me, woman!"

Uncle Stan always said things like that, but he was just being funny. He was right about one thing, though, it did smell good in our kitchen. Mom handed Stan an apron and a carving knife.

"You could start with the roast. The geese can wait until I get the gravy finished."

While he was knife-sharpening, I showed him my platter of devilled eggs. I'd worked hard at them, and Aunt Marg said they were perfect, but Mom said a speck more salt wouldn't hurt. Then she made me cut stuffed olives in half and stick one on top of each egg. It seemed like a lot of fiddling around for an egg that would take a lumberjack about half a second to eat. Mom told me to garnish them with celery leaves so the platter would still look pretty after some of the eggs were eaten.

"Nobody will eat the celery leaves," she told me. "It's not proper to eat the garnish."

Oh yeah, like McLaughlin's lumberjacks cared about proper. But Mom was happier than she'd been for a long time, so I stuck celery leaves wherever they'd fit. Uncle Stan said they were definitely the most beautiful devilled eggs he'd ever seen, and it would be a crime to eat them.

At six-thirty everything was ready, but Mom said dinner couldn't start until seven o'clock. I figured she meant we couldn't start until Freddy got there, so I went around with my devilled eggs. Dumas the Trapper hogged in right away and ate four eggs before I could move along to the next guy. McLaughlin's boys cleaned up the eggs, then they ate the celery leaves. I stored that up to tell Mom later.

Chris Stinson was making the rounds behind me, filling glasses with his special holiday Matilda. The men raised their mugs and said, "Here's looking at you, Chris," and then they'd take a big swig. "Damn, that's smooth," they'd say, or "Don't that just put a curl in your tail!"

At ten minutes to seven we were still waiting for Freddy.

Stan had carved everything there was to carve and kept looking at his watch. Aunt Marg said the natives were getting restless, and didn't Mom think it was about time to turn them loose on the food? People were hungry, she said.

Then Mary Leski, who'd had quite a bit of Matilda, said maybe Freddy and his little wifey were having a wee nappy and were too busy to come to the party. Maybe they're having their own pah-tee, she said.

Mom gave her a dirty look and told me to start putting things on the table. It was seven o'clock. I figured maybe Su Li was still getting dressed or something, and I heard one of the McLaughlin boys say to Chris Stinson, "If I had that little chinky gal in my bed, I'd be late for the party too," and they both went hohoho, except Chris got his hoho cut short because Kay heard him, so he said, "Whoops, I think I'm needed at the stove."

"Here they come," yelled one of the Swedes, who had his nose pushed against the window, watching. At exactly two minutes to seven Freddy and Su Li walked through the door.

Su Li handed me her coat, and I thought Mary was going to drop the gravy boat when she saw what Su Li was wearing. Everybody else just stopped whatever they were doing. Stopped talking, stopped drinking, stopped everything. We all gawked at Freddy's wife. Even my mom.

The dress we had watched her unpack the day she came to Trout Creek looked a whole lot different when she was in it. It was made of shimmery silk the colour of the reddest sunset you ever saw. When she moved, the colour seemed to change, red, red-orange, back to red, like a flame. It was really tight, from the high stand-up collar all the way to the floor, except for that long slit on one side, from the hem to the top of Su Li's leg. A flock of gold butterflies flitted from the collar down across her chest and kept going, ending just where the slit started, kind of at the top of her leg.

Uncle Stan whistled.

Georgie-the-enemy stood there with his mouth open, looking really stupid.

Mary swallowed hard and said, "Jeez Louise, that's quite a dress!"

My mom smiled, but her mouth looked kind of stiff at the corners.

"Su Li, you look, uh, lovely," and then she ran her hands over her apron. Su Li's hair was piled high and fastened with a comb, and she looked exactly like a picture in a movie magazine. Better, maybe.

"Plum sauce," Su Li said, handing a small jar to my mother.

"My amah sends it from Vancouver. Is not so good, I think. She is not such a good cook as you, Joanna. I hope you like."

That was how she talked. She'd always tell you that whatever you did was special, but whatever she did was just ordinary. I guess you'd say she was modest.

Mom took the jar and handed it to me.

"Do something with this, Hope," so I opened it and dipped a blob on my pinkie finger because everybody was so busy looking at Freddy's wife that I could have stood on my head and nobody would have noticed. The plum sauce was thick and sweet-sour, like ketchup, only yellow. I gave it a good spot, right beside the roast geese.

Su Li was carrying a fan. When she unfolded it, the air in the warm kitchen suddenly smelled of the same perfume she'd worn the night she got off the train. Mom noticed too because she gave Su Li a funny look, and after that the fan stayed closed.

Finally, we were ready. Mom lit the candles, and when Uncle Stan turned off the lights, even Mary was impressed. I could hear people whispering, "It's beautiful! Beautiful!"

Stan banged a spoon on a glass.

"Ladies and gentlemen, dinner is served."

The food was so good, and everybody oohed and aahed and said they hadn't seen such a table for so long, not since Mick left. Then my mom stood up.

"I'd like to say something."

Everybody shushed everybody else, because Mom was usually so quiet, and we all wondered what the heck was coming.

"Friends, I know we all loved Mick, and this year I thought, Well, it's time to bring back Mick's Christmas, and celebrate together as he would have wanted us to do."

Mom raised her glass in the air.

"Ladies and gentlemen, friends, to the man we all loved, and we all miss. To Mick Keegan! Merry Christmas!"

Everybody in the room raised their glasses and yelled things like, "To Mick! Yes, Joanna! To our Mickey, God bless him," and stuff like that. Then they were all laughing and clapping, and Aunt Marg hugged Mom. It felt like Christmas was really here.

Except that Freddy didn't seem to be having any fun. He laughed a lot, and loud too, but it wasn't his real laugh so I knew he was just pretending. The more Matilda he drank, the louder he got.

All this time Su Li was sitting on a chair beside the Christmas tree, looking beautiful, but in a sad way, if you know what I mean. The soldier with all the ribbons didn't seem to know anybody but Al the brakeman, and he ended up standing beside Su Li's chair. After a while he sat on the floor, close to her knees, and they started talking. Her voice was always so soft, I guess he had to lean close to hear what she was saying.

I saw Freddy watching them. He'd filled a plate for himself, but he didn't bother to get one for Su Li. Then he plunked himself down beside Mary on the piano bench and ate his supper. The English guy brought Su Li a plate with some roast goose and cabbage rolls, which she hardly touched. Maybe she wasn't hungry.

After supper had been cleared away, Mom went to the piano and played "White Christmas," and we all sang. Everybody wanted Freddy to play his mandolin, so he and Mom played a couple of carols, but while the Swedes were still waiting for "Silent Night" and Dumas the Trapper was getting primed for *De Stove Pipe Hole*, Freddy decided to change the program.

"Is this a party or a goddamn funeral?" he yelled and laughed a crazy loud laugh. "Hey, it's my goddamn birthday! So let's party!"

Freddy picked up his mandolin and started a song. He leaned close to Su Li, but he sang too loud, and he had a miserable look in his eyes, like a dog getting ready to bite somebody. The song was about a hard-hearted woman and a soft-hearted man. I didn't like it.

People weren't talking anymore. Everybody was watching Freddy and Su Li. My stomach felt like there was a big hole in it, all the way up to my throat. I felt Mom's arm go around my shoulder, tight, like she was hanging on to me in case of a high wind. Mary and George looked at each other, and Stan got off his chair and stood extra-straight, like he was waiting for something to happen.

Freddy finally stopped singing his stupid song. It wasn't a good song anyway, it was just drunk Freddy, being mean. Su Li had her head down, but I guess everybody saw the big tear fall on her shiny red dress.

The English soldier put his hand on Su Li's arm and started to say something to Freddy, but he never got a chance to finish.

Freddy threw his mandolin on the floor and grabbed the guy by his jacket. He yanked him onto his feet and started to shake him so the guy's head wobbled back and forth.

"You puffed-up Limey sonofabitch, strutting around here in your fancy uniform! Get your bloody Limey hands off her!"

Then Freddy swung at him. I heard his fist connect with the English guy's jaw, and he staggered, but he stayed on his feet.

"I did four years in Jap hell so a miserable little rat-bastard like you can come sniffing around my wife?"

Freddy hit the English guy again, but he still didn't fall down, so Freddy got him by the throat. Uncle Stan tried to grab Freddy's arms, but one of the guys from Dogrib jumped on Uncle Stan, and then George yelled, "Okay, my turn," and tackled the Dogrib guy around his middle.

That's when Freddy, the Englishman, Uncle Stan, the guy from Dogrib, and George Leski all went crashing into our Christmas tree.

With all the other noise, hardly anybody heard my mother's beautiful Christmas ornaments breaking into a thousand pieces.

△   △   △

ON BOXING DAY morning, after Joanna and Marg had swept up all the broken glass, Stan took the tree outside. As he was going out the front door, Freddy came in the back. He hadn't shaved, and he looked as though he hurt all over.

"Joanna. I'm sorry. I don't know why I did that. I guess I had a few too many."

"I guess you did." Joanna's voice would have cut glass.

"Jo, Christmas is the worst day of the year for me. I thought I could get through it this year. I shouldn't have come to your party. I didn't want to. I can't explain it."

"Maybe you should try," she said, her voice like ice.

He sighed heavily.

"Just too many memories." His voice broke, and normally she'd have forgiven him, poured him a cup of coffee, offered him aspirin. But not today. Not anymore.

"You aren't the only one with memories, Freddy. I have memories too. I just finished sweeping some of the best ones I ever had into the garbage!"

She was shouting. He looked around desperately, like a trapped animal looking for an escape route, but he tried again.

"I never meant to hurt you, Jo. I'd never hurt you on purpose. Don't you know that? I'll buy you new ornaments. I'll replace everything I broke."

"You can't replace them," she told him, her anger quiet now, with deadly control. "Mick bought them for me, before he ever knew you. Those ornaments were Mick's. And mine."

Freddy stayed sober all week.

Tom Cat and Hope went to the cookshack once, but Freddy was too busy for visiting, and he said Su Li was asleep, so they went home again.

SIX: Freddy's New Year

IN TROUT CREEK, JUST BEFORE midnight at the turning of the year, all the men would get out their guns: .303, .22, .410, and whatever else they had. They'd go outside and wait until somebody declared that it was twelve o'clock. Then they'd all fire their guns into the sky, potting away at the moon.

Even Georgie had his own .410 shotgun. He got it for Christmas, a rabbit-hunting gun with a big red bow on it and a card that read *Ernie's Pawn Shop, Wpg., Man.* on one side and *"With Love, from Santa"* on the other. Mary remarked that Santa had definitely lost his marbles, giving a kid a shotgun, but George said it was about time his son had his own gun. He sure didn't want him turning into some pansy who couldn't shoot straight.

So there they all were in the icy dark, blasting away at the moon, when suddenly some of the shots were no longer aiming at the sky. Somebody was firing in their direction.

It was Chris Stinson who raised the alarm.

"Somebody just shot at me!"

"What's the matter, Chris? Been into your homemade hooch?"

Stan had asked the question, and the men chuckled appreciatively. He was wearing a slouchy felt hat at the time, and the next bullet whizzed right through the crown.

"Take cover, boys, my hat's been hit," he yelled and dove behind an empty gas barrel just as a third shot pinged off the rim.

They were rifle shots, and they were coming from the direction of the cookshack.

"Freddy!" Stan had been halfway expecting something like this ever since the Christmas Eve debacle. "He must be drunk again."

229

By the time Stan and George Leski managed to get around behind the shack where they could see Freddy through the north window, Chris Stinson had shepherded what he would later describe as "all the women, children, and livestock in town," into Joanna's kitchen. There were actually five women, two kids, and Tom, the cat, and although Joanna's kitchen put them well out of range of Freddy's rifle, Chris insisted they stay flat on the floor "until the sniper has been subdued."

Through the small north window of the cookshack, Stan could see Su Li, face down on the floor beside Freddy, who was on one knee. She was struggling to get up, and she seemed to be pleading with him, but he shoved her back down, never taking his eyes off his target. He'd knocked out a pane of glass in the south-facing window and was holding a Lee-Enfield .303 and aiming across the tracks in the general direction of the Popoviches'. They heard the double click as he pulled the bolt back. He squeezed the trigger once, and once more. The shots echoed through the silence.

"I wish I knew how many rounds he's fired," Stan whispered when he and George had belly-crawled through the snow to the cookshack door.

"Counting the one that went through Chris's hat, I'd say five," George whispered. Stan had eased the door open a crack.

"That clip holds ten cartridges. He's got five rounds left. When he stops to reload, yank the door open. I'll jump him."

▲   ▲   ▲

FREDDY ENDED UP in handcuffs that night, shackled to a freight wagon in the shed beside the CN station, the wheels padlocked so he couldn't go anywhere. Around 4:00 AM, Kay Stinson brought in a pot of black coffee and Stan unlocked the cuffs and gave Freddy a sleeping bag and a pillow.

Freddy couldn't even keep the coffee down.

"Such a mess," clucked Kay the next morning when she was the centre of attention at Mary's kitchen table. "That boy was as sick as a dog and twice as sorry."

Stan had spent the night sitting upright in one of Chris's office chairs, huddled into his buffalo coat, watching his prisoner shake and shiver. He knew it wasn't all from the cold.

By morning, Freddy was calm and rational.

"Where's Su Li? Is she all right? Jesus, did I hurt Su Li?"

"She's fine. She's at Joanna's. She'll stay there until I figure out what to do with you."

Stan listed possible charges.

"Dangerous use of a firearm, unlawful confinement. Attempted murder! What the hell did you think you were doing last night? These people are your friends, Freddy. I don't understand you."

Later that morning, Chris Stinson had a talk with Stan.

"I figured it out. It was our gunshots that set him off. Boys like that, they never forget what happened over there. He's not crazy, he's just remembering too much."

Chris sucked on his pipe before he continued.

"In my war, it was the horses that bothered me the most, when they were gut-shot. I'll never forget that sound.

"They scream, horses do. Just like a wounded man, only worse. I can still hear it. Worse things too. Sometimes a fella has nightmares. And my war was a long time ago. But you take young Freddy there. We don't know what happened to make him go so crazy, and he can't tell us."

Chris paused, sucking on the pipe.

"That's his trouble, maybe. He can't tell anybody."

Stan decided not to file charges, but he made Freddy promise to see a doctor in Winnipeg as soon as they could get an appointment. The following Tuesday, Freddy left Trout Creek.

When he got off the train in Winnipeg, he checked himself into Deer Lodge, the veterans' hospital where Tony Cecci had lived ever since he'd been repatriated, early in the war.

Freddy had gone to see Tony a few times, whenever he'd been in Winnipeg, but the visits hadn't been a success.

His missing legs were only part of Tony's problem. As a result of the explosion in the bunker, he'd lost the sight in one eye and had only partial vision in the other. He suffered from terrible headaches, which his doctor could not treat.

"Tony, we have a visitor," chirped the young nurse, leading Freddy into a sunroom painted mud-beige. A dozen wheelchairs were arranged in a semicircle, their occupants wearing identical blue housecoats.

Somewhere a radio played, a man's voice, deep and sonorous, reading the news. Freddy wondered why somebody didn't change the station or turn the damned thing off.

The men in the wheelchairs were silent. A few heads lolled forward or sideways, like they hadn't the strength to sit up. Some of them seemed to be asleep. The rest stared straight ahead, looking at nothing, doing nothing. Tony sat among them, wearing dark glasses, the bandaged stump of one thigh propped on a board that stuck out in front of him, the other a blunt bulk under his housecoat. A cloth urinal bag was slung over one of the handles of his chair, and yellow liquid bubbled through a plastic tube from somewhere under Tony's housecoat.

"Hey, Tony. Guess who?" Freddy pulled a chair beside him and patted his shoulder awkwardly. "Good to see you're still alive and kicking!"

The instant the words were out of his mouth, he could have bitten his tongue off. Kicking? Christ, how could he be so insensitive? He tried again.

"You look good, Tony," he lied. "That little nurse has eyes for you. I can tell." Then he added, "You always were a lucky bugger."

Again, he wanted to bite his tongue. Too late. Tony's voice was bitter, grinding.

"You call this luck, Fredo?"

Freddy didn't mention luck again.

The silence was finally broken by Tony.

"What're you in for?"

"Oh, just a checkup. The shrink wants to have a look at my brain. See if it's still there. You know how it is . . ."

These headaches are getting worse, Tony. I get black spots in front of my eyes, and sometimes when people talk to me I can't understand what they're saying. Their lips move, but I can't hear them.

And I went crazy, Tony. Tried to kill my best friends.

But he didn't tell Tony. They were quiet again until an orderly wheeled in a stainless steel cart with mugs of weak tea and a plate of arrowroot biscuits. Freddy started to lift the cup for Tony, but he swatted his hand away.

"I'm not helpless."

Freddy was relieved when a nurse came in looking for him.

"Mr. McKee? Doctor will see you now." She swished out of the room, starched skirts rustling importantly, expecting him to follow her. But as he got up to leave, Tony's hand fastened over his arm.

"Not so fast, Fredo. I gotta ask you something."

Freddy bent over the wheelchair, listening.

"What happened to Mick?"

It was the question he'd been waiting for, the one he'd been dreading for years. He'd rehearsed the answer a thousand times in his mind, but how could he tell Tony the truth? How could he tell anybody when he didn't know himself?

He sat down again.

"We were on Mount Butler, east of the Gap. Remember? Got ambushed. There were Japs everywhere. They were throwing everything at us. Mortars, grenades, rifle fire, everything. Mick took one in the leg. He was hit pretty bad."

Tony made a rasping sound, half chuckle, half cough. "A leg wound? C'mon. The medics would've picked him up!"

No. I picked him up, but then I lost him. Left him for the Japs.

Freddy tried to leave, to follow the nurse, but Tony held on. "A leg wound wouldn't kill him, Freddy. Hell, no. They keep you alive without legs, Fredo. No legs, no balls, a dick that dribbles all the time, they keep you alive! Legs? Hell, who needs legs?"

He slapped the protruding stump.

"You can still feel them, even when they're not there. Did you know that, Fredo? It's the nerves. Pain receptors, the doc says. That's why they keep me stupid with morphine. Lucky me, eh Fredo? Lucky old Tony, with a million-dollar wound. I got to come home, didn't I?

I got to spend my war in this place, in this goddamned chair. So you tell me, Fredo. What happened to Mick?"

Freddy dropped his head into his hands.

"I don't know, Tony. I wish to God I did, but I honestly don't know. Maybe he crawled away. He could have been taken prisoner, but the Japs shot wounded men. I tried to find him. I tried! But when I got back to where I thought I'd left him, he was gone. He was just ... gone."

There was a long silence before Tony spoke again.

"Well, Fredo, you just keep telling yourself that, if it makes you feel better. Now get the hell outta here. I don't expect I'll be seeing you again."

Freddy stayed in the hospital for three weeks, saw a parade of doctors, endured dozens of tests, answered hundreds of questions, took enough aspirin to swamp a rowboat. He paced the hallways alone, ate alone, sat alone in an eight-bed ward leafing through six-month-old copies of *Life* and *Reader's Digest*.

For as long as he stayed, he avoided the half-circle of wheelchairs in the sunroom.

SEVEN : Spring

LATE MAY. LIKE THE ANIMALS, the people are hungry for sunshine and the smell of green in the air. Here in the north it comes first to mossy places along the creek bed, a smell so delicate that only those with the most acute senses ever notice it.

Stan often sees Deaf Gilbert walking the track, heading for the trestle on some mysterious mission or other. Some people say he has a still out in the bush, but Stan ignores that possibility as he ignores Stinson's quiet bootlegging of Matilda.

"The old guy is anxious for spring," he says when Mary Leski speculates about Deaf Gilbert's mysterious treks. "He and Dahlia have been shut up in that little house since November. Maybe he needs some space."

At first, Freddy had avoided Gilbert's company because trying to talk to a deaf guy was damn near impossible. Deaf Gilbert was always waving his hands: he didn't talk, but he wasn't a mute either. He made these crazy sounds, grunts and yelps that only Dahlia could understand. It was embarrassing just being around the guy.

But now Freddy begins to watch Gilbert carefully, trying to figure out how the lip reading works.

Freddy knows he's going deaf. The doctors in Winnipeg shrug it off. They say it will happen slowly, and he won't be totally deaf for some time, maybe for years. Then they slap him on the back and tell him not to worry, he's lucky to be alive and walking.

He'd like to give them a good head-kicking, bust those little bones that let them hear, bust their eardrums, and keep on kicking until their stupid ears blow up like a softball and ache so they want to cry, and their brains feel like they'd been scrambled.

Just so they could feel as lucky as he did.

Now an ordinary speaking voice has a muffled quality, and he finds it easier to understand what people are saying to him if he's looking at them, watching their lips move.

▲ · ▲ ▲

PEOPLE IN TROUT Creek thought it strange that Deaf Gilbert loved music, but Bertha Yellowquill knew why. It was like the drums, she said. Out on the reserve, when there was a celebration and the drums beat for the dancers, the old ones still felt that rhythm, even if they couldn't hear the singing. Gilbert heard music with his feet, she said.

That spring, the meltwater from the Dogrib Hills and the late spring rains came down together. Trout Creek was neither wide enough nor deep enough to handle a flood, so the excess water tore along at ten times its usual speed and volume and the placid little creek became a torrent. It ripped off dead trees and scooped up debris until at last it reached the gorge, where it pitched its full fury at the old wooden trestle. The CN roadmaster who came out afterwards said it was as though a dam had burst somewhere upstream.

Deaf Gilbert was on the trestle. He couldn't hear it coming, but he felt it in his feet, and it was the wildest, craziest crescendo of his life. He was halfway across, and when he turned sideways to see what it was that was making him want to dance, the wall of water was almost on top of him. Instinctively, he wrapped his arms over his head and ducked, so he was in a crouch position when the water picked him up and tossed him off the trestle. Deaf Gilbert hurtled through the air, tumbling and looping like a bird in a down draft.

Three days. It took three whole days before Stan could get the RCMP diver from Winnipeg to help them bring Deaf Gilbert back. Freddy was in the police boat with Stan when the diver signalled that he'd found the body. It was wedged under a rocky ledge at the mouth of the gorge, where Trout Creek dumps into Steeprock Lake.

That night Freddy got drunk again, but instead of yelling and smashing the furniture as he often did these days, he curled up like a baby and whimpered. Su Li held him in her arms, rocking his quivering body back and forth, but he could tell her nothing. Freddy's well of sadness was growing too deep even for her.

▲　▲　▲

IT WAS STILL the middle of the night when the guards pulled Freddy out of the sleeping hut at North Point Prison. There was a black car in the prison yard with its motor running.

"You, white boy. Get in."

They shoved him into the back seat.

"Where are we going?"

Nobody answered. Wedged between two silent, beefy Japs in military uniforms, he recognized familiar streets, ones he'd briefly known with Su Li. They stopped in front of a graceful three-storey building with a large central dome. In the bright moonlight, he recognized it as the Supreme Court Building.

"Why are we here?"

For the first time he got a response from one of the Japs.

"You are at Kempei Tai headquarters. You understand? You smart Canadian boy! You understand?"

The Jap grinned at him.

Freddy felt his stomach lurch. Everybody knew about the Kempei Tai. They were the Japanese secret police who operated under the War Ministry. They had complete authority, both civil and military, and they specialized in torture.

There were three of them in the room with Freddy. One in an officer's uniform directed the other two, a pair of goons in dark suits who never spoke. The officer, an older man with an intelligent face, asked his questions in slightly accented English, never raising his voice above a soft, reasonable tone.

He kept asking about an escape. Freddy denied any knowledge, but denial was to be expected. It was part of the game these foolish boys insisted on playing. Too bad, really. It wasted his time, and so many of them failed to survive.

When Freddy stubbornly insisted that he had no information to give them, the officer tired of his non-cooperative attitude and turned the goons loose. He left the room. Torture was effective but not to his taste.

Freddy's arms were bound behind him, but his feet were free, and they made him stand up. They started on him with two square clubs about the thickness of a baseball bat. They worked on his ribs and his shins, and when he was on the floor and couldn't get back on his feet, they abandoned the clubs and started kicking. They kicked his ribs and his groin. The pain curled him into a ball and they kicked him in the kidneys. They kicked his head like it was a football. Whenever he passed out, one of the goons threw water on him. It stank of gasoline, and in a lucid moment he thought they intended to set him on fire.

Eventually they tired of beating him, and one of the goons bound his ankles together and dragged him across the room, to what looked like a gas barrel with a wooden lid. One goon took the lid off and smacked his hand into the full barrel, playfully sloshing water at Freddy and laughing.

They lifted him off his feet, and when he saw what they were going to do with him he gulped greedily at the air, twisting frantically to get out of their grip.

Holy Jesus, they're going to drown me!

They intended that he should go in headfirst, but he fought so hard, twisting and bucking, that they finally pushed his feet into the barrel, forcing his body into a crouch, back and knees straining against metal. They shoved his head under, and water sloshed over the top so there was only the thin film of gasoline left floating. They slammed the wooden lid down hard.

His first terrified seconds in the cold black water were silent, but then his ears roared, his blood pounded in his head. His lungs ached. His final scream came to nothing but a burst of bubbles as his breath, held for so long, exploded into the water. The involuntary inhalation was immediate, as gasoline and water was forced into his stomach and lungs.

The drowning had begun.

For his interrogators, the water treatment was almost routine and invariably effective, no matter which variation they used—the barrel or forcing water through a man's mouth and nostrils with a hose. Once their victim lost consciousness, one of them would jump on his stomach, forcing the water back out. When he came to, they'd repeat the process. The victim either talked or he drowned.

But this one had been too stubborn, and they'd tired of him. They didn't try to revive him and start again. When the Kampei Tai lifted the lid and yanked the Canadian fool out of the barrel by his hair, he was apparently dead. Just as well. They'd been at this for hours, and they were hungry.

In the morning the black car drove back through the gates of North Point Prison, and Freddy was pitched out of the back seat and left in a heap on the ground. For the rest of that day, nobody dared touch him.

After dark, two men picked up the inert body and carried it into a building. Almost as a formality, a medic searched for a pulse.

"He's still alive," the medic said. "Barely."

The gasoline that reached his lungs had almost killed Freddy. His nose and left cheek had been reduced to pulp, his left ear was caked with dried blood and swollen to four times its normal size. The camp doctor figured he had damage to the temporal bone in both ears, as well as to the three tiny bones of the middle ear. In Freddy's fourth grade health text these bones had been labelled: the hammer, the anvil, and the stirrup. Serena helped him memorize them for the final exam, and he'd even drawn a little diagram so he'd never forget. Fat lot of good that knowledge did him, in the end.

A doctor at Deer Lodge, the veterans' hospital in Winnipeg, gave him the final verdict: he was going deaf.

So on that spring morning in Trout Creek, he wakes up ice cold and sweating. The bastards had been drowning him. Held him underwater until his lungs were ready to burst. He feels death coming, the way Deaf Gilbert must have felt it in his final terrible silence, trapped under the rocky ledge in Steeprock Lake. He crawls away from Su Li, from the pillow where she has fallen into warm, flower-scented sleep, and he huddles in a corner until dawn. She finds him there on the floor, shivering.

EIGHT : Hairstyles by Mary

WHEN MARY GAVE MY MOM her semi-annual home permanent, Su Li was sitting there too, at the other end of the table. They were all drinking coffee, even Su Li. Tom Cat and I were underneath the table, staying out of sight.

I was supposed to be studying, but I was a lot more interested in what they were talking about than anything in my stupid science book. Who cared if radios had been invented by some old guy named Macaroni?

Mary was winding Mom's hair around some pink and blue plastic curlers that looked like chicken bones, and Tom Cat and I were trying not to inhale the fumes. It was an awful stink, but I didn't want to leave, in case I missed something important.

After she was finished winding Mom, Mary got one of her bright ideas.

"Why don't we cut Su Li's hair?"

My mom didn't think so.

"Su Li's hair is beautiful, Mary. She doesn't want it cut."

"Oh c'mon, don't be such a stick-in-the-mud. Su Li, your hair's too long anyway. You look like you're in the Salvation Army with that big bun in the back. All you need is a bonnet. Let me cut your hair, sweetie! Give it a little pep! I'll even give you a perm!"

Su Li never seemed to talk much during those coffee sessions with Mary and my mom. If they asked her a question she'd say yes or no, but mostly she just listened. Mary kept on yakking at her about her hair, and finally she gave in and pulled out the long pins so it spilled down her back. I remember how shiny it was.

My mother said once more, "Mary, I don't think you should cut her hair."

But when Mary started a project, she didn't mess around. She just yanked Su Li's hair back behind her head like my mom did when she braided me. Then snip, whack, all that beautiful hair started falling into a soft, shiny pile on Mary's linoleum.

My mother had a funny look on her face, as though she didn't like what was happening but didn't know how to stop it.

"Mom, what's wrong with Su Li?" I whispered close to her ear so nobody else would hear me. "She's crying, Mom. What's wrong?"

"Nothing. It's this awful smell. It makes my eyes water too."

Sure enough, they were. Mom picked up Su Li's hair where it had fallen, smoothed it into three long shiny strands, and began weaving it into a braid.

As the perm progressed, the smell got stronger. Su Li's eyes were really watering now, and she was wiping them on her sleeve.

"That's the ammonia," said Mary. "It always does this. Makes me bawl like a baby."

When Su Li's new perm had been timed and rinsed and dried, Mary started taking the plastic chicken bones out of her hair really fast, dropping a few and not even bothering to pick them up. Mary was freaky about neatness, so I knew she must be anxious or she'd have been scrambling around on the floor, picking up curlers.

When they were all out and Su Li's hair washed and towelled, she took a brush to her masterpiece, but it seemed to be standing up a lot more than Mom's ever did after a home perm. Su Li's hair acted like it had been starched. So Mary went after it with a comb and turned it into little corkscrews. She said it looked so darn cute. "Doesn't it look cute, Joanna?"

My mom said hmmm, but she didn't sound convinced, so Mary looked at me.

"Hope, what do you think?"

Like Mary ever cared what a kid thought, especially me. I wasn't supposed to lie, but I wasn't supposed to be rude either, so I was stuck both ways.

"It's really curly," I said.

That was the truth. Su Li looked like Little Lulu when she sticks her finger in a light socket and yells, "Yoikes!" and her hair goes *sproing* and stands up like springs. I had a comic book where Little Lulu did that, and Su Li's hair looked just like hers.

Mary handed her a mirror, and she looked at herself for a long time. Her expression didn't change at all. It was just solemn, like always.

"I go home now," she said. "I go home to Freddy."

And she left.

"Jeez, she didn't even say thanks," Mary said. "How do you like that? Maybe chinks don't say thanks, eh?"

My mother didn't answer, but she stood up really fast and said, Hope, we're going home, and we left right away.

Mom bawled me out all the way, like I was the guilty party here.

"Don't you ever use that word, Hope. Never ever!"

"What word? Curly?"

"You know what word I mean! Chink! It's rude, and crude, and it hurts people."

▲   ▲   ▲

FREDDY GOT DRUNK that night. Plastered, Mary said. It was late at night, and Su Li was at our door, knocking loud and fast.

"Joanna, please, I must come in!"

Freddy was there too, yelling in a voice that didn't even sound like him.

"Goddamn little chink! Goddamn little whore!"

I heard my mother talking, fast and low. I couldn't understand what she was saying, but all of a sudden Mary was there, and Stan. Pretty soon the whole town seemed to be in our kitchen, so Tom Cat and I climbed out of bed and went to see what was happening.

Stan had Freddy pinned against a wall with his arms over his head so he couldn't move. Su Li was sitting on a kitchen chair, hugging herself with both arms, and her head was down low, almost on her lap, so I couldn't see her face.

But her hair, or what was left of it, looked weird. There didn't seem to be as much of it as there was when she left Mary's place. Most of the corkscrews were gone, and in some places, I could see her scalp sticking out. I couldn't believe anybody would be that mean.

My mother was kneeling in front of Su Li, talking to her. She had her arms around her, rocking her back and forth like a baby.

"It's all right now. Su Li, you're safe. Everything will be okay."

Mom saw me then and told me to get back to bed *this very instant*!

The next morning the door to the guest room was closed, and when I opened it so Tom Cat could have a look around, Su Li was there with her head on Mom's pansy-embroidered pillow.

Except it didn't look like her face. Her skin had dark blue patches. Her lips were swollen so big, and looked like they'd been bleeding. But the worst thing of all was her eyes. You could hardly see them. They were purple and so puffed up I figured she'd never get them open again. Tom Cat brushed past me and jumped onto the pillow, meowing. I grabbed him, and the face on the pillow groaned, but it didn't sound like Su Li.

She stayed in our guest room for three more days. On the morning of the fourth day, even though it was Sunday, Freddy got drunk again. Only this time he didn't roar and break furniture and hit people. He just sat at our kitchen table and cried. Giant, terrible sobs came out of him, and a lot of muttering I couldn't understand because I was stuck outside the window and my mom closed it all the way so it was really hard to hear. Mom stood at the cupboard, leaning against it and watching him, like she didn't want to get too close. Su Li stayed in the guest room with the door closed.

On Tuesday, Mom and I walked over to Freddy's cookshack and went in the back door, to the room where Su Li and Freddy lived. I watched Mom pack Su Li's clothes in a suitcase, even the beautiful red dress. Then she wrapped the little statue of Kuan Yin in an old towel and took the little shrine apart with a tack hammer. She saved all the nails, so it could be put back together, and put it all in the suitcase.

Su Li was going to Winnipeg to see a doctor, and Stan had arranged for her to stay at the YWCA after that, until she decided what she wanted to do.

The last thing Mom packed was a tissue paper package that was soft and smelled of sandalwood. It was Su Li's braided hair.

NINE: Long Cold Season

THAT WINTER, FURIOUS BLIZZARDS HOWLED through Trout Creek, and the temperature dropped to forty-six degrees below zero. At night the wolves joined the howling of the wind, and daylight, when it came, was a poor excuse, with low cloud obscuring the few hours of sunlight that such northern places are allowed in winter.

One Thursday night when the train came in, Su Li was on it. Freddy had followed her to Winnipeg and persuaded her to come home with him. Su Li's hair had grown back, and she seemed well enough, there in the back room of Freddy's cookshack.

But Freddy had changed. Hope no longer sought him out for tea and brown sugar sandwiches during the afternoons. When he wasn't drinking, he was withdrawn and silent, and his binges were more frequent.

Sobering up, he was like a contrite dog who'd messed on the floor. He spent an entire day painting Joanna's kitchen cupboards white and screwing on new brass door handles. Having coffee at Mary's, he paid Su Li compliments, telling everybody how she was learning to roll pastry like a pro.

As she began to spend less time with Freddy, Hope spent more time with Su Li. Both of them turned to Joanna for comfort and companionship.

Gradually, the snow melted and the air began to smell of spring, but it brought them no joy. They were like three women on the bank of a river, watching helplessly while the man they all loved was sucked into a whirlpool. If their shared sense of loss drew them together, it was pity that finally took away their love for Freddy.

Sometimes in the afternoon when she knew he was busy baking his pies, Hope would slip in the back door and visit Su Li.

The Chinese woman was fond of the little girl and her big orange cat and would hold Tom on her knee, stroking his head while he purred himself to sleep. Sometimes she'd brush Hope's hair for her, just for something to do, for her days were empty.

"Beautiful hair," she told Hope.

"I hate my hair," Hope replied. "My mother always puts it in braids. Did you have long hair when you were a kid?"

"Yes." She measured with her hands, so Hope could see that her hair had hung past her waist.

"Did your mom make you wear braids or stupid ringlets?"

"Braid. Like you."

"When you were a kid, did you ever get your hair cut?"

"Once. My amah cut off all my hair. I was angry!"

"What's an *amah*?"

Su Li thought hard. How to explain to this western child? Finally, she remembered Marg, the woman who came and went so often.

"She is like Auntie Marg, but very old."

"Why did your mom let your auntie cut off your hair?"

"Mother die. My amah makes me look like small boy, so soldiers will not hurt me."

"Why would they hurt you? Didn't the soldiers like little girls?"

"There was war. I cannot explain."

Hope wondered if it had been anything like the time Freddy chopped all Su Li's hair off, after Mary gave her the permanent.

"Is something wrong with Freddy?" Hope asked.

Su Li looked down at her hands.

"I think he is sick."

Hope didn't like him that way, so sick and miserable.

She and Tom Cat stopped visiting Freddy for good.

Meanwhile, Trout Creek watched and waited. All quiet on the western front, Chris Stinson said. Finally concluding that things had righted themselves, the community breathed a collective sigh of relief.

Except for Stan. He wasn't sure.

"Do me a favour, Jo."

Stan was having coffee in her kitchen one morning just before Easter.

"Keep an eye on Su Li. Tell me if you spot anything unusual."

"Like what?"

"Like bruises. Things you might notice, things she'd hide from me."

"Why are you so hostile to Freddy? He suffered so much in that prison camp. We can't expect him to act like a normal man."

"Right. Maybe he's not a normal man, Jo. Maybe he never will be, and maybe that's his problem."

"But they tortured him. You don't know what he went through. He'd never tell you, but he has scars all over his body. I've seen them . . ."

She stopped in mid-sentence. Stan let the silence lengthen before he replied.

"No doubt you have, Joanna. That doesn't excuse the beating he gave Su Li. Whatever you knew him to be in the past, he's a violent, angry man now." He paused, looking out the window, away from Joanna. "He's dangerous."

Stan stood up and shrugged his long arms into his parka. It was Tuesday, and he was heading for Winnipeg for a few days.

"Just watch her, okay? She needs a friend."

TEN : Another Season

I GUESS MY MOM DIDN'T watch close enough. The very next weekend, Freddy got drunk again and beat up Su Li. He hurt her a lot.
When she left him this time, we all knew she wouldn't be coming back.

Two weeks after Easter, Freddy got on the Thursday train without
even saying goodbye. I thought that was a mean thing for him to do.
Mom and I had loved Freddy a lot, and maybe we still did. Especially
my mom.

He should have said goodbye.

A couple of months later, Dahlia Rempel came huffing over to our
place to deliver a parcel. It was a funny shape, bigger on one end than
the other, wrapped in brown paper. It was addressed to my mother,
and the writing was all squiggly, like it had been written by an old,
shaky person. Dahlia and I watched while Mom opened her surprise
package.

It was Freddy's mandolin. Whoever wrapped it had padded it all
around with copies of the *Winnipeg Tribune*, but there was nothing
else, not even a note.

"No return address either," Dahlia pointed out. "I guess he doesn't
want anybody to know where he is."

So my mother was the last person in Trout Creek to hear from
Freddy McKee. After that he just sort of disappeared from our lives
for a long time.

"What a piece of work he turned out to be," Mary said to my
mother, when we were all in her kitchen. Mom didn't say anything, but
Mary pushed it, like always.

"You were lucky, Jo. That little chink did you a favour, turning up the
way she did, just when you and Freddy were getting involved like that."

Mom's face got red, and I could tell that she was mad enough to spit. You could almost see the smoke rolling out of her ears.

"Mary, whatever was between me and Freddy is none of your business. And will you please stop calling Su Li by that crude, ignorant name? She is not a chink! She's a woman, just like you. She happens to be a Chinese woman, and *she is not a chink*!"

And we stomped off home. I put my arm around my mom while we walked. I just felt like it.

The next Christmas Su Li's card came from an address in Edmonton. She had moved and was working in a restaurant called Elite Eats.

The year after that, her address had changed again. This time she was living on East Pender Street in Vancouver with her auntie, the one she called "amah." The old lady had had a stroke and needed somebody to look after her.

▲　　▲　　▲

AT THE END of March, Stan stopped in to see Joanna. He had some news: he was being transferred to D Division, in Winnipeg. Joanna sat across from him at the kitchen table.

"Transferred? But you haven't said a word. Were you expecting a transfer, Stan?"

There was a small silence before he answered.

"I asked for it."

Joanna winced.

"When will you go?"

"Probably early summer. They need to find a replacement. Strange as it may seem, Trout Creek isn't high on the list for a young single guy."

She folded her hands together, avoiding his eyes.

"We'll miss you. A lot. You've been like a second father to Hope."

He reached across the table, but before he could touch her hands she jerked them out of his reach. Seeing the hurt in his eyes, she pretended to brush something off her sleeve. He tried again.

"You could come with me, Jo. Hope could go to a good school in Winnipeg. I could be a real father to her."

"Stan, no. Stop this, please." She heard the sharp edge in her own voice, continued in a softer tone, hoping not to hurt again.

"You're my very dear friend, my best friend, but we both know it would never work as anything more. Too much has happened. To me. To all of us."

▲　　▲　　▲

STAN STAYED UNTIL June. Mom and I and Mary Leski threw a farewell shindig for Uncle Stan the night before he left. It was early for Mary's Summer Solstice event, but she said, "Close enough, let's do it!"

It was a terrific party, but I felt sad all night long. So did my mom. I could tell because she had her chirpy voice on, the phony one she always used when she felt bad about something and didn't want anybody to know.

I figured it out that night, after everybody finally left and we went to bed. So many things had ended for us, and this was another ending.

I think endings are the saddest thing of all.

In September, a big brown envelope arrived at Dahlia Rempel's post office. It was addressed to Miss Hope Keegan, and Dahlia called me into her living room so she could hand deliver it. "It feels like a photograph," said Dahlia. "See this? It says DO NOT BEND." Dahlia wondered if I needed scissors, and I could tell she wanted me to open it. She was right. It was a photograph. Uncle Stan, wearing his dress uniform. The red serge, Dahlia called it. Beside him stood a pretty woman in a long white dress, holding a bunch of flowers. They were both smiling, like they were the happiest two people in the world. When I looked at it I got kind of a funny feeling in my stomach. I handed it to Dahlia.

"Oh, my," she said. "I guess this'll rattle the teacups at your house, won't it?"

There was a note. I decided Dahlia didn't need to read, so I thanked her and left.

I read it on the way home.

Dearest Hope,

Now I have two best girls—you and Janice. We were married in August. Janice is a physiotherapist, working at Deer Lodge Veterans' Hospital here in Winnipeg.

I know you'll love her as much as I do.

Give my best to your mom.

Love and kisses, Uncle Stan

P. S. Janice knows Freddy. He's in and out of Deer Lodge as a patient. I thought your mom might want to know.

ELEVEN: Endings

THE FOLLOWING SUMMER, MOM AND I left Trout Creek and moved to Winnipeg so I could go to a real school. We shared an apartment with Aunt Marg, and that fall Mom registered me in the Royal Manitoba Academy for Young Ladies. Mom called it her Alma Mater.

"You'll be a day girl, just like I was," she told me, like being a day girl was some big deal and I should be thrilled to bits.

I wasn't. It was a snotty school full of snotty girls, and we had to wear stupid uniforms. Black stockings, plaid skirts, white shirts, and a tie like guys wear. The headmistress, Miss Elkhorn, was a total witch, and she smelled.

I hated everything about the place, but my mother loved it. She told Aunt Marg that the academy would smooth off the rough edges from Trout Creek, and at least I'd know a fish fork from a salad fork when I got married.

"That will be really useful, Jo," said Aunt Marg. "Won't it, Hope?" She winked at me.

For my birthday, Mom gave me a set of *Encyclopedia Britannica*. I knew they must have cost a lot, so I pretended to be grateful.

"They're an investment in your future," she told me. "An education is the best insurance policy a girl can have. Your father knew that. He wanted you to have an education."

Aunt Marg gave me a bottle of Evening in Paris cologne in a dark blue bottle with a silver tassel on top and a pair of nylons. I tried them on with my new high heels, and she whistled.

"Gorgeous legs, Hope. That's almost as good as knowing which fork is for fish, eh?"

Then the doorbell rang, and a delivery boy handed me a long white box tied with a pink satin ribbon. Inside were fifteen pink roses. They were the most beautiful flowers I'd ever seen.

Aunt Marg and Mom oohed and aahed.

"I'll bet they're from your Uncle Stan," Mom said.

They weren't.

For Hope on her 15th birthday.

Love, Freddy.

Mom said they were exquisite, and wasn't it thoughtful of Freddy to remember. That was Mom's big trouble. She didn't know how to stay mad.

"You want them? Here!"

I slammed the box on the table with both hands.

"You keep them! I don't want his damn flowers! Freddy can go to hell, and take his roses with him!"

"Hope!" (Mom, all shocked and bothered.) "Language!"

I didn't care what she said. I hated Freddy for what he had done to us. To me, to Su Li, to Mom.

"How could you still love him?" I yelled. "How can you be such a pushover, Mom?"

My mother didn't say anything else, just looked somewhere between hurt and scared. I didn't care.

Two more Christmases went by without a card from Su Li, and one October night when I got home from school, Uncle Stan was sitting in our kitchen, having coffee with Mom and Aunt Marg, just like the old days. He was wearing his new uniform. The gold bars on the shoulder pips had been replaced by a crown. He was an inspector now, and he was handsomer than ever.

We'd seen him a few times, and we'd been invited to his house to have dinner with him and his wife, Janice-the-therapist, but my mother was too busy, she said. She was still too busy when they asked the second time. After that they stopped asking.

Anyway, I could tell by the look on Mom's face that something was wrong.

"Stan has some bad news, Hope. It's about Su Li. There's been an accident."

"How? What happened? Is she okay?"

Mom looked at Uncle Stan, but he stayed quiet so she kept talking.

"Hope, Su Li is dead."

"What?"

"There was a gun," she whispered. "It went off."

My mother ran out of words.

▲   ▲   ▲

UNCLE STAN HAD spent some time ferreting out the truth, about how Freddy had pursued Su Li, followed her from Winnipeg to Edmonton to Vancouver, where he finally found her living in Chinatown, in a tiny room above the Silver Dragon on Pender Street. She'd been alone after the amah died, for Su Li had nobody else except Third Uncle, and she was now too sick to work in the restaurant, so she seldom saw him.

For three months Freddy had stayed sober, looking after Su Li day and night. He nursed her, doled out her medication, cooked her special dishes in an electric frying pan. During the day they'd take a bus to English Bay and go for walks in Stanley Park. If it rained, which it often did, they'd go to the library. At night he'd lay beside her, reading out loud until she fell asleep.

One evening he went out for cigarettes and didn't come home. Su Li walked the streets of Chinatown all night, looking for him.

Eventually she found him, crumpled in an alley, too drunk to stand on his own feet. Somehow she got him home, and that night he beat her so badly that Third Uncle called an ambulance and then the police.

Freddy spent the night in the drunk tank. Su Li ended up in emergency at Vancouver General. It took twenty-seven stitches to close the gashes on her face and scalp, where he'd cut her with a broken bottle. In the morning, when she persuaded Third Uncle to bail him out, he refused to see her.

Then Freddy disappeared again.

Su Li went back to their room. She housecleaned. Washed the walls and windows. Packed all her things into two small boxes, each item carefully labelled, with one package ready for mailing. She brushed her hair as well as she was able, considering the stitches in her scalp, and carefully dabbed at her bruised face with makeup. She put on her best dress, the red silk cheongsam.

Su Li lay on the bed and arranged the silk skirt neatly over her legs. In her mind she carefully reviewed each step of what remained to be done. Concentrating hard, she wrapped both hands around the amah's pistol.

Downstairs in the busy restaurant, the dim sum crowd was in full voice. But everybody heard the shot.

▲　▲　▲

STAN STOOD UP and put his arms around Hope. She was crying into his starched shirt, but he stroked her hair, rocking her back and forth.

"Hope, do you know what suicide is?"

She pulled away indignantly and blew her nose.

"Uncle Stan, I'm seventeen years old! I know everything about everything!"

He looked at her and sighed.

"Yes, I guess you do. Well then, maybe you'll understand what happened. Su Li took her own life," Stan told her. "She was depressed about a lot of things. You understand depression, Hope? She'd been very sick for almost a year."

Hope's face had lost its colour.

"At the end, I guess she couldn't help it," he finished lamely.

Aunt Marg was sniffling and my mom was crying out loud, little hiccupping sobs. So was I. Mom wiped her eyes, sniffled a couple of times, and then asked the question we were all thinking.

"Does Freddy know?"

"Not yet. We're still looking for him. He was in and out of Deer Lodge Hospital here in Winnipeg for the past couple of years before he went to Vancouver, where he seems to have pulled himself together and honestly tried to look after Su Li. But he's a sick man. You know that, Jo. Better than most of us."

Stan stood up to leave. He had his hat in his hand, and he brushed the gold braid with his fingers.

"What I'd like to know is where she got that gun. It was a Radom. A pistol used by the Polish army. The only people who own them now are collectors. There were two bullets missing, but we only found one. The other had been fired a long time ago. I'm surprised the gun fired at all."

A couple of days later, a parcel arrived by special delivery. It was the little china statue of Kuan Yin, the Goddess of Mercy, and it was addressed to Joanna.

▲   ▲   ▲

WHEN THE TIME came, Hope decided on a university far away from Winnipeg. She wanted to try the coast, she said. The University of British Columbia had a good law faculty, and with her marks and Uncle Stan as her reference, she'd get in easily.

She met David Chu her first day on campus. He bumped into her, literally. Sent her armful of books flying.

"Have coffee with me," he pleaded. "Please, it's the least I can do."

In her second year, when they moved in together, Hope didn't tell Joanna.

Instead, she dumped it on Stan, who was in Vancouver on business.

"Stan, what will Mom think?"

"About what? David being Chinese? Or your living arrangements? I doubt she'll approve of her only daughter living with a guy, if that's what you mean. But does it matter? After all, your mom wasn't always as conventional as she is these days."

"You mean about Freddy?"

"Yes. About Freddy."

"Do you know where he is?"

"Probably here, in Vancouver. Your mom told me you'd seen him."

"Maybe. But he looked so awful. So grubby and sick. I know I should have done something, but I didn't know what to do."

"It's okay, Hope. I don't think he wants to be found."

TWELVE: Ghosts

FREDDY'S GHOSTS ARE ALWAYS HOVERING, but they're worse when he isn't expecting them. In a too-small elevator, in a thunderstorm, in a sudden fume of coal smoke, they sneak up on him.

It's an evil stink, coal smoke. He won't go near the docks where they load the coal for Japan.

He doesn't sleep much, especially if he's sober. He's afraid to sleep. That's when he hears the voices. They whisper, but he can hear them, even with his bad ears. He could sure use a drink.

Sometimes his ghosts are so real. A Chinese girl, hair like black silk, body as fragile as a child's. She reaches for him and he tries to take her hand, but she floats ahead of him. His feet are heavy, too heavy to run. Like they're stuck in deep mud.

He sees a man sprawled on the ground. Too still. Hears his own voice, *Wait here, Mick, I'll be back . . .*

He's falling again. Always falling. Wakes up screaming, hears the fist banging on the wall, voices yelling from another room, *Shudup, godammit, people are tryin' to sleep.*

He's wide awake now, watching the rhythmic splash of neon from the all-night restaurant, red, yellow, red, green.

Down in the street the sirens shriek, but he doesn't mind. They keep him from his nightmares. Police, ambulance, another stabbing in the alley. Night noises. Funny, the things a nearly deaf man can still hear.

The sirens were different then. Air raid sirens started low, built up, fell off again, never quite finished that rising note. Nobody paid attention after a while, when the bombing got so heavy and the Chinese began hiding their daughters behind secret panels, in dark cellars, between hollow walls. Waiting.

He's so tired. Maybe he'll doze off again, hopes to hell the nightmares don't come back. He pulls the blanket up, covers his ears. In the morning, he'll find a drink somewhere.

If he wakes at all. If morning comes.

A DOZEN QUESTIONS FOR FURTHER DISCUSSION

The best bit about reading a book is often the discussion that comes afterwards. *Freddy's War* is based on a real event in history, but the story itself is fiction and could have been written with many different plots and outcomes. Here are a dozen questions to get the discussion started:

1. Originally this book had a different ending, in which Freddy died. What do you think might have been the reason for his death? (Accidental? Natural causes?) Why would the author have chosen the second ending instead of the original?

2. If Freddy hadn't appeared in Trout Creek after Mick's death, would Joanna eventually have married Stan Novak, and could it have been successful? Why or why not?

3. Among the secondary characters are Chris Stinson, Bertha Yellowquill, and Deaf Gilbert. Would this story have been as compelling without their roles? Why or why not?

4. In what ways is Hope's boyfriend, David Chu, important to this story? What about Stan Novak?

5. Freddy's welcome home party at Elite Eats and the violent death of Deaf Gilbert are two events that cause Freddy to suffer horrific flashbacks. Would his problem have been different in any way if Freddy's war had been Vietnam or Afghanistan?

6. When Hope tells her story as a child, secondary relationships within the community are revealed with surprising insight. Given that she's so young, how do we explain her insightful comments?

7. Is Freddy's growing affection for and dependence upon Mick a natural side-effect of war or does it go deeper than that? If Mick had survived, what might have happened to their friendship?

8. Hope really believes she has seen her father in the woods. Is there a supernatural element to this story, and if so, does it have anything in common with other "ghost" stories?

9. Hope and Freddy are both drawn to Vancouver's Chinatown district. Discuss the reasons for this, and the eventual effects, if any, in Hope's life.

10. At no point in the book does Freddy profess love for Joanna. If Su Li had not reappeared in his life, would his relationship with Joanna have continued, or would the memory of Mick have interfered?

11. Joanna's friendship with Mary Leski seems like an odd match. What drew the two women together? Or was it just a friendship of convenience?

12. Among the supporting characters in this book, does Yip or Serena have the greater influence in Freddy's life, and why?

Acknowledgments

WHERE DOES AN AUTHOR BEGIN to say thank you?

To my publisher, Ruth Linka, for taking a chance on first-time fiction.

To my wonderful editor, Dr. Lynne van Luven, for respecting my words while firmly guiding my text.

To Anna Wong, for introducing me to the ladies of the Tuesday night mah-jong group, and for translating their shared memories.

To Lila Mah in Guangzhou, for hospitality and history lessons.

To Hong Kong Tourism, for their assistance with itineraries and access to battle sites.

To the history master and staff of St. Stephen's College, Hong Kong, for access to archives and buildings.

I am grateful for the assistance of Veterans Affairs Canada for access to information on battles and battle sights in Hong Kong, and to The Memory Project, for personal stories from Winnipeg Grenadiers during the Battle of Hong Kong.

JUDY SCHULTZ IS a nationally renowned travel and food writer, the author of ten books, and the winner of numerous awards. Her publications include *Looking for China: Travels on a Silk Road*; *Mamie's Children: Three Generations of Prairie Women*; *Nibbles and Feasts*; and *Jean Pare: Appetite for Life*. She co-authored *The Food Lover's Guide to Alberta, Volumes 1* and *2*. Judy divides her time between Alberta and New Zealand, and devotes her attention to travelling, cooking, and writing.